# The Cowboy Code of the West

Live each day with courage.
Take pride in your work.
Always finish what you start.
Do what has to be done.
Be tough, but fair.
When you make a promise, keep it.
Ride for the brand.
Talk less and say more.
Remember that some things aren't for sale.
Know where to draw the line.

# The Cowboy Code

A novel by Linda Ellison

© Linda Ellison 2019

Linda Ellison asserts the moral right to be identified as the author of
*'The Cowboy Code'*

Cover photography by Linda Ellison

Design and typeset by Green Avenue Design

Published by Cilento Publishing, Sydney Australia

ISBN Paperback: 978-0-6483932-8-3

ISBN Australian Paperback: 978-0-6483932-7-6

ISBN Kindle: 978-0-6483932-9-0

This novel is entirely a work of fiction. Any resemblance to actual persons, living or dead, is entirely coincidental.

*Instagram: lindaellison.author*

*For my mom x*

# Chapter One

His mind was racing away from him, so he breathed in deep to pull back his thoughts and gain some control. It was the day that he never expected to happen. The day that had been playing on his mind for quite some time, and as he wandered around his bedroom, he began to feel anxious.

He walked over to the wall and looked closely at the handcrafted display box his father had made. With the buckle he won at the show in Dallas filling the last space, it was now complete. It took him back to the ride on the filly, the ride that gave him back his title as the best cutting horse trainer in the country, and it made him feel satisfied. Not only was his career back on track, but he had Double J Ranch restocked with cattle and it was profitable again.

It also made him think of Raylee, the girl who had stolen his heart and had run away with it, leaving him constantly thinking of her. He knew that she was the reason for his latest success and he owed all of it to her.

It was their flirtation and their love for the same horse that had quickly turned their friendship into an intense love affair, and the events that followed resulted in his successful comeback in the cutting arena. She had helped him through the lowest and most difficult time of his life and Cutter knew that without a doubt, she completed him.

He had often wondered why he'd been dealt such a bad hand, constantly questioning what he had done to deserve it. To have lost his mom under tragic circumstances, then nursed his dying father to his long drawn out end, was something that most people would never recover from. To top it all off, when everything was said and done, he had been left without his colt, without his career and with a ranch sinking deep in debt.

After meeting Raylee Tremayne, he never questioned again why these things had happened.

When Cutter returned home from Australia alone, he felt lost. He went to countless shows over the summer and into the autumn, with some outstanding results that only added to the filly's status as well as his prize money. With his impressive win at the show, he'd bought a new horse truck to cater for the new clients that he now had onboard, as the three-angle horse float just wasn't going to cut it anymore. He had also picked up two new sponsors and everything from that show in Dallas was finally falling into place. What a remarkable restart to his career and he couldn't have asked for anything more, except maybe one thing.

As the months were rolling on, the outlook on his personal life was plunging down. A complete contrast to his work life on Double J Ranch and his career in the cutting pen.

He pulled on a fresh pair of jeans and a long sleeved black shirt, and he stood in front of the mirror while he did up his buckle. It was the buckle that he won on the colt many years ago. It was his favorite. He still wore it every day, not only as a reminder of his win, but the colt was also the connection he had to Raylee.

A closer inspection of the lines around his eyes revealed that nothing in his appearance had changed since he last saw her, even though he had a birthday just the other week.

He celebrated it after a long day at work with his neighbors and best friends, Johnny and Emma, who had invited him over for supper, knowing that he needed to be away from the ranch for a while. Emma had surprised him by baking a cake, and while they sat on the porch and shared it over their late night coffee, when Cutter looked out and stared at the sky, they could tell that he was still low.

So much had changed since then.

While still standing in front of the mirror, he traded in his old work hat for his black one, and when he pulled it into position and sharpened the front, he was ready to go. As he stood in the doorway, he took one long look around his room. It had changed since Raylee had first come to visit there almost twelve months ago. She'd hardly recognize it now with a repaint, a new quilt and new curtains. But the bed was the same and he stared at it, remembering the last time they had shared it together. He switched the light off, pulled the door closed and went downstairs to the kitchen.

The house was quiet without Marnie. She was gone and Cutter had been on his own for a couple of days now, hating every minute of it. Every room in the house felt empty. No Marnie and no Raylee. There were no delicious smells coming from the kitchen, where Marnie had baked and cooked every morning of his life since he could remember, and it wasn't the same. It was in darkness. He opened the fridge door and looked inside. Although it was full, there was an instant uneasy feeling in his gut, which made him close it again and he walked outside to the porch and pulled his boots back on.

It had been an early start and a long morning at the barn, and now he was back there again, taking the mare out of her stall and throwing a saddle on. He'd already worked seven horses and was now feeling it. The foals had been broken in and he'd started working with them soon after his return from Australia. He'd taken a look at another six prospects from clients he'd met during the show in Dallas, and agreed to train just two, while the filly was now in her Derby year. He could have taken on more, except that he was without help and he needed to focus on the ranch as much as his training. He wanted to be selective and give his clients a fair deal, taking on a limited number of horses. It was Raylee's idea. Take on less, charge them more. It was a win win situation between Cutter and his clients and although he was busy, he needed to be.

The barn was peaceful and the quietness echoed in his head as it had done every day since he was on his own. It had been driving him beyond crazy for quite some time.

"What're you looking at?" he asked the mare, just to break the silence, then he untied her and put the bridle on. With his boot in the stirrup, he grabbed the horn on the saddle and pulled himself up, throwing his leg over. He used his spurs ever so lightly as the mare was responsive to his pressure, and he rode out of the barn past the day yards towards the first pasture.

When he reached the gate, he took his usual long look back down at the barn and the house. Smoke was barely coming out of the chimney now as it had turned out to be an unexpectedly warm day and he was letting the fire burn out. With his need to keep busy, all the maintenance around the immediate house and yard was done and it looked like a picture, while the barn was looking fresh from a new coat of paint.

He took it all in. He loved it, and he knew that after today, it would never look this way again.

Riding over the first rolling hill, he was picking up the pace and the mare was feeling strong. She knew the ranch as well as Cutter did, and had only improved in her ability on the ranch in front of cattle, which was reflected in her talent in the cutting pen. With his training taking up all of the morning, this was his first ride over the ranch for the day. He now looked at everything as he rode past, checking the fences, the water levels, and doing his usual head count of stock as best as he could.

Even today would not stop him from going through his daily routine.

The calves that had been weaned were now in the middle pasture while the cows were back in calf, grazing freely out the back. The rest of the cattle were overindulging on the good body of feed and the cycle of the ranch was back to normal.

As he rode on, he had a flashback of his last trip to Australia. It was the one time in his life that he needed to cowboy up outside the cutting pen and rodeo arena, to face Allan Tremayne and convince him that he was the best man for his daughter.

But things didn't go as well as he'd planned...

When Cutter and Raylee returned to Australia and arrived at the vineyard, they decided to go straight to the complex and avoid the house, wanting to take their time and ease their way in. Cutter wanted to catch up with the boys and Raylee was desperate to see the horses again. When they walked into the stables, they received a big welcome back from everyone and it was like no time had passed at all.

"You been bull riding again?" Ryan asked, when he saw the stitches on Cutter's face.

Cutter touched his cheek and grinned. "No sir... I just had some trouble last week at the show."

"What, did you have to fight for first place?" Jesse asked.

"You're more right than you know," Raylee said quickly, taking over the question. "And if you think his bull ride was good, you should've seen him in the final when he won on the filly." Raylee was very proud of Cutter's win at the show in Dallas and she hadn't stopped talking about it since.

They all looked at the new trophy she was wearing. It was rather large for a frame as small as hers and it was difficult to miss it. "Nice buckle," Ryan commented.

"Thanks," Raylee said shyly, now that the focus was turned to her. "How's everything going here?" she asked, to get an understanding of what she had missed in the last three months while she'd been in Texas, before going to the house to see her father.

"Apart from your parents fighting, the budget cuts, and Tyler leaving, everything's exactly the same," Randall said, to give her a quick overview of the downside.

"I hope you didn't get into too much trouble over the colt," she said, since it was Randall and Jesse who had arranged for him to leave.

"Your dad was pissed off when he found out the colt was gone," Jesse stated, giving her a warning of what had been a very sore point over the last couple of months.

"But not as pissed as he was when he found out how it was paid for," Randall added.

Raylee hesitated. "You heard about that?"

"Everybody heard about it," Jesse said with annoyance. "And we've heard about it every day since."

Raylee was angry that her father had shared those details with everyone. "Well, there's more to it than that. Trust me," she said.

"There always is," Randall agreed, not wanting to be in the middle of their family drama. "Anyway, it's good to see you both. Welcome back."

They all stood around the tack room catching up on the last three months. When Raylee had left for Texas, Randall took over the complex, making all the decisions and delegating to the boys the new programs that were put in place. Raylee had insisted that they continue with the kids' riding school each month, since she was so fond of the children and they remained close to her heart.

Allan Tremayne was so annoyed with how things turned out, that he cut the training and breeding budgets down. Everything had to be re-evaluated and restructured, especially with the colt gone.

When Raylee's parents separated, they each took their share of the business. Evelyn kept the vineyard and restaurant, while Allan took over the complex and the cattle. Together they still owned the family company that operated the property development, since it was too big and too successful to pull it apart, and they wanted to pass it on to their children one day. There were often times when they had to put their personal issues aside and work side by side, although it was mostly Allan who drove the business forward.

It left the three boys to divide their time between the complex and the vineyard. Allan and Evelyn agreed to share the costs between them, allowing everything to stay as normal as they possibly could for the sake of the boys. And they couldn't complain. A job like theirs was hard to come by and they devoted all their spare time to rodeo when they could...

As Cutter rode through the field of flowers on the ranch, his thoughts came back to the afternoon ahead of him. He pulled the mare up and decided to take a walk through them, brushing his hand over the colorful wild flowers as he leaned down. Raylee had been the one who would pick a bunch for the graves and since she left the ranch, Cutter had only been to the resting place once, for his mother's birthday.

He tied the mare up to the fence that overlooked the graves and walked through the squeaky wrought iron gate. Although it had been a sunny day and it was peaceful, the place was starting to look unloved and not at all cared for as the weeds were popping up everywhere in tiny clusters. He laid the fresh flowers at the bottom of his mother's headstone and read it, like he did every time he visited. He looked at Macca's grave. He missed them both. It was a case of being given life's lessons the hard way, and he'd learnt those lessons without a choice. He stood up. It was all the time he had, but he needed to go there, if only for a short while.

As he stood there looking at the graves, his thoughts went back to Australia...

It had been more of a hope than a positive thought when Cutter and Raylee left the complex and drove to the house. They knew it wasn't going to be easy but they were going to do this together, and while they were both scared of the outcome, it wasn't as scary as the thought of being apart.

When Cutter pulled the hire car around the roundabout, they could see her father's black BMW parked outside the garage and knew that he was home. It was tempting to turn the car around and leave, but Cutter picked up Raylee's hand and gave it a squeeze, and confirmed that no matter what happened next, they would let nothing come between them. Although with the time that had passed over the last three months, Raylee was feeling slightly more confident than Cutter was.

As they walked up the path to the front door, Raylee was looking around at everything and she began to feel anxious. It was spring and the grounds were in perfect order as usual, with not a leaf on the ground or a twig out of place. Raylee knew the front door would be unlocked, but she wondered if she should knock first before going inside. But this was her home, the house she'd lived in for the past ten years and knocking on the front door seemed like a strange thing to do. She reached for the handle, then carefully and slowly walked in, looking around to see who was home.

"Hello?" she called out hesitantly, taking one steady step into the room at a time. "Is anyone home?"

There was no answer.

Raylee walked into the kitchen, then wandered over to the window that overlooked the pool and back deck. Cutter stood still, looking around the house while reliving his very first days there. Not much had changed, and he wondered if Raylee had missed her home.

"Raylee?" Cutter heard Allan Tremayne's voice before he saw him. He came out of his sitting room and walked straight to her and he was more than happy. "You're home."

"Hey, Dad," she said, giving her father a smile in return, and he pulled her in and hugged her tight.

"When did you get back?" he asked, when he pulled back to look at her.

"A couple of hours ago. I've been down at the barn."

"Your mother will be so pleased to see you," he said. "I'll give her a call."

Allan turned towards the phone and saw Cutter standing in the kitchen. There was a strain of silence that was deafening, and Allan Tremayne looked embarrassed that his reunion with his daughter had not been a private moment...

Cutter looked at his watch and untied the mare. It was time to keep riding. He left the resting place and rode through the back pasture, checking the cows from a distance. He didn't want to be late. Everything was looking good and he rode towards the eastern boundary, aware that the minutes were closing in and revisiting that dreadful day...

Allan stood up straight and puffed out his chest. "What the hell are you doing here?" he asked Cutter abruptly.

"Dad," Raylee said severely to intercept the question.

"No. It's alright," Cutter said, raising his hand slightly towards Raylee. "Maybe I should've waited outside." He turned to walk towards the door.

"Wait," Raylee called out loudly for him to stop. "We're not going to do this again. We need to talk about this."

Cutter hadn't made it to the door before he turned around.

"The only thing we need to talk about it why he's here," Allan said to Raylee.

"Dad, you're going to hear what we've got to say whether you like it or not," Raylee said strongly to pull her father up.

Cutter walked back into the room. It had been less than a week since his fight with Tommy Parker at the show. While his blackened eye had started to settle down, it was the cut on his lip and the stitches on his cheek that were the obvious signs he'd been in some sort of trouble. He looked all messed up.

"Alright then. Let's talk," Allan said smartly, although Cutter could tell that he was far from interested in listening to what either of them had to say.

Raylee felt relieved. For the first time, she believed that her father was prepared to listen and maybe he would begin to understand.

The three of them sat opposite each other on the couch. Cutter and Raylee sat on one side and Allan on the other. The start of this conversation was going to be a sticking point and Cutter wasn't really sure where to begin, even though he had rehearsed it so many times in his head while on the long flight over. It was awkward, and he discreetly rubbed his ribs for a bit of comfort, in case they were the reason for his sudden shortness of breath.

Raylee looked at Cutter. She could tell that he wasn't sure of what to say first. He only had two words he had to address. Sorry, and marriage. But neither of those words were finding their way out of his mouth. He knew they were the last two words that Raylee's father wanted to hear. He'd tried to apologize to her father before, when he caught them in bed together the day after the rodeo, but his apology was quickly dismissed. Cutter guessed that the last thing Allan wanted to hear now, was that he loved his daughter and wanted to marry her. Except that it was the one and only reason he was there.

"Well, let's hear it," Allan prompted, as he sat back with his arms stretched out either side of the couch and his boot crossed over his knee.

"Mr Tremayne," Cutter began, and Raylee started to feel at ease now that he had found his voice. She was just hoping that he chose the right words. "I've already tried to tell you how sorry I am the last time I was here. And I'd tell you again if I thought it would help. But for you to forgive me, sir, you need to wanna hear it."

Cutter was off to a good start, although Allan didn't say a word. He just listened, and Raylee wondered what was really going on inside her father's head.

"So much has happened in my life. Things that you'll never begin to know or understand until you get to know me. But I'm the man I am today because of your daughter. She helped me get my career and my life back on track and

I couldn't have done it without her." He gave Raylee a quick smile while he squeezed her hand. "And I need you to know that I love her, and I want your permission to marry her."

Raylee was relieved to hear those words and she looked at her father, expecting the same response. The stare between Cutter and Mr Tremayne was intense, then Allan leaned forward on the couch and rested his elbows on his knees and put his head down momentarily...

As Cutter rode the mare along the boundary fence, he came across the gate that joined his ranch to Johnny's and he swung it open enough to ride through. When Cutter and Johnny were younger, it was how they would get to each other's house. Often they'd saddle their horses and out they'd ride, meeting at the gate where they would make a plan on which ranch they'd ride over and what they were going to do next. Two young ranchers, full of adventure and pretending to know exactly what they were doing, looking over everything as they rode past.

As they grew up, the gate was rarely used. It was faster and more convenient to go there by truck, especially when they would head into town on a Saturday night and hang out at the local diner where they caught up with the girls from school.

Cutter hadn't used the gate to Johnny's ranch for some time and it made him feel like a kid all over again. He knew Johnny's ranch as well as his own. It was a reminder of his childhood as he rode through the open pastures and headed for the house, inspecting Johnny's cattle as he went by. Mostly it was out of habit.

When the house came into view, Cutter could see there was a lot going on. It was more than busy. He rode through the last gate and straight into the barn where he unsaddled the mare. After giving her a quick brush, he put her into an empty stall, making sure she had enough hay and water. It was never unusual for Cutter and Johnny to use each other's barn like their own, since they had shared so much time there together growing up.

He straightened out his shirt when he stood tall and repositioned his hat after running his hand roughly through his hair, then he left the barn and walked to the house. With his hands deep inside his pockets, Cutter looked down at his feet as he walked.

Johnny caught sight of him. "Here he is... We were just talking about you," he said, and he left the guests and gave Cutter a brotherly hug that was well overdue.

"What... Did you think I wasn't gonna turn up?" Cutter asked.

"I knew you'd be here. I just wasn't expecting you to be on time," he joked.

Cutter looked around. Many people from town and some of the neighbors had gathered and he noticed how well dressed everyone was.

"How do I look?" Cutter asked, when it struck him that maybe he was a little underdone.

Johnny laughed. "Like you always do."

Cutter took a moment to admire how the place looked. "You've been busy," he said.

"Let's just say that the last two days have been out of control here," Johnny stated, and Cutter believed it.

"Then you'll be glad when it's over."

"And so will you," Johnny agreed, and he reached for Cutter's shoulder. "Now, just give me a minute and I'll be right back."

Johnny left in a hurry and went inside the house. Not wanting to get caught up in the crowd, Cutter walked over to the table when it was clear of people to pour himself a glass of water. He didn't want to dehydrate even though the warm day had cooled down in the afternoon. It had been a long time since breakfast and he was now starting to regret missing lunch. As he held the glass under the water dispenser, he began to stare at nothing and his thoughts drifted back to Australia again...

Allan Tremayne was sitting silently on the couch with his head down, in deep thought. What was going through his mind was anyone's guess, leaving Cutter and Raylee anxious for his response. He looked up, giving Cutter the death stare that he had seen a few times before. "Over my dead body," Allan said in a controlled voice.

"What?" Raylee said sharply, deeply surprised by his reaction.

"I said, over my dead body," her father repeated more sternly.

"I heard what you said, but aren't you listening?" Raylee asked. "We're going to get married," she announced.

"Like hell you are." Allan stood up to intimidate them both. "And you," he said, pointing to Cutter arrogantly. "You're nothing but a lying thief."

Cutter got to his feet quickly to defend himself. "Excuse me?" he demanded, expecting a full explanation. Raylee stood up too and held onto his arm.

Allan was fired up and ready to go to war. "You come here as a guest of this house and you take my daughter home with you," he said aggressively. "When I go to the stables, I find the horse you trained had mysteriously disappeared and then I find money stolen from my credit card." Allan was furious and he let Cutter have it. "And let's not forget what else you've taken of Raylee's that wasn't yours to take." He was talking about her innocence, although Cutter didn't need reminding about that.

"I'm sorry you feel that way, but we've already decided whether you like it or not," Cutter said in a matter of fact way.

It was at that point that Allan reached over and pushed Cutter on the shoulder with a force to direct him towards the door. Cutter didn't like that he was being manhandled that way and in defense, he grabbed Allan Tremayne by the shirt while Raylee stood there and yelled for them to stop...

Cutter's flashback was interrupted by Johnny's return when he touched him on the shoulder again. "Where are you?" Johnny asked.

Cutter looked confused. "What do you mean where am I? I'm right here," he said, as if it should have been obvious.

"I mean your head. You looked like you were somewhere else."

Cutter had a vision of being face to face with Raylee's father. "Yeah, I guess I was. But I'm here now," he confirmed, to let Johnny know that he was alright. "If there's enough time, I think I'll go for a walk."

"Sure. But don't be long," Johnny said.

Cutter took a walk over to a small yard with a mare and young foal, just to be on his own again. When he leaned on the rail, the mare walked up to him while the foal hesitated and held back. Johnny had already discussed with Cutter that he needed the foal broken in when it was old enough. Cutter leaned down and stepped through the rail and into the yard. He rubbed the mare down all over, while edging the foal closer as he held out his hand to make contact. Within no time at all, he had the foal standing still and enjoying his touch. His presence was gentle and he was soon all over it.

The guests that had gathered were standing in front of the house, watching Cutter with the foal, while he was miles away. Thousands of miles in fact, while he was reliving his run-in with Allan Tremayne...

"Stop it," Raylee yelled to no avail, as Cutter and her father were so riled up now and were in each other's face. "What do you think you're both doing?"

The scene was reminiscent to the fight Cutter and Tommy had at the show, and she knew how that had ended. The last thing Raylee wanted now was for Cutter to throw a punch at her father. Surely it wouldn't come to that?

"Get out of my house," Allan demanded.

Cutter released Allan's shirt slowly when he realized what he had done. He knew he'd just stepped over the line and the return from that point would be all but none. At least he didn't throw a swing. "Alright. If that's how you wanna do this. But Raylee's coming with me."

"Well, the way I see it," Allan said in a very controlled manner as if he'd given it a lot of thought. "She's staying with me. We all know she can't get back on that plane with you until she applies for another visa. And who knows how long that will take. So it looks like you'll be the one leaving, and she's got nowhere to go." Allan looked satisfied when he delivered the final blow.

Cutter and Raylee both knew this and it seemed that her father was using it to drive a division between them. Cutter looked at her. "I'll be at the barn," he said to Raylee, and he left the house to let her see what she could do to resolve it…

While Cutter was making a good connection with the foal in the yard, it was suddenly spooked and ran behind the mare again. Cutter turned around to see Johnny leaning on the rail, watching him.

"You scared her," Cutter said. "I don't think she likes your hat."

"Or maybe you're not as good as you thought you were," Johnny teased.

"Now that's bullshit and you know it."

"Yes sir, I know it. I was just trying to convince you of it," Johnny said, and he looked towards the house. "Everyone's waiting to start… If you're ready?"

Cutter looked around again at the house and the guests as if he was nervous, and he took another deep breath. "Yeah, bro. I'm ready," he said. "I'm more than ready."

# Chapter Two

As the sun was sinking low towards the west, it cast long shadows across the yard. The warm air from the day lowered in temperature to a subtle coolness as a slight breeze picked up, swirling tiny buds off the trees.

It had a hazy look to it that reminded Cutter of his younger years and he wondered where all those years had gone. From a little boy riding his horse without a care in the world, to a man who had the sole responsibility of the ranch now and was about to embark on a new chapter of his life. He began to feel anxious again. It had been a long nine months on his own and it had been without a doubt the loneliest time of his life. Spending every night alone, listening to the stream in the silence of his own misery, and every day spent busily working to avoid the uncertain heartache. It had been wearing him down gradually and he wasn't sure just how much more he could take.

He looked to the house and shifted his focus. Everything he had felt over the last nine months was now gone. Knowing that the girl he was going to marry was about to walk through the doors of the house gave his nerves a twitch to the next level.

When Cutter finally received the long awaited phone call from Raylee to say that her visa had been granted, she immediately booked herself on the next flight out of Sydney, much to the disappointment of both her parents, who had done everything they could to keep her there. Even trying to buy her contentment.

Her father had traded in her car, buying the next model up and stacking it with so many features that it was like sitting at the controls of a cockpit. With the colt gone and no sign of him coming back, he bought her a nice young mare, although she could feel nothing for her compared to the colt. Allan Tremayne had tried everything he could to get Raylee's mind off Texas, but when her visa came through, she all but had her bags packed and was ready to go.

Out of the deepest love for her parents, she gave them one last invitation to go with her. Raylee's disappointment was realized when both her mom and dad declined to take up the offer and didn't want any part of it. She cried all the way to Sydney until she boarded the plane, while the flight to Dallas was a chance to rest and unwind.

Once Marnie knew that Raylee was on her way, she insisted that Cutter didn't see her before the big day. She dropped everything and headed to the airport to pick Raylee up, spending the next two days in Dallas with her shopping for a dress. It left Johnny and Emma at home to plan a wedding, and Cutter back at the ranch training the horses and working on the cattle. The days were long, and knowing that Raylee was only a short distance away made the nights stretch out too. She was close, yet she was so far away and three days to Cutter felt like an eternity.

Cutter stood at the front next to Johnny, taking in every detail. He was sure that nobody had any sleep in the last few days, as everything looked perfect. Dozens of chairs were lined up, lights hung from the trees, and tables were set for the celebration afterwards.

"Thanks for being here with me, bro," Cutter said quietly.

"Hey, I owed you this one," Johnny replied, as Cutter had been his best man when he married Emma years ago.

When the Pastor called everyone in, people took their seats. For the first time, Cutter saw Pete, Beth and his two sisters, Aimee and Cassie. He made eye contact with them and felt their need to reach out to him. He scanned the guests further and saw familiar faces all looking at him, and he suddenly felt another rush of nerves.

All those anxious feelings he had about returning to competition, his fight to keep the ranch from going under, and the reservations he had about meeting his real dad and new family, were nothing compared to what he was feeling now.

This was it. As he put his hands up to his face, he took a deep breath in, then let it go and straightened out his shirt for the fifth time that afternoon, before he adjusted his hat. He was fidgeting while he was staring at the door of the house, not wanting to miss anything.

Johnny noticed, and it wasn't until he looked down at Cutter's boots and saw that he'd not even remembered to take off his spurs, that he knew just how nervous Cutter was.

"Is this really happening?" he asked Johnny, just in case he was dreaming again as he'd done so many times before, and Johnny could only laugh.

When the door of the house opened, Cutter's heart gave another rush. It was only Marnie, and he relaxed and breathed easy again. She stepped out onto the porch and walked down the steps towards him. Cutter hadn't seen her for a couple of days and it surprised him just how dressed up she was. When she neared the front, she gave Cutter a huge smile then took the front seat.

Everyone was now seated.

Cutter took another deep breath and pulled at the collar on his shirt when the music began. Coming through the front door and onto the porch was Emma, and Cutter could hear Johnny sigh as if it was the first time he'd ever seen her. Cutter looked at him, although Johnny was too engaged with his wife to even notice. That's what he loved about Johnny and Emma. They were so close and so right for each other.

She walked down the steps in a long flowing dress, carrying a bouquet of flowers in shades of pink and ivory that hid her large tummy. Cutter did admit, he'd not seen her look that way very often and even at five months pregnant, he thought she looked beautiful.

His eyes went straight back to the door of the house and he saw Doug walk out with Raylee holding onto his arm. They stopped at the edge of the porch while Raylee looked to the front, wanting desperately to see him.

"Woah," Johnny said when he first laid eyes on Raylee, except that this time there was no sigh. "You lucky son of a bitch," he said quietly to his best friend, and while Cutter couldn't speak, he was thinking exactly the same thing.

Her strapless and tightly fitted dress hugged her waist in and fell to a full skirt, which was finely beaded with silver thread. Her skin was tanned and her long blonde hair was pulled up, revealing her bare neck and shoulders. She held tightly onto Doug's arm as they carefully walked down the steps and made their way behind Emma to the front of the aisle. When Emma reached the front, she looked at Johnny, throwing him her loving eyes. Although they had been married for almost six years, they were still like newlyweds and Cutter admired every part of their relationship. She stood on the opposite side next to the Pastor and she turned around to watch Raylee and Doug do the long walk.

That's when Emma lost it, and Cutter could hear her sob which could have easily brought it out of him too, if he wasn't so happy to see Raylee walking down the aisle towards him. He beamed. When they reached the front, the music died down suddenly and Cutter took Raylee by the hands when Doug stepped back to sit in the front row next to Marnie.

For the first time in nine months, Cutter and Raylee faced each other. Their eyes were drawn into each other's and before the Pastor had a chance to begin, Cutter leaned down and kissed her. He let go of her hands and held her in an embrace that should have been left for the end of the ceremony. He couldn't help it, while everyone whistled and applauded in complete support and approval. This kiss had been a long time coming. This moment had been on his mind for months and he pulled back to look at her momentarily, before he reached down and kissed her again.

"I missed you," he said to her, over the noise of their family and friends.

"Not as much as I missed you," she said softly in return.

"Are we ready to begin?" the Pastor asked, since he wasn't sure if he should interrupt their very private but public moment.

Cutter couldn't take his eyes off her. "Yes sir… We're ready now."

While the Pastor spoke of love and marriage, Cutter was lost in thoughts of her. He wasn't as interested in what the Pastor was saying, the details of her dress or the way she had done her hair. He was lost in the thought that they were finally together and nothing or no one could do anything to change that now.

He did notice though, that she was wearing the white gold and pearl drop earrings that he had bought for her the last time he was in Dallas visiting his sisters. They had gone shopping and the girls helped to pick them out. He'd kept them locked away in his top drawer for months, waiting for this day. He'd only sent them over yesterday, when Johnny was used as the messenger.

Raylee looked up into Cutter's face. The cut on his cheek from the fight at the show last year was healed and had left a faint line that was only visible if you were up close as they were now. His smile was natural and she could see that loving sparkle in his blue eyes, which deepened the fine lines on the sides of his face that were otherwise unnoticeable. Raylee could tell that he was happy.

When the Pastor asked for the ring, Cutter turned to Johnny and he passed it to him. He held it in his hand and looked at it. Just as he'd promised, he'd bought Raylee a ring of her own. She had worn his mother's ring every day while they were apart and it was now time for Cutter to give Raylee the gift of his heart. He held her hand and pushed it onto her finger, remembering the day that Macca and his mom had done the same thing. Raylee hadn't seen the ring until now and when she looked at it, her happiness turned to tears. She didn't want to cry and had promised herself that she wouldn't, but Cutter had bought her the most beautiful diamond ring and it was perfect in every way.

When they were pronounced man and wife, Cutter looked to the Pastor for permission. "You may kiss your bride now," he said, and Cutter didn't need to be told twice. He put his arms around her and pulled her in close, kissing her accompanied by an eruption of applause from their guests.

When they turned around and looked at everyone, Raylee threw her arm in the air, still holding her flowers as the celebrations were just beginning.

When they walked up the front steps and onto the porch, Raylee turned around to lean on the railing and she looked out at the sky. The breeze was blowing the clouds in front of the moon and the stars were coming out at intervals. Cutter leaned in behind her and kissed her softly on the neck.

"Welcome back, Mrs Jones," he said warmly, now they were back at the ranch and alone for the first time.

"I like the sound of that," she replied. "It's so good to be home."

"And I like the sound of that." Cutter was still snuggled in behind her when he found the zipper at the back of her dress and pulled it down.

Raylee wriggled and turned around laughing. "What are you doing?"

"Well, looking at the size of this dress, I didn't think it would fit through the front door," he said, and he let it fall to the floor. She was standing on the porch in the dark, wearing her white satin knickers and matching corset. When he looked down, it was her brown cowgirl boots with white lacy topped socks that Cutter noticed. He held her hand for balance while she stepped out of the dress which was now sitting in a heap on the floor, and he was totally entertained.

"I knew there was a real cowgirl under there somewhere," he said, and he swept her up and carried her to the front door.

"What about my dress?" she asked, looking back over his shoulder.

"I promise you, Raylee Jones, you'll never need to wear that dress again," he stated, and he left it there, meaning every word.

He carried her upstairs to the bedroom. When Cutter turned the light on, Raylee looked around. The first thing she noticed was how different the room looked and she tried to figure out everything that had changed. Cutter put her down and she wandered around the room, running her hand over everything. The trophy saddle that had sat in the corner for many years had gone down to the barn and was now replaced with a reading chair. She had her own wardrobe in the opposite corner, waiting to be filled up with her clothes. The curtains were colorful and fresh, and the new quilt was suited to them both. But it was the change of color on the walls that Raylee loved the most.

"Did you do all this for me?" she asked, while she was still looking around.

"Yes ma'am. I hope you like it."

"I love it. Everything is just perfect," she said, and Cutter could tell that she meant it.

It had never occurred to Cutter to settle down until he met Raylee Tremayne. This day had been a long time coming and it was finally here. All that was left to do now, was to show her just how much he loved her. When the room fell dark, Raylee looked around to see where he was.

Standing by the door, he had switched the light out and was walking over to her while he was unbuttoning his shirt. There was enough light from the moon to see that his eyes had locked onto hers, and he threw his shirt to the floor. He picked up her hands and placed them on his bare chest and he closed his eyes when he drowned himself in her neck. He was kissing his wife, absorbed in her perfume and soft skin and he suddenly wondered if this moment was real, until her hands wandered with intent and he felt his buckle loosen.

She laid back on the bed and he leaned over her. "Aren't you going to take your hat off?" she asked, looking up into his face.

He kissed her again. "I would... but I don't think there's enough time for that," he said seriously, and she laughed at how truthful he was.

"Good morning," Cutter said, when Raylee finally made it downstairs the next day.

She had no concept of the time and had woken up to the smell of breakfast cooking. For a moment, she thought that Marnie was back home, until she wandered into the kitchen and saw Cutter standing by the stove cooking up a big breakfast. She was wearing nothing but his black shirt with the sleeves rolled up, and she walked up behind him and wrapped her arms around his waist.

"Wow, I'm so hungry and that smells amazing," Raylee stated, and she stood on her toes to look over his shoulder into the frying pan. "You know, this could be your new job now."

He turned the stove off and spun around and held her. "Oh no... Don't get too used to it. You've got me for a full week. But after that, I've gotta get back into some training."

It was now going to be just the two of them, since Marnie had already packed her bags before the wedding and was going on a road trip with Doug. Just as she'd promised, Marnie had waited for Raylee to arrive back at the ranch and now it was time for them to hit the road for a well deserved vacation. They had no set direction or time plans in mind, and they would only come home when they'd had enough of living out of their suitcases. Although Cutter and Raylee were both pleased for them, they knew they would miss Marnie's company and her cooking.

Raylee looked at the table. It was already set and she could see that Cutter had put a lot of thought into it. He picked her up and sat her on the kitchen counter, then pulled her in close to kiss her.

"You were amazing last night," he complimented, while he was nibbling at her neck.

"I know," she said, then she started to giggle. "I had no idea that I'd not get you to the full eight seconds... I've seen you ride a bull longer than that."

He couldn't disagree. "You know the first one didn't count... Right?"

"Well all I can say, is that you were lucky you scored well in the second go-round."

"Hey, and what about the final?"

Raylee laughed some more. "You always save the best for last," she said, then she kissed him again.

The honeymoon was well underway.

While Raylee was still sitting on the kitchen counter, they heard a door slam shut and the sound of a truck outside. They went out to the front porch to see who was there. They were greeted by the mare, who was tied to the fence with her saddle off which was sitting on the top rail. Johnny had ridden her home while Emma drove the old green truck to pick him up, and they were both waving out the windows as they drove off up the long driveway, the horn blasting all the way.

"Hey, look," Cutter said.

Raylee's dress had been picked up off the porch and was laid out nicely on the swing and her bags were placed neatly by the door. She laughed. "Oh, I can only imagine how that looked... They'll be talking about us all the way home for sure."

They leaned on the rail and watched as the truck reached the top of the driveway and fell silent. "Now, how about that breakfast?" Cutter said, and they went back inside, taking a bag each.

They spent the next hour talking over breakfast about the last three days. Raylee couldn't believe that no one had told her about Emma's pregnancy. Emma had wanted it to be a big surprise and it was. Cutter admitted how nervous he was in the lead up to the wedding, and that he was tempted to sneak over during the night, just to make sure she was really there. They talked about the day, how it was thrown together at the last minute and how perfect it was. There was not one thing that either of them would change, except for the very noticeable absence of Allan and Evelyn Tremayne.

It had broken Raylee's heart that her parents were not in support of her decision, since she had truly believed they would stand their ground to wear her down until they eventually realized that nothing was going to hold her back. Even her brothers had given it their best shot to convince Raylee to stay at home and make her life there, trying to line her up to go out on a date with someone from her own town and of the same age.

But they all fully underestimated the love Raylee had for her Texan cowboy.

"You know, I have such a big family back home with my parents, brothers and two sister-in-laws. I've got nieces and nephews, uncles and aunties and my grandparents are still alive on both sides. I've got so many cousins that I don't really know half of them... And you. You've only got me." She looked at him lovingly. "And I want you to know that I'll never let you down. I'll always be your family and even though you don't think so, it seems that you're the only family I've got left too."

Cutter loved that. It was so true. It seemed that the only close family they both had, was each other.

"And that's why I promise you that I will do everything I can to make you happy," he said in return. "Anyway, who needs a big family? It will just be me and you and a couple of kids. Right?"

"Right," she agreed, without going into a full blown discussion about when and how many. There would be time for that later. For now, they were both needing and wanting the undivided attention of each other.

"You wanna go to the barn?" he asked.

"Absolutely."

After a quick clean up in the kitchen, they went upstairs to get ready for the day. Cutter took Raylee's bags up to their room and she opened them, looking for something to wear. He spread out on the messed up bed and watched her sort through her jeans and shirts, looking for her favorites. With so much lost time to catch up on and no one around, they found a few distractions that were not at all planned, taking up most of the morning.

It was closer to lunch time when Cutter was downstairs waiting for Raylee, and she came down looking like the real cowgirl he remembered. "Now that's better," he said, and he sharpened the front of her hat before stepping out onto the porch where they pulled their boots on.

The day was warming up and the sun had a sting to it that was early for the season. They untied the mare and Raylee walked her to the barn while Cutter carried the saddle. It was exactly as she remembered it. Nothing had changed. She was keen to see the colt again and meet the young horses that Cutter had taken on for clients.

He led the first one into the barn. A blue roan filly.

"She's from the Blue-Jean Renegade bloodlines," he announced proudly.

"Wow, that's impressive... She's beautiful," Raylee stated. "I've heard of that horse but I've never seen any of his lines."

"Just wait 'til you see her move."

"So what do you call her?"

"I don't call her anything... I haven't needed to."

Raylee looked the filly all over. "What about Bluey?"

Cutter didn't care what the horses were called. He was there to train them, not to give them silly names. But with more horses now, it was something that they needed to do. "Okay," he agreed. "Predictable, and very Australian, but Bluey it is."

Raylee found her saddle in the tack room while Cutter brought the next horse in.

"Recognize this boy?" he asked.

It was the colt. Raylee left the saddle on the rail and went up to him, fully pleased to see him again. She rubbed him between the eyes and down his nose while the colt responded to her presence.

"I think he knows me," she said with excitement.

"Well he should... I've been talking about you every day. In the end he was the only one who would listen."

Raylee was not amused. "Very funny," she said, giving him that look.

Together they threw their saddles on and went for a ride. Raylee stopped on the peak of the first rolling hill and looked back down at the house. She had missed the ranch more than she realized. It had a fresh new look to it that could only be explained by it being her new home now.

They rode through the open pastures and Cutter gave Raylee a rundown on the current stock situation. He gave her an update on which cattle had been used in the cutting pen already, what part of the cycle they were at, and how long it would be before they reached their targeted weight. All the cattle were at different stages and Raylee could see that Cutter had the program working well.

The cows in the back pasture still had a few more weeks before they were ready to start calving out. They were in good buckle, shaded well with plenty of water and feed.

On the way home, they rode along the side boundary, checking the fence lines and stock that were only a couple of weeks away from finishing.

"And in this mob," Cutter said, "somewhere," he added reluctantly, "is Lucky."

It got Raylee's immediate attention. "Lucky's in that mob?" she asked, anxious to see her again.

"Yes ma'am, she sure is. They all look the same but I know she's in there somewhere," he teased, and Raylee knew that Cutter could easily have picked her out of the herd.

Lucky was the first calf that Raylee had pulled out. When Cutter had to put the mother down, Raylee took it upon herself to raise her. She gave her a name and the lucky little calf followed Raylee around the barn like she was her new mother. When Raylee had to go back to Australia, she expected that Cutter would take exceptionally good care of her. As she looked into the open pasture, it was clear that Cutter was taking very good care of her... the cowboy way.

They rode along steadily side by side, wasting time and soaking up every bit of the afternoon. When they reached the last gate, the barn came into view in the distance. The colt was feeling good, while the roan was still young and was getting used to the routine of the ranch.

"Can I ask you something?" Cutter said without hesitation, though it was with a slight sense of uncertainty as if he was treading lightly.

"Sure. What is it?" she asked.

Raylee could tell that whatever Cutter was going to ask, he'd already given it a lot of thought. "What do you think about us getting some help... with the ranch?"

"But I'm here now. I'll help you," she said quickly, as if it were the obvious answer to his unnecessary dilemma.

"But you do realize that I've got two young ones in training, plus another three that have only just been broken in and need handling, as well as all the others. And there's more cattle now."

Raylee could see that they were going to be busy.

"And with Marnie away, there'll be so much work to do at the house and the office still needs tending to," he pointed out.

She could see where he was coming from and was just thinking as they rode home.

"I don't wanna put all this extra pressure on you, and I still want us to have our time together," he added.

"Who'd you have in mind?" she asked, while she immediately started her own thoughts on the matter.

"Well, I've got a couple of ideas, but I really need to think about them and talk to you about it first."

It made perfect sense. With more horses, more cattle and no Marnie, Raylee was starting to see the workload mounting up and it was only her first day back.

"Alright. As long as you promise me that we have all of this week. I don't want to see anyone before next Sunday."

"Agreed," he said, and they rode into the barn and began to unsaddle the horses.

Raylee picked up the routine as if she had never been away. When Cutter wasn't watching, she began to straighten everything up in the tack room. It wasn't that it was messy, it was more that she liked everything to be organized and in order, exactly how she left it.

Cutter introduced her to the rest of the horses and they spent the next couple of hours before sunset, going over everything in the barn and yards, finishing with a tour of the new horse truck. Raylee spent the day surrounded by everything she had missed in the last nine months and she was happy to be back. Happy to be home.

As Cutter sat on the swing and began to sway, the squeak from each motion was beginning to annoy him. He looked at Cooper's empty basket by the door. She had made it well into the early winter months, until her arthritis, blindness and good old age kept her down. Marnie often moved her into the house on the cold nights and put her in front of the fireplace, then returned her back outside for a few hours through the day, much to Cooper's disgust.

It was when Cutter had come home from a three day show on a sunny day and seen an empty basket by the front door, that he knew Cooper was gone, and he couldn't bring himself to take the basket away just yet.

The porch door opened. Raylee came out holding two cups and she handed one to Cutter. They were halfway through their first week and it was going fast.

"I've thought about what you said. About getting some help and I think that I have the perfect answer," Raylee said when she sat down.

"But you don't know anyone here," Cutter stated. "How could you possibly come up with someone to help us?"

"Well, who did you have in mind?" she asked.

"You first. Who did you have in mind?" he responded.

"Someone you know well."

"Well I've thought of someone you know well too. Maybe we're thinking the same person."

Raylee sat sideways on the swing and they looked at each other, trying to read each other's mind. It was almost a game.

"Aimee," Cutter said, at the exact same time that Raylee dropped Jesse's name as her choice.

"Aimee?" she said, totally surprised. "But she doesn't know anything about horses."

"But it won't take her long to pick it up. I'll teach her how to ride, wash them and feed them. It's not that hard. And she's already asked me about having some time here before she goes to college," he explained. It was at the show last year that Cutter found out he had sisters and Aimee was now desperate to visit the ranch.

"But what about your training? I thought that if Jesse came over then we could set up the loft for him in the barn, and he knows everything already. Although not as much as you, but you can teach him. I'm sure he'd be more beneficial to your training."

Cutter hadn't thought about one of the Australian boys coming over. He'd racked his brain and thought of everyone he could think of, and knew that they'd already be tied up with other trainers.

"Do you think he'd come over?" he asked.

"All I can do is ask him. He can always say no," Raylee said. "But I'm sure he'd love the opportunity to take another step up in his career."

"He'd have to know he was here cutting, not bronc riding," Cutter half joked.

"Well with you as his boss, he'd have to do whatever you tell him."

It may have been a long shot, yet there was no harm in asking. When Cutter sat back and thought about it, it really was the perfect answer. Jesse had grown up on a small cattle property and had been working with cutting horses for the last three years at the Tremayne complex and had ridden at a few local shows. He wasn't tied down to any responsibilities in Australia, so why wouldn't he think it was a good, life changing, great idea?

"Leave it to me. I'll make the call tonight," Raylee said, and they finished their coffee in the quietness of the front porch.

# Chapter Three

Being confined to the house, the barn and the ranch for an entire week, without the interruption of phone calls, drop-in visitors or training sessions, was exactly what Cutter and Raylee both needed.

Every week apart had been torture, let alone nine full months. While one week back together was flying by like the blink of an eye.

"I can't believe he said yes," Cutter exclaimed over breakfast the next morning.

Raylee had made the phone call and without giving it a minute's thought, Jesse said he'd go and pack. The boys were having a miserable time at the Tremayne property after Raylee had left, with Allan and Evelyn at each other's throats, arguing over their irrational daughter's decision to leave, and the running costs of the vineyard and the complex. It wasn't a happy place to work anymore and when Jesse received the phone call from Raylee, he was all but leaving anyway. It only helped to make his decision easier.

They had also agreed that Aimee could come and stay for a while. She wanted to spend some time with her brother and new sister, and get to know them both better. They made up the bed for her in the spare room, a small bedroom opposite their own. Raylee gave it a fresh coat of paint while Cutter took the boxes of personal belongings of his parents down to the garage for storage. The room was coming along nicely, and they finished it off with a new quilt that Raylee had picked up one afternoon when they slipped into town unnoticed.

Standing back looking at the room, both thought that it was a job well done, even though it had taken up the last two days of their week alone.

"You know, I always thought this would make a good nursery," Cutter stated, and he put his arm around Raylee's shoulder.

"One day it will make a perfect nursery," she agreed. "But right now, the only baby going in there is your baby sister," she said. "What time are they arriving?"

Cutter looked at his watch. "Damn it. They'll be here in less than an hour," he said in a panic, as they were both far from being ready.

They cleaned up quickly and changed in just enough time to see the car coming down the driveway. They stood on the porch and watched it pull up in front of the house. All the family were there. They'd never been to Double J Ranch before and while Cutter had let down a lot of those barriers he'd spent his whole life putting up, he was now feeling nervous that his father was at his house, on his ranch, in his space.

The girls were both excited to see them again and they took a long look around at everything in the distance when they stepped out of the car.

"Wow, it's so pretty here," Cassie stated as if she was jealous. "You are so lucky," she said to her sister.

Aimee was taking it all in, admiring the view silently. They all stood around the car and exchanged their greetings before they made their way to the house. Pete and Cutter carried Aimee's bags inside and they all settled around the table, catching up on the last nine months. Raylee made lunch for everyone and it was relaxed, while they talked about the wedding, learnt about the ranch and laughed at Aimee's inexperience around the barn. She still wasn't sure what she'd got herself in for.

"She'll do a good job, and you won't recognize her when she's finished here," Cutter said in a positive way. "Just ask Raylee... She'll tell you."

They all looked at Raylee. "Yep... He's the best," she agreed, even though that was not what he meant.

"I must say, that I was surprised to get the call from you," Beth said. "I thought you'd want to be here on your own."

"To be honest, we do," Raylee replied. "But we can't do it all by ourselves and we've got more help arriving tomorrow anyway."

After lunch, Cutter took everyone to the barn to show them around. It was more of a quick look, since he would need to go into more detail when he had Aimee there on her own. They walked out past the day yards and Cutter introduced everyone to the horses.

"I can't believe they're worth so much money," Cassie said.

Cutter agreed. "Yes ma'am... This one here is worth four times your college fund I'm sure."

It was an unfamiliar world to them all, yet it was good for Pete and Beth to see what Cutter's life had become and to know that whatever happened after Pete's separation from Mary-Ann, that his son had been well cared for by Macca, who loved him like his own. Pete was quietly thankful for that.

It was getting late into the afternoon and was time for Pete and Beth to hit the road, much to the disappointment of Cassie, who would have been more than happy to stay with her sister. Aimee leaned on the porch rail and waved to her family as the car drove away and she watched them until they reached the road and went out of sight. She looked out at the view again while Raylee stood back, remembering her first look at the ranch. It was overwhelming for her back then, and now Aimee was feeling that same way.

Instead of looking across the street into the neighbor's front yard, she admired the barn and yards, thinking it was straight out of a movie scene. There were no city noises. No traffic. The only sounds were from the horses and cattle in the distance and the air was crystal clear, making her close her eyes and breathe it in. With the house set back from the road, there was a peacefulness from the rest of the world.

After she settled into her room, Aimee changed into her jeans and boots and came back downstairs to the kitchen.

"Wow, you look ready to start," Cutter stated.

"Ready when you are," she replied.

"Actually, I won't be starting 'til Tuesday. I'm picking up Jesse from the airport in the morning while Raylee takes you shopping in town."

"What are we shopping for?" she asked.

Raylee was equally curious and joined in. "Yeah, this is news to me," she said, as the word shopping got her attention immediately.

"Well, you're gonna need more than one pair of boots and one pair of jeans if you work here," Cutter informed her. "Trust me. Raylee knows all about that."

Aimee looked at her.

"I sure do," Raylee agreed. "If your jeans are clean and your boots have too much shine, he'll make you shovel shit all day," she said from personal experience.

Aimee then looked back at Cutter.

"True story," he said. "I've been known to turn ladies into cowgirls... It's my specialty."

"And after you become a real cowgirl, you won't ever want to go back to city life again," Raylee added.

"Well I'm not so sure about that," Aimee said confidently. "But we'll see."

Cutter looked at the time. "I'm going to the barn to feed up for the night."

"And I'm coming with you," Aimee said, and she jumped to her feet quickly and was only two paces behind him.

Raylee watched as they left the house to go to the barn. She had enjoyed a full week of being alone together, locked up on the ranch and not sharing their time with anyone. But with Aimee wanting to be Cutter's shadow, Raylee felt that the honeymoon was now over.

When Aimee wandered downstairs the next morning, she found the kitchen empty. She looked around. It was quiet, when she was expecting it to be alive and bursting with people, with the radio blaring and the morning activity in full swing, just like it was at her own home. She looked at the photos hanging on the kitchen wall and for the first time, she saw a picture of Cutter's mom. It gave her a strange feeling, as it just dawned on her that this woman was once married to her father.

She went out to the front porch and looked over at the barn and yards and couldn't see anyone. The blue truck that was parked at the side of the house yesterday was gone. Surely they haven't thrown her in the deep end so soon, expecting her to look after the ranch on her very first day? She pulled her shiny boots on and went for a walk.

She slid the barn door open and walked in. The smell hit her instantly and she could have easily dry retched, if she hadn't covered her mouth and nose with her hand. She walked in and found every stall empty. Looking over the gate into each stall, she found exactly where the stench was coming from.

"Yuk," she said to herself out loud, even though no one was there to give her a reply.

She wandered around some more, looking in the tack room at all the saddles, straps, ropes and pieces of leather that looked like they were useful for something, yet she had no idea what.

Next to the tack room was the feed room. It did have a nicer smell to it with bags of chaff and grains sitting on the floor waiting to be emptied into the feed bins. Bales of hay were stacked three bales high and a drum of molasses sat in the corner. Aimee thought that this would be the best room in the barn to work in.

She looked around. The smell of the barn was beginning to settle and she was getting more used to it now, especially with the door left open and a gentle breeze floating through. Then, something moved and she caught sight of it out the corner of her eye. It was her curiosity that made her hesitantly take a step closer towards the bag of chaff. She couldn't see anything. She gave it a soft kick and something ran out from behind the bag, over her boot and hid behind one of the feed bins. Aimee screamed and ran out of the feed room and out the barn door to escape.

Raylee had just arrived back at the barn to hear Aimee's calls of distress. She launched herself off the horse to see what was going on. She held the reins of the colt and rushed up to Aimee, who was panting uncontrollably.

"What is it?" Raylee asked in a panic.

Aimee couldn't answer. She looked whiter than a sheet and was gasping for each and every breath. She leaned over with her hand pressed tightly against her chest.

Raylee didn't know what had happened so she didn't know what to do for her. "Are you alright? Aimee. Talk to me," Raylee said.

"I... I... just... saw a... a... a mouse," Aimee struggled to get out.

Raylee laughed. "A mouse?"

"Yes," Aimee panted, followed by more gasps of short breaths that she pushed out hard.

Raylee laughed some more and put her hand on Aimee's back for unnecessary comfort. "Well, you'd better get used to that around here," she said without any sympathy.

When Aimee gained some control back, she stood up and managed only half a smile. She suddenly imagined how that must have looked and she was quick to be thankful that it was Raylee who was at the barn and not Cutter.

"Promise me you won't tell him," Aimee begged. Although Raylee was not prepared to make a promise like that, since it could always be saved for a good story over dinner.

"What are you doing down here anyway?" Raylee asked.

"I was looking for you. There was no one at the house, so I thought you must have been at the barn."

Raylee walked the colt towards the tack room. "Well, you missed your brother by about four hours," she said.

Aimee looked at her watch. "But it's only nine o'clock."

Raylee laughed again. "Exactly. You need to be up at five if you want to see him."

"As in five in the morning?" Aimee asked innocently.

"As in yes. He's up every morning before daybreak."

Aimee looked disgusted at the sound of it. "Why would he do that?" she asked.

"I'll tell you what. You give it a week, and you'll have the answer to that," Raylee replied.

Raylee unsaddled the colt and replaced his bridle with a halter, then led him to the wash bay. It was a good time to show Aimee how to wash a horse. Raylee explained about the different products they used and what the process was. Luckily for Aimee, the colt stood still like a big baby and they scrubbed him with suds all over. They talked and laughed about the mouse, and Raylee could see that Aimee was a city girl through and through.

After they threw a rug over him and put him back into his stall, the two girls went to the house to change out of their wet clothes. All the horses were fed early and Raylee had already taken a quick ride over the ranch before Aimee showed up at the barn. All they had to do now, was head to town to do some serious shopping and treat themselves to breakfast.

Aimee loved spending time with Raylee. She was like a big sister and was someone Aimee could talk to, when the last person you want to have those embarrassing conversations with is your mother. Raylee had come into Aimee's life at exactly the right time.

"What time will they be back?" Aimee asked about her brother, when they sat down opposite each other at the diner.

Raylee checked the time. "Not too much longer. He said he'd call me when they're back on the road," she explained.

"So how do you know Jesse?" Aimee asked.

"We went to the same school. But he's worked on our property for the last three years, handling horses and working in the vineyard."

"Does he cut too?"

"He's been to some shows back home and done quite well, but he leaves the training to the professionals," Raylee said. "But his specialty is broncs."

Aimee looked lost. "What's that?"

"You know... Bucking horses. You see them at every rodeo," Raylee explained, before she remembered that Aimee was a world away from any kind of horse or rodeo event.

"I've got so much to learn, haven't I?" she stated, without needing the obvious answer. "Is he any good?"

"Well, the last time I saw him ride, he rode the full eight seconds and won the event. So yeah... he's pretty good I suppose."

"But not as good as Cutter?"

Raylee looked at her with pride. "Aimee... No one is as good as your brother."

After a leisurely breakfast they went shopping. Raylee picked out some jeans, shirts and new boots for Aimee to try on. In fact, she picked out an entire new wardrobe. Everything that she would need and plenty of it.

When the boys called to say they were on their way home, Raylee hurried their shopping time along. "We'd better get going. We've got some stalls to clean out before they wonder what on earth we've done all morning."

They talked all the way home which at times was easy and other times awkward, with Aimee full of questions about Cutter and his life. She was wanting to know more about Mary-Ann and what really drove her father to his lowest point. Although Raylee would only fill her in on limited detail, since it wasn't her place to share that personal information and Aimee didn't need to know the ugly details anyway. She would have to ask her brother those questions when the time was right.

When Aimee walked back into the barn, the smell of horse manure hit her hard and she immediately put her hand back up to her face. She was looking at the ground for any sign of sudden movement as the mouse had her on high alert.

"How do you do it?" Aimee asked.

"Do what?" Raylee asked back.

"Put up with that smell?"

"What smell?"

It was clear that Raylee was so used to the smell of the barn that it didn't register to her that it was unpleasant. She laughed at Aimee, who was now pulling faces at the sight as well as the smell. Raylee took a rake and showed her how to pick through the straw for the manure and place it in the trolley.

Aimee was as much curious as she was naive. "Does this have to be done every day?"

"Don't worry... After a week of this, you'll be a professional."

"There's such a thing as a professional shoveler?"

Raylee tried hard to contain her laughter. "Not exactly... And just for the record, it's called a stable hand."

It was slow going, since Raylee was only working at a pace that Aimee could keep up with. They refilled the feed bins and tidied the tack room, all the while Aimee was on edge. Raylee showed her all the different products in the tack room and explained what they were used for. She made up a feed mix for the colt and explained what each grain was and how much was needed. It would take Aimee some time to know the routine, but with three of them working alongside her, Raylee was confident that she would pick it up quickly.

As the last halter was being hung up, Aimee heard the truck pull up outside the barn. "They're here," she said, as if it was a good reason to drop what she was doing and go out to meet them, and Raylee followed her out.

Jesse climbed out of the truck and looked around while Cutter went straight for his wife and gave her a good morning kiss. It had been less than a fortnight since Raylee had last seen Jesse back in Australia, and she greeted him with a hug as if he was family. Aimee stood back and waited for an introduction. Although Jesse was looking worn out from the long journey, he had an instant spark about him when Cutter introduced his sister.

"Hey," Jesse said, and he reached out with his hand. "Looks like Raylee's had you cleaning out the barn."

"How can you tell?" Aimee asked.

Jesse pointed to her face. She had a smear of something across her cheek that resembled what she had been shoveling out of the stalls. She wiped it away and looked at her hand while everyone laughed. She was embarrassed, and decided that it was better to laugh at herself than to show everyone what she was really feeling.

"No wonder that bad smell kept following me around," she stated.

Jesse found it quite cute at the same time as it was very funny. He also found her blue eyes and cheeky smile easy on the eye, while the colored streaks in her long hair had him confused. Jesse couldn't tell if Aimee was a blonde trying to be a brunette, or a brunette trying to be a blonde, until he lined her up next to her fair-haired brother.

"Let's get you settled upstairs then we'll go to the house for some lunch," Raylee said to Jesse, like the good host she was.

The afternoon was spent around the horses. It was the third time in a week that Cutter had to go through the introductions of the horses and explain their breeding and training programs, and while Jesse was taking it all in and was throwing endless questions his way, Aimee just tagged along and had no idea what any of it meant.

"And this girl comes from the legendary stud, Blondie's Rattle and Roll," Cutter explained, when he brought the palomino filly into the barn for exhibition. "Her owners run an oil company here in Texas and this is their first cutting horse."

"She's gorgeous," Aimee stated, and she rubbed her hand down the filly's neck.

Jesse was less complimentary. "Really, you think so?"

"Yeah... She's got more talent than good looks," Cutter agreed. "And you wanna be careful around this one. She's the boss around here and she'll let you know it," he said to Aimee.

While Aimee didn't know one good horse from another, she did recognize that she had a lot to learn. Listening to everyone talk was a good way to pick up as much knowledge as she could, without interrupting to ask the most ridiculous questions that would make her look completely stupid. What she didn't know, she would figure out over time.

When the sky was barely dark, Cutter called an end to the long day. Much to the disbelief of Aimee, who had never been to bed so early in her life. She climbed into bed and listened to the silence of the ranch. Only the night noises and the stream were helping the seconds tick by. She closed her eyes. It wasn't helping. She was still awake and was restless, tossing and turning, hoping her body would find a comfortable position that would settle her runaway mind. Bored and completely annoyed that she couldn't get to sleep, it was well past midnight when she last checked the time, and no sooner had she drifted off, than it felt as if it was time to get up again.

Five a.m. comes around quickly on the ranch, as Aimee soon found out. The alarm was making a revolting noise in her ear and she dragged herself out of bed and wandered over to the bathroom door, blurry-eyed. It was locked. She made her way back to her bed with her eyes only half open and she crashed back down again, pulling the covers up over her.

"You've got to be kidding me," Aimee said, when she made her way downstairs and saw everyone sitting around the table having a coffee and looking fresh, ready for work. "The sun's not even up yet."

"Good morning," Cutter said cheerfully. "Actually, we're running a bit late today... Lucky for you. Now we don't have to start without you."

Aimee grabbed a bowl down from the cupboard and found the cereal and milk. As she took the first spoonful, Cutter, Raylee and Jesse all stood up from the table and made their way to the door.

"Hey, hang on," Aimee called out with a mouthful. "Where are you going?"

"To work," Cutter announced, as if it should have been obvious. "Now, are you coming with us or should we meet you back here at lunch time?"

Aimee scoffed her cereal down quickly and ran for the porch, pulling her boots on while she watched them walk over to the barn. By the time she caught up, Cutter was already giving Jesse another rundown on the breeding of the young blue roan.

"Now, that's a nice type," Jesse said to Aimee, and while she totally agreed with him, she really couldn't tell the difference.

They found two more saddles in the tack room and when Cutter brought Macca's horse in, he gave the job to Jesse to show Aimee how to saddle her up.

Jesse stood close behind Aimee, helping her to put her boot into the stirrup. She held onto the horn and when he counted to three, he pushed her up and she threw her leg over the mare and landed in the saddle. After placing her feet into the stirrups correctly, he gave her some quick and easy instructions on the rein control. All she had to do now, was sit still and follow.

As they rode towards the gate, Aimee was squashed between everyone. Cutter rode out in front with Raylee and Jesse on either side, while Macca's horse just plodded along. The mare was quite old now, but she was safe and she knew the ranch better than any other horse.

Riding over the ranch, Raylee was so familiar with every pasture and fence line and it took her back to her very first ride there last year, while she listened to Cutter explain everything to Jesse as they rode on. The sun was breaking through the early morning mist and was hitting them on the back as they rode in and out of the shade, through the trees. The way Cutter spoke to Jesse was different to how he had explained everything to Raylee in those early days, since Jesse didn't need it given to him in simple terms like she had. Aimee was concentrating so hard on balancing and keeping up, that she didn't hear a word they said.

The ranch was looking good. Every pasture was in good shape and every fence was now in good repair. They could just focus on the training of the horses each day and which herds they would bring in for their next training sessions.

By the time they reached the back pasture where the cows were freely grazing, Aimee was starting to get the hang of it. Raylee willingly shared with everyone her first calf delivery experience, as they sat on a log in the shade under a tree and let the horses pick at the grass while they rested. They all laughed at her, and it made her realize just how far she'd come since that very first day.

Aimee stood up a little too quickly. "Ouch," she said, and she grabbed the inside of her legs. "That hurts."

Cutter laughed. "You just wait 'til tonight," he warned her ahead of time.

"Why?" she asked, thinking it was a reasonable question.

"Because you've gotta get home yet," he said, and he stood up and laughed at her some more while he untied the horse.

Although she struggled, Aimee pulled herself up and over the horse again without anyone's help while everyone else did the same. "I hope you're all having a good time, are you?"

It was clear that Aimee was completely out of her depth.

"Like I said, a week of this and you'll be a professional," Raylee encouraged.

"Now come on, Raylee, be fair," Cutter said. "Give her at least two."

The ride home was steady going. As they rode through each pasture, Jesse looked around. He could see why Cutter was an all round cowboy with the ranch giving him what many rodeo riders back home don't have. The real thing.

Back at the barn, Jesse helped Aimee off the horse. Her legs felt unstable from holding on so tight and he held her until she found her feet firmly on the ground and regained her balance. "Thank you. I think I've got it," she said, and he slowly let her go. Jesse showed her how to unsaddle the horse and together they prepped them all for the wash bay.

After a quick clean out of the stalls and four horses through for a wash, they headed to the house for breakfast. Cutter put his arm around Aimee to help her walk and he kept teasing her all the way to the front steps, making her feel quite useless.

"So, what are we doing after breakfast?" Aimee asked enthusiastically, when they all sat down around the table together.

"Well Aims," Cutter said lightly, "that's when the real work begins."

# Chapter Four

Every day Aimee was learning something new. Every ride, every stall cleaned and every horse washed and fed, she was becoming more efficient and more confident. Cutter sent her out on the daily ride over the ranch while everyone else took it in turns to go with her. She needed the experience in the saddle and everyone else needed the break so they could concentrate on their other chores.

With Marnie away and four of them living on the ranch now, Raylee had to keep up with the running of the house. Her daily routine consisted mostly of washing everyone's clothes and keeping everything tidy, while she would spend up to an hour in the office of an afternoon. The kitchen was no sooner cleaned up then it was time to prepare the next meal, with everyone piling into the house for breakfast, lunch and dinner.

Raylee wouldn't give up her time at the barn though, and she managed to squeeze in a couple of hours each day so she didn't miss out on anything. While Cutter and Jesse devoted all their time to training the horses, Aimee was making herself useful in the barn, becoming familiar with the tack and reading the labels on all of the products when no one was watching.

There were plenty of moments when Cutter found the time to give his wife a sneaky kiss, pinch or affectionate touch when the others had their backs turned, and with Jesse going out over the ranch every third day with Aimee, there were fun and games going on at the house or in the barn. It was safe to say that a couple of hours alone for the newly married couple was rare and they never missed an opportunity.

Their picnic dates by the stream was something they kept private, not sharing their special time with anyone. As Cutter stood outside the barn, he made sure Jesse and Aimee reached the first rolling hill on their way to the back pasture before he'd race to the house to find Raylee waiting for him on the porch with the picnic basket ready.

Every time Cutter found himself alone with Raylee, it reassured him that it was a great idea to bring both Jesse and Aimee to the ranch to share the load.

He needed Raylee to be that sneaky little distraction that put the spark into his training, and she was.

After a couple of weeks of daily riding, Cutter thought that it was the right time to fit Aimee with a set of spurs. He took her into the sand yard and taught her how to apply the pressure to the horse. She picked it up quickly, although Macca's horse was steady to begin with. It was more of a concern to him how she would use them while riding over the ranch, and Cutter took her out on the daily ride to see how she managed.

"Be careful not to dig them in, or you'll need to hold on," he warned her.

Aimee was extremely careful and lucky for her, the horse just plodded along next to his.

While Aimee loved spending time with Cutter when it was just the two of them alone, it was becoming less often with so many people around. She thought that her brother was something special and she put him at the top of her list of favorite people. The ride gave her the time to talk openly about anything that was on her mind, including family.

"What do you remember about our dad?" she asked, while they were riding side by side casually.

Cutter looked at her. He didn't want to crush Aimee's ideals of a perfect parent. After all, Pete was a hero to her like every father should be. He just wasn't a hero to Cutter.

"What did he tell you?" Cutter asked.

"Not much," she replied quickly.

"The truth is, Aims, that I don't remember everything. But the things I do remember aren't worth thinking about."

"Did he hurt you?" she asked, and it surprised him that Aimee was so open about her father and his situation.

He looked at her again. "No ma'am, not in the way that you think," he said. "But he hurt my mom and I can remember that well."

"Is that why she left?"

"To be honest, I think she left to protect me... Before he did do something to hurt me, and because it was the only way he was gonna get some help."

They were on their way to the back pasture and they sidetracked away from the field of flowers. Aimee couldn't help but comment on them. "It's so beautiful," she said, as they rode past the gate like she had done every day since she arrived.

"And one day, I'll take you there."

"Is it part of the ranch?" she asked.

"Yes ma'am… That, and the next pasture near the roadside," he half explained.

After checking the cows in the back pasture, they rode home along the eastern boundary. When Cutter picked up the pace to a trot, Aimee applied more pressure and began to feel the uncomfortable rhythm again.

"Lift your butt," he said, and she watched Cutter show her how it was done. "That's it… You've gotta move with the horse," he explained.

"You make it look so easy."

"That's because it is easy," he stated.

They made it home in good time, as they trotted on and off. When they rode past the day yards, they had slowed down to a walking pace. Aimee was feeling more trusting of the horse every time she went out, although it was helping that she was receiving the best tuition from everyone. She was around the horses from morning until dark, either feeding and washing, or in the saddle riding. Her aches and pains had subsided, and her knowledge of everything from tack to grain had increased. She was starting to talk the same language as everyone else.

Both Jesse and Aimee were getting used to the daily program and were understanding the way things worked around the ranch. Aimee couldn't believe that this was actually a real job, that she got to ride horses and ride over the ranch while Jesse was handling the young foals and helping with the training. Who wouldn't love this life? Jesse and Aimee didn't mind spending time together either, since they both recognized Cutter's need to spend time alone with his new wife.

Raylee, on the other hand, was finding it more difficult. She was dividing her time between the house, the office and the barn, with so much more to do than she'd expected. For the first time in over forty years, the ranch was without a housekeeper, and Raylee was beginning to see just how much work Marnie really did. While she was trying to keep everything up to date just like Marnie had always done, the workload was depressing and was wearing her down. It was nearly a full time job on its own. She was thankful, however, that Cutter had the help in the barn and the cutting pen, so that it took the pressure off him.

When Cutter came up to the house after a training session, he took his boots off at the door. Raylee was standing at the sink and he came up behind her and slipped his arms around her waist, kissing her on the side of the neck.

"What're you doing?" Raylee asked with a smile from the tickling sensation he was giving her. "Where is everyone?"

"I sent them out the back to check on the girls. They'll be a couple of hours at least," he said in a suggestive way, to let her know they were finally alone again.

She turned around and kissed him. "Well you know it doesn't take you that long," she said, and she gave him a teasing look. "I don't know what you'll do with the hour and fifty-five minutes you'll have left."

"You're so funny," he said. "Actually, with the time we've got left, I thought I'd take you out to lunch."

Raylee had done so much work in and around the house while Cutter had been so consumed with the horses and the ranch. Even with the time they found to have those secret moments together, they still hadn't taken the time to do the most simple things in life, like go to town for lunch. For Raylee, the thought of going out the front gate on their own was almost as exciting as their wedding day.

"I'll just change my shirt," he said, and he headed to the bottom of the stairs.

"Do you need some help?" she flirted.

He stopped in his tracks and looked at her. "No ma'am... But if you insist, then I'll never say no," he replied, and she followed him up the stairs.

With every ride, Aimee was becoming more confident in the saddle, even with the spurs. She was starting to sit right and get some good control over the reins, something that she didn't have in those first couple of weeks. Every time she messed up, either Jesse or Cutter was there to talk her through it and they could see that, in such a short time, she had come a long way.

Aimee loved spending the time with everyone. She loved going on the ride with Cutter, as they would talk about her family and his. She was getting to know more about his mom and Macca and she started to understand how his life had played out. On her rides with Raylee, they shared family stories and girlie talk, and on her rides with Jesse, she flirted and carried on with him and he was more than happy to play along. Their connection was growing fast in a direction that no one saw coming.

As they rode towards the back pasture, Aimee stopped at the gate that led to the field of flowers. She got off the horse to undo the latch.

"What're you doing?" Jesse asked.

"It's alright. It's part of the ranch," she informed him.

"Have you been through this gate before?"

"No. But it will be okay."

"I don't know, Aimee. If Cutter wanted us to go there, then he would've taken us already."

"Are you afraid?" she asked.

He laughed at her. "Afraid? Of what? It's just another pasture." Jesse was not worried about going through the gate as much as he was worried about Cutter finding out.

They closed the gate behind them and rode the horses through the flowers. They were full and at their best bloom. The gentle breeze made a slight ripple over them as they rode through. There was a calmness and a fragrance that filled the air and it lingered until they rode out the other side towards the road. They rode side by side, just soaking up the time and feeling relaxed in each other's company, when the wrought iron fence of the resting place came into view.

"What's that?" Aimee asked.

"It looks like a graveyard," Jesse replied, and he immediately felt like they shouldn't be there. "Maybe we should go back," he suggested.

"Let's take a look first."

"I think we should go."

Aimee rode on, ignoring Jesse's idea to leave. She tied the horse to a tree while Jesse did the same, since he didn't want to leave her there on her own.

The wrought iron gate squeaked when Aimee opened it which put a shiver up Jesse's spine. He figured that if he gave her the time to have a quick look, then they'd be out of there soon and on their way to the cows where they were supposed to be.

Aimee walked past several graves when she came across the headstone of Bobby McKenzie Jones. The headstone looked newer than all the others.

"I think that's Macca's," she said, looking down at it.

Jesse was feeling uncomfortable about being there, but he looked closely at it too. "I think you're right," he said. "And that looks like Cutter's mom," he added, and he pointed to the grave next to it.

Aimee looked and read the name. Mary-Ann Jones. She didn't feel it coming on, but an emotional rush hit her suddenly. She wiped her eyes when the first tear started to appear.

"Are you crying?" Jesse asked. Her hat fell off when she turned and buried her face into his shoulder so that he couldn't see her eyes. "What is it?"

She straightened herself up and gained control. "I'm sorry, it's just that... this is Cutter's mom."

"And?" he asked, as if he didn't understand what the big deal was.

"And, a long time ago, she used to be married to my dad."

She wiped the remains of the last tear, gave a sniffle and took a deep breath. Jesse still had his arm around her for comfort. They both looked down at her hat sitting in the grass and both bent down to pick it up at the same time, bumping heads.

"Ouch," Aimee said, and she stood up holding her hat in one hand and rubbing her head with the other.

Jesse laughed. "Sorry," he apologized, and he looked at her head and also rubbed it for her, while he was straightening his hat.

He looked at her closely and without any more hesitation, he reached down and kissed her. He pulled her in by the waist and held her close to his body. It was so sudden that it caught her by surprise. It wasn't a friendly comforting kiss that would have been more appropriate standing in that graveyard. It wasn't a kiss to say let's be good friends and I want to get to know you some more. It was a kiss that was reflective of their closeness at that time and the result of all their flirting. It was a kiss that said I want you.

Aimee's heart and head was taking it all in, kissing him back and touching his face, until he pulled away, looking into her eyes.

"What did you do that for?" she asked.

Her question stunned him. "I'm sorry... I couldn't help it, and I've wanted to do that for a couple of weeks now... And I thought you wanted it too," he explained.

"I mean, what did you stop for?"

Jesse gave her a smile. It was clear to him that she felt that same way and without giving it a second thought, he reached down and kissed her again.

When Cutter and Raylee sat in the diner, they took their regular table by the window in the corner, away from all the other customers. While they waited on their lunch, it gave them some alone time to talk.

"I love being married," Raylee announced.

"And I love being married to you," Cutter replied.

"I just wish we had more time to do this."

"I know we haven't had much time since the wedding, but that's why we needed the help. And I think it's been working out okay. Jesse seems to know the ranch now and Aimee's picking up everything she needs to know in the barn."

"And I'm becoming a good housewife," Raylee added, just in case it was going unnoticed.

"Which you won't always be doing. It's just while Marnie's away. She needed this vacation and she'll be back before you know it."

They caught up on the training progress, when the next load of cattle would be going out, and reminisced on the events from the previous year when Raylee had first arrived in Texas.

Over lunch, they focused more on their friends and personal life.

"Emma looks great, doesn't she? I wonder if she'll have a boy or a girl," Raylee said.

"I don't know. But either way it's gonna be amazing for them."

"And life changing."

Cutter agreed. "It will certainly be that."

Neither of them were committing to the topic, even though Raylee was dancing around with some leading questions.

"Do they have names picked out?" she asked.

"Not that I've heard. But you know Emma, she'll be organized," Cutter said. "In fact, I think that's the hardest part."

"Choosing the name is the hardest part? Are you joking? It might be the hardest part for you but for the woman, I'd say it's a walk in the park compared to what she has to go through."

"Then I'm so glad it's you and not me," he teased.

Cutter wasn't catching on quickly enough, so Raylee felt that she should just blurt it out, to get it off her chest and see if Cutter was thinking in the same direction. "When do you think we should have a baby?"

He was less committed to answering a question like that than what Raylee would have liked. "When you're ready."

"But you must have an opinion."

"Look, we only just got married and you're so young. I want you to do all the things in your life that you wanna do first. Right now, I'm just happy being in training for it."

"And if I was ready now?" she asked.

It made him nervous to think about it. "Then I would be too... Are you ready now?" he asked cautiously, almost unsure of her answer.

"Hell no."

Cutter laughed at her and he silently agreed, feeling quite relieved. He'd like to spend more time together before they dived into that territory. There was plenty of time for a family later. Without a doubt in the world he wanted a family. He just wasn't in any hurry and neither was Raylee.

Looking at her across the table, he didn't want to put an end to their lunch date, yet it was all the time he had to give. "It's time we got back. Jesse and Aimee will be back by now and he might have her in the cutting pen on the mechanical cow if I'm not careful."

They made their way to the truck and headed home to the ranch. It was a relaxing afternoon and Raylee not only needed the break from the house, but she also needed the time alone with Cutter. She loved that he was thoughtful enough to know it and to realize that he needed it too.

When Jesse heard the truck pull up outside the barn, he immediately ran out of the feed room leaving Aimee to straighten herself up, while he tried to look busy with a horse.

"How do the cows look?" Cutter asked when he walked into the barn.

"I'd say they're only a few days away," Jesse informed him, leaving Cutter looking pleased.

It was straight back to work. "Let's get the pally and the roan saddled up and we'll bring in a few steers."

Although the girls had gone to the trouble of naming all the horses, Cutter was having difficulty calling them by their new silly names. If Bluey wasn't bad enough, he'd have no chance on calling them Spot, Flirt and Sandy. It was easier and more cowboy-like to just call them by color or by their breeding and Jesse agreed.

They spent the afternoon in the cutting pen with a few steers from the mob. With Aimee wanting to be part of the action, she saddled up Macca's horse and went in also, watching from the corner and keeping out of the way. She was impressed with Cutter's training methods, and she listened while he was talking to Jesse, explaining in detail what the filly was doing right and what she was doing wrong. It seemed that Cutter was interested in advancing Jesse's cutting experience and that maybe one day he'd become a trainer himself.

Cutter waved Aimee in. He put her in position in the corner and explained what to do if a steer moved from the mob. Unbeknown to her, he was teaching her to be on the team.

Raylee came to the pen, although this time, it wasn't to ride.

"Hey, you should saddle a horse and come in for a cut," Cutter invited her.

"Can I talk to you for a minute?" Raylee asked.

"Sure. Jesse, take a break," he called out, and he rode over to the rail that Raylee was leaning on. "What is it?"

"I just had a call from Emma. She's feeling uncomfortable and she's asked me to go over," she said.

"Is she alright?"

"I hope so. The doctor's coming out and she wants me to come over too."

"Is the baby okay?"

"I don't know." Raylee was doing her best not to concern him, but he could see the look of worry on her face.

"Should I come too?" he asked.

"There's nothing you can do and I'm sure she'll be fine. But I don't know what time I'll be back, so you might have to take care of dinner for everyone."

"Don't you worry about that. We'll survive. You just give Emma a big hug for me."

Raylee drove away in the truck while Cutter picked up his training again. After a couple of hours in the pen with the steers, his concern for Emma was playing on his mind and he couldn't think straight. He couldn't focus. Raylee still wasn't back and it worried him even more. He cut the afternoon short, leaving Jesse and Aimee to finish in the pen and feed up for the night. While he thought about calling Johnny, he decided to take the old Ford truck and drive over there for himself.

When Cutter arrived at Johnny's house, the doctor was just leaving in his car. Cutter felt a sudden sickly feeling and hesitated as to whether he should go inside. He sat there for a while and stared at the house. What was he going to be faced with? He was fully supportive when everything was going well, yet he'd always been on the receiving end of tragedy and he was always the one being supported.

He couldn't sit in the truck all night and he gained enough courage to get out and walk up the front steps. Raylee was right. Maybe choosing the name was the easiest part. His protective instinct took over, thinking that he didn't want Raylee to go through this.

He didn't knock on the door. Instead, he went straight in and called out. "Johnny?"

Johnny came down the stairs casually. "Hey, bro. What're you doing here?"

"Is Emma alright?" Cutter asked reluctantly.

"She's good."

"And the baby?"

"The baby's fine too."

Thank goodness, he thought, and he breathed a sigh of relief. Johnny could see his concern and appreciated his best friend being there. "Do you wanna come up and see her?"

Cutter followed Johnny up the stairs to the bedroom. He'd rarely been upstairs in their new house, never having a reason to venture beyond the kitchen and sitting room. Raylee was sitting next to Emma on the bed and they both smiled when the boys walked into the room.

"You've got another visitor," Johnny announced unnecessarily.

Cutter sat on the side of the bed next to Emma and couldn't believe the size of her tummy. "Woah, look at you," he exclaimed. He hadn't seen Johnny and Emma for a few weeks now and she was looking like she was about to pop. "What did the doctor say?" he asked.

"Everything's okay. There's no need to worry," Emma said, to give rest to his concern.

"I'll fill you in later," Raylee added to cover for Emma, so she didn't have to go through it all over again and embarrass him with the intimate details of a pregnant woman.

"Oh... It's moving," Emma said, while she held her tummy low. Cutter could see a wave of movement through her shirt and everyone laughed at how freaked out he was. "Do you want to touch it?" she asked, and before he could answer, she picked up his hands and placed them on either side of her tummy.

Cutter looked into Emma's face and gave her a smile when the baby moved. He looked at Raylee. She was laughing at his reaction. It was an amazing feeling and he was quietly excited at the thought of new life. He'd seen this hundreds of times before with a cow and a calf, and in the barn with a mare and a foal, but a woman and a baby was a whole different experience. One he'd never known about.

The four of them sat on the bed and talked for a couple of hours. Johnny went downstairs to the kitchen and came back with the ice cream, and they all shared it out of the tub, polishing it off in no time at all. They caught up on everything that was going on with both ranches and both families. With the baby not due for a couple of months, Johnny's parents had decided to take a short vacation and would be back in time for the arrival of their first grandchild, weighing Johnny down with the extra workload in the meantime.

Raylee knew the feeling. The house chores were weighing her down too. As every week passed, she almost wished Marnie was back from her road trip, to take the pressure off her. Except that she knew that was selfish and that it wouldn't be fair on Marnie.

It was getting late into the night and it was time to let Emma rest. Raylee loved the time they all had together. She had missed that over the last while, with the training taking up most of Cutter's time, while she was silently suffocating under the mountains of work that the house demanded.

"I'll come back tomorrow," Raylee promised, not thinking twice about putting the housework on hold to spend time with Emma. "But you need to get some sleep now."

Cutter reached down and gave Emma a kiss on the cheek. "You just keep smiling and you do what that doctor tells you," he insisted.

Johnny led Cutter and Raylee downstairs to the front door so he could lock up the house when they left.

"She'll be alright, won't she?" Cutter asked Johnny for a little more reassurance.

"She just has to rest as much as possible, and if she does that, then the doctor said she should go to full term."

Cutter and Raylee took both trucks home and parked them at the side of the house. They walked up the front steps and onto the porch which was in total darkness, as no one had thought to leave the light on.

"They must've gone to bed," Cutter said referring to Jesse and Aimee, and he pulled Raylee by the hand and leaned her against the rail. He reached down to kiss her, letting his wandering hands find their way all over her, while he was whispering his intentions into her ear.

She kissed him back, loving the attention and his need for her. She giggled from his suggestions and welcomed his touch. "Let's go upstairs and I might let you..."

Squeak. There was a squeak from the swing, followed by a chuckle of laughter. It frightened them both. It was Jesse and Aimee, sitting on the porch in the late hours of the night in the dark.

Raylee squealed loudly and hid behind Cutter, her heart skipping a beat or two. "Damn it, Jesse and Aimee... You frightened the pants off me," she said.

"Actually, I thought that Cutter was doing a good job of that," Jesse said, and Aimee laughed along with him.

"What're you doing sneaking around?" Cutter asked, and he walked to the end of the porch where they were.

"We aren't the ones sneaking around in the middle of the night," Aimee pointed out. "We've just been sitting here talking. It's you that's been caught out."

"Well we're allowed and you're not. So I think that everyone needs to go to bed now," Cutter insisted.

Jesse agreed. "Yeah, the morning sure comes around fast."

Everyone said their goodnights and Jesse wandered off to the barn while Aimee stood at the front window in the dark and watched him.

"Now... where were we?" Cutter asked, after he had a shower and pulled back the quilt.

Raylee didn't answer.

He snuggled in behind her and gave her a soft kiss on the neck.

She didn't stir.

He was gentle with her, tangling their feet together and running his hand up and down her body to provoke a reaction.

She didn't give him one.

"Raylee?" he whispered.

She was silent. He looked at her. She was totally exhausted and had fallen asleep.

## Chapter Five

As the days were warming up, the training sessions were taking place earlier. To beat the heat of the day, everyone had to get out of bed a half hour earlier to get through as many horses as they could before breakfast. Cutter gave Jesse the job of handling the young horses and was letting him do it his way. Standing back, Cutter watched from a distance and was impressed with Jesse's methods.

Aimee was watching silently too, admiring Jesse from a completely different angle. When she first asked to come to Double J Ranch to spend time with her big brother before she went to college, she never expected that it would be an Australian cowboy that she was wanting to run around with. Now Aimee was secretly scheming for every opportunity to get Jesse on his own, even coming up with the lamest excuses and most mischievous plans to pull him into the barn and out of sight, where he found her hard to resist. She was good at it, while Cutter remained focused on his training and never noticed Jesse's sudden disappearing acts.

Needing to get out of the kitchen and go for a ride, Raylee put the housework on hold for a couple of hours. It had been depressing to know that everyone was outside working around the barn, while she felt chained to the boredom of domestic chores.

She saddled up and began riding in circles at one end of the sand yard, getting the horse warm. After Cutter finished his session, they adjusted the length of the stirrups and exchanged horses. Raylee gave the horse a warm down while Cutter reset the program on the mechanical cow. He strapped the remote control to his arm and as soon as the cow zipped up the wire, the horse followed it until it stopped.

When Aimee had the stalls cleaned out and the tack room organized, she wandered over to the rail and watched. Cutter was working the palomino filly to an irregular pattern and was taking the time to correct her mistakes. He was firm with her, and for the first time, Aimee recognized that this was where his talent really lay. He had a stronghold over the filly and was not letting her cheat or lose focus, and while her owners had very high expectations, Cutter felt that she still had a long way to go.

Everything to do with the horses and training program was flowing along smoothly and the ranch was running like clockwork. Everything was right on track and was going exactly as planned, just the way Cutter wanted it.

After Raylee finished cleaning up from breakfast and had put a load of washing on, she wandered over to the barn. She could hear Cutter working in the sand yard, as the zipping noise of the wire from the mechanical cow was a dead giveaway.

To keep herself sane, she had been trying to get out of the house as much as possible, and now she felt the unexpected need to go for a ride.

She looked around for Aimee, to see if she wanted to go on a ride with her, but she was nowhere to be seen and neither was Jesse. Raylee wasn't purposely trying to sneak up on them, except that her suspicions were justified when she heard them laughing quietly together in the feed room. Then it fell silent. Raylee took her hat off and peeked around the door to see what they were doing.

Pulling back quickly out of sight, Raylee closed her eyes and pinned herself against the wall while she held her breath. No... this isn't happening, she thought, while her heart was pounding fast. She kept silent and moved slowly, taking another sneaky look just to make sure.

She pulled back immediately. Yes... they are.

Now she was caught in a situation that she had to get out of. Very quietly, she tiptoed out of the barn before she walked back in again, calling out loudly to make sure she was heard.

"Jesse, are you in here?" Raylee said, as if she had no idea.

After a suspiciously quiet scuffle, Jesse wandered out of the feed room. "Hey, Raylee. I was just making up some feeds for later."

Sure you are.

"Where's Aimee?" she asked, feeling stupid that she already knew the answer.

He was quick to reply. "She's in here helping me," he said, just as Aimee lifted her head up from the feed bin.

"Do you need me?" Aimee asked.

"I thought we'd go for a ride. Let Cutter and Jesse deal with the training," Raylee said, making it up as she went along.

Jesse intercepted the plans. "Actually, I think it's my turn to take Aimee out." Sure it was.

Raylee was desperately trying to be a wedge. "But you went two days ago, and anyway, it looks like Cutter needs some help out there."

Neither of them were letting Raylee interrupt their plans. "Well why don't you go and help him," Aimee said more abruptly than was needed.

"Yeah. You're newly married and haven't spent much time together. Cutter would like that," Jesse added, to soften Aimee's comments.

Sure he would.

They were being manipulative, not realizing that Raylee already knew too much. She left the barn to watch Cutter on the colt. She sat on the top rail and kept silent and he was unaware that he had an audience. When he finished, he turned around to see all three of them had been watching. "How long have you been sitting there?" he asked.

"Long enough to be impressed," Raylee replied. "Do you need Jesse to give you a hand? I could go out with Aimee if you like."

Aimee gave Jesse a jab in his side to let him know that now would be a good time to cut in and rearrange Raylee's plans, before Cutter turned it all upside down.

"Actually, you can all saddle up. We're all going," he announced.

Cutter wanted to bring in a mob of cattle to the cutting pen and thought it would be a good idea to take everyone on the roundup. While everyone was saddling up and getting ready, Raylee couldn't get close enough to Cutter on her own to tell him what she'd seen. By the time they were all ready, it hardly seemed the right time to break that news to him in front of Jesse and Aimee.

As they rode through the first gate, Raylee held back, wanting to keep a close eye on the new loved-up couple. She was sure that she was feeling more uncomfortable about what they were up to than either of them were.

"Hey, come on, Raylee," Cutter called out from the front. They had not been on the daily ride together since the first day they all went out, and he was wanting his wife to be by his side, not trailing behind. She spurred the horse to pass them and when she caught up with Cutter, it seemed that Jesse and Aimee started to lag behind even more.

"What's wrong with you?" he asked, when they were safely out of earshot.

Raylee quickly glanced behind her to see where they were. They were having a happy time back there, riding close together and laughing among their whispers.

"Don't worry about them... They can't hear you," Cutter said for added reassurance, although Raylee was still looking unsettled. "What's wrong?" he asked again, now sounding concerned.

"I'm fine," she assured him. "It's them I'm worried about."

Cutter gave a quick look behind him and could see their closeness. "Jesse and Aimee... You're worried about them?" The tone in his voice gave her the sense that he was far from worried.

"Yes."

He looked again. "Well I don't think you've got anything to worry about there. They look like they're good friends who are having a good time. And besides, they probably just want us to spend more time together," he said, to try and convince her that her suspicions were unnecessary. "And trust me, if there was anything going on, Jesse would be on the first plane outta here tomorrow and Aimee would be going home to Dallas." Cutter was making fun of the situation even though his comments were completely serious.

Raylee wasn't sure now how to tell Cutter what she'd seen. She knew that he would flip out, and the roundup was hardly the right time or place to bring it out into the open.

When they reached the pasture of weaners, Cutter opened the gate. Everyone rode through and then he explained the game plan. Jesse and Aimee were to ride along the fence line and come in behind the mob, while Raylee was to come in from the side. Cutter would wait halfway so that he could apply the pressure from the other side and direct them to the gate, leaving Jesse to pick up any strays that had broken away.

This was second nature to Cutter. He'd done this thousands of times before and it was something that he really could have done on his own without any help. Aimee, on the other hand, was inexperienced in this situation, which was shown by her waving arms and the strange noises she was making to get the mob to move, even though she was having a great time.

They moved them slowly through the different pastures, keeping clear of the other herds. Cutter and Jesse were working well as a team to keep control, while

Raylee and Aimee held back and applied pressure to keep them moving forward. It was only a small mob of thirty-six that needed to come into the yards ready for Cutter to use in the cutting pen, and then they would be treated and put back out to graze again.

The sounds of the cattle in the quietness of the roundup was what Cutter loved most about the ranch. This was the true cowboy spirit coming out in him and he'd never trade his life for anyone else's. When they reached the cattle yards, he looked at the team. They had done a good job and for Cutter, they were his family, including Jesse, who was almost like a brother to Raylee.

When the last calf was in the holding yard, Jesse closed the gate. The girls took the horses away to unsaddle them while the boys checked the water and gave the calves some feed. Lunch was on everyone's mind after everything was done, and as they all wandered to the house, Raylee still felt uncomfortable. Jesse and Aimee were walking far behind them and she was frustrated that she couldn't see or hear what was going on.

She was desperate to talk to Cutter alone, yet she didn't find the chance, as the four of them sat around the table for a quick bite to eat.

Cutter spent the afternoon in the sand yard with Aimee, giving her some extra time to build her up to where she needed to be, while Jesse was busy in the barn and was keeping on top of the maintenance around the yards. There was no time for any sneaky, playful games, as Cutter unintentionally had them both busy until dark.

Raylee made sure that she was the last one to bed that night. When everyone was settled into their rooms and the house was locked down, she went for a shower. By the time she pulled the quilt back, Cutter was sound asleep. Like everyone else, he was tired from the long day. She wasn't quiet about it, hoping that her closeness would wake him. It didn't, and Raylee lay her head on the pillow and stared at the ceiling.

Although she was tired too, her mind was racing away with thoughts on what to do. How would she break the news to Cutter, and she wondered what his reaction would be. She didn't want Jesse or Aimee to go home, since they needed the help desperately and she loved to spend time with them both. Even though she was wanting to spend more time with Cutter, she wasn't about to push the two of them together so that she could have that time with him alone.

Raylee didn't hear the door open in the hallway, but she did hear the floor-boards creak and she opened her eyes and sat up on her elbows to listen. There was no sound. Maybe it was in her imagination. She lay back down and could hear Cutter breathing heavily in his sleep. He hadn't moved at all.

Creak, creak. There it was again. She sat back up and listened some more. Raylee was confident now that it was Aimee outside their door and that she was now going down the stairs.

Raylee touched Cutter on the arm. "Wake up," she whispered.

He stirred. "What is it?" he asked, still three parts asleep.

"Do you hear that?" Raylee asked. "It sounds like Aimee's out of bed and is going downstairs."

He tried to sound interested, except that he really wasn't. "She's probably gone to the kitchen... Go back to sleep," he said, totally unaware of the time and that she had only gone to bed ten minutes ago.

Raylee lay in the silence of the room and was sure that Aimee was tiptoeing, not out of politeness so that she didn't wake the house up, but so that she could sneak out of the house without getting caught. It got the better of Raylee, who was convinced that Aimee was up to something, and while she could tell that Cutter had immediately fallen back into a sound sleep, she got out of bed and went to the window to look, pulling the curtain back.

Again, her suspicions were confirmed when she saw Aimee running to the barn in the dark.

"Oh yeah," Raylee said loudly. "And since when was the kitchen in the barn?"

"What are you talking about?"

"Aimee... Your sister. She just snuck out of the house and is now in the barn," she announced.

Cutter rolled over in bed and looked at her. "You're kidding me. Why would she do that?"

Raylee looked at him and was silently entertained by his naiveness. "Do I really need to spell it out for you?"

He sat up on the side of the bed and rubbed his face and the back of his neck. He looked at her with a confused look on his face, determining the situation. "Jesse?" he asked.

Raylee didn't reply. She didn't need to, when it started to sink in and his reaction was the answer to his question. "Where's my jeans?" he asked, and he stood up and wandered around the room in the dark, feeling unsteady on his feet. He found them.

"What're you going to do?" she asked, while he was buttoning them up and reaching for his shirt.

"I'm gonna find out what's going on... There could be a reasonable explanation."

Raylee knew that was more of a hopeful thought than a realistic one. She knew what he was going to walk into and it saved her having to tell him.

Cutter was not as silent as Aimee when he went down the stairs to the kitchen. He took a drink of water quickly at the sink, mostly to help clear his mind and to get his thinking straight.

He was, however, quieter when he slid the barn door open enough for him to slip through the gap. He looked around in the dark. Aimee was nowhere to be seen and he walked quietly through the barn, thinking and listening. He could hear voices, voices that were coming from upstairs and he immediately knew what was going on.

Pacing back and forth, he was thinking fast. What to do? What to say? This can't be happening. He paced some more and put his hands behind his head, beginning to feel quite nervous, even though he had nothing to be nervous about. This was his ranch, his barn and his sister. So why was he the one feeling uncomfortable?

"Jesse?" he called out so loud that it even surprised himself, as the tone was more aggressive than he intended. It was silent upstairs. "Jesse... One of the fillies is out and is running with the colt." His voice was loud and controlled.

There was a scuffling of footsteps upstairs on the floorboards and Cutter knew that Jesse was now scouring around for his clothes. Thump. Thump. That was his boots, and Jesse flew down the stairs with his jeans still unbuttoned and was pulling his shirt on over his head.

"Which filly?" Jesse asked, looking around frantically and breathing heavily from the rush.

Cutter was leaning up against the post with his arms crossed, staring at him. Jesse asked again. "Where is she? Which filly?"

Cutter didn't reply and walked past him to the bottom of the stairs.

"No," Jesse called out. "You can't go up there." He was still catching his breath when he unsuccessfully tried to get ahead of Cutter, who stopped suddenly and turned to look at him, gripping the handrail tight. They were now nose to nose and Cutter noticed Jesse's young fresh face was now full of fear. There was something almost angry in Cutter's eyes, and Jesse knew then not to challenge him.

He took his time as he opened the door of the loft and flicked the light on, keeping in control. Jesse was only two paces behind and they both looked at Aimee, who was sitting up in the bed and seemed unsurprised at being caught. The room was so small with only a wardrobe, two side tables and a bed, that there was nowhere to hide even if she wanted to.

Cutter returned the look that she was giving him, and he stared while he was thinking. From what he could see, she was mostly dressed, although she was partially covered by the quilt.

"This filly," he announced, giving her a disapproving stare. "Go back to the house, Aimee," Cutter said firmly, although she didn't move. Their stare was intense and neither of them were going to give in, until Cutter spoke again, this time with a severity that shook her up. "I said, go back to the house... now."

She didn't speak. She threw the covers back and got to her feet, pulling her boots on and straightening out her clothes. She walked past them both to the door and left.

"I know how this looks," Jesse began to say, and Cutter put his hand in the air to silence him, and he turned around. "I didn't know she was coming up here until she knocked on my door," Jesse went on to explain.

Cutter was barely listening. "I trusted you," he said, confusing anger with disappointment while friendship wasn't even coming into it, and Jesse wasn't sure what was coming next. "We'll talk about this tomorrow," he added, and he left the room. Cutter wasn't ready to get into that discussion right then and there. He was more interested in talking to his sister first.

When Cutter closed the barn door behind him, he could see Aimee had already made it to the porch and he heard the screen door shut. His thoughts were running wild. His sister was in his care, on his ranch, and he was responsible for her. How could she let him down like that? More importantly, what was he going to say to her and how was he going to deal with it? He wasn't a parent. He'd never had to deal with a situation like this before. It had caught him by surprise that it had happened under his roof, on his watch. It had been happening right under his nose but he hadn't noticed. They had been hiding and sneaking around in plain sight.

He paced around the kitchen for a moment while he was gathering his thoughts. The house was silent when he walked up the stairs and he could have easily gone back to bed and ignored what had just happened, if he didn't feel the responsibility he owed to Pete and Beth to take care of their daughter.

He knocked on Aimee's door. She didn't answer. Not to let that stop him, he opened the door and walked into her room. She was under the quilt and he could hear her quietly sobbing. He hated making girls cry. It softened him straight away when they did. Right now, he had to be strong and firm with his sister, and let her know that she was way out of line.

When he sat on the side of the bed, he gently pulled the covers back and looked into her face. The room was dimly lit and his eyes adjusted quickly. She wiped her face but still wouldn't speak. This was the moment that Cutter needed to keep calm and choose his words wisely. He was out of his depth where teenage girls were concerned, and although Raylee was only four years older than Aimee, it immediately struck him that maybe she was better qualified for having this conversation than he was.

"Are you angry with me?" he asked cautiously.

"No... I mean yes... I mean, I don't know," she answered, confused by his question.

He knew he had to tackle this carefully or he could end up with all the drama of a teenage meltdown. He didn't want that.

"You know what you did was wrong, don't you?" he asked, expecting a reply. He didn't get one. "You know you can't go sneaking around with boys in the middle of the night, especially when you're at my house." There was still no reply. Aimee wasn't giving him anything to work with so he wasn't sure what else to say. "Do you wanna go home?"

"No. Please don't send me home," she said quickly.

"Then you have to talk to me."

"I like Jesse. And he likes me. So I don't see what the problem is."

"I'll tell you what the problem is, Aimee. Your mom and dad trusted me to look after you. That means I have to know where you are, who you're with and what you're doing."

"So now you know." Aimee thought that it was as simple as that. As far as she was concerned, the problem was now solved.

"But it doesn't make it right. It's not my position to let you to spend the night in some boy's bed... And Jesse... he shouldn't have allowed it."

Aimee defended Jesse immediately. "It's not his fault. Please don't send him home," she pleaded.

"Why shouldn't I? He's as much at fault here as you are. I trusted both of you and you've both let me down."

"Because we really like each other." There was something in her remarks that told Cutter that there was more to her feelings for Jesse than she was letting on.

He looked her in the eyes and would expect a truthful answer. "Have you and Jesse already crossed that line?" he asked, to get a clear understanding of the situation.

"Only twice," she admitted.

Cutter jumped to his feet. "What?" His tolerance level just went through the roof and he began to pace again. "Twice. Are you serious? How could you let this happen? Actually, when did this happen?" It was now Cutter who was having the meltdown, not Aimee. "On second thoughts, don't tell me. I don't wanna know."

He wasn't sure how to react. It blew his mind that he hadn't seen it coming and if it wasn't for Raylee's observation, then he may never have known. A million thoughts ran through his head. "Your dad is gonna kill me," he said, although it was more of a statement to himself.

As he was pacing, he was trying to keep calm and steady himself down to gain control. He took a deep breath and was thinking fast. His head had nearly spun off his shoulders and as he paced some more, he finally started to settle.

"He's not my first," she announced, which really threw Cutter into a spiral of madness that he wasn't expecting.

"What?" he said aggressively. "No... You've gotta be kidding me, right?"

"I've had a boyfriend before. I'm nineteen, you know. I'm only four years younger than Raylee and she's married." Aimee was trying to justify her situation through a typical teenager's explanation.

Cutter looked at her. It had finally sunk in. He sat back down on the side of the bed and changed the course of his questioning, deciding that his fury was going to get him nowhere.

"Do your mom and dad know?" he asked.

"Of course not. I'm not going to tell them everything I do. Did you come home and tell your parents the first time you'd been with a girl?"

Aimee was right and he knew it. It wasn't something that you just waltzed in the front door and announced to your parents when it did happen, as if it was the best news they were expecting or wanting to hear.

"You should've waited," he said, trying to be soft with her again. "You're so young."

She quickly turned it around. "So you waited all these years for Raylee, did you?"

"No ma'am, I didn't," he admitted.

"And you were much older than me?"

"No. I wasn't."

"And you regret all those times..."

"Alright, I get your point. But my point is that you're here in my care and I'm responsible for you. And besides, how do you know Jesse is right for you?"

"I don't. But I do like him a lot and I know he likes me. So I'm begging you now, please don't send him home."

Cutter had a lot to think about. This had not been on his mind when he went to bed earlier that night, and now he had to deal with the fact that his sister and Jesse were getting it on together in the barn. If it wasn't right from a brotherly point of view, then it certainly wasn't right that he had them both there to work and he didn't need either of them being distracted while on that job.

"I'm going to have to think about everything you've told me tonight. But right now, I need to sleep." He gave her a kiss on the cheek and walked to the door.

She knew that he was disappointed in her and she called out before he left the room. "I love you," she said almost desperately, to make things better.

Cutter wasn't expecting it. He looked back at her and could see from the look in her eyes that she meant it. "I love you too," he said, and he closed the door behind him and went back to bed.

Four a.m. came around more quickly than Cutter would have liked. He couldn't get back into a sound sleep, as the thoughts of Jesse and Aimee frolicking around in the barn kept spinning in circles in his head. After another fifteen minutes, he decided to get up and get an early start. It would give him the extra time on his own and he needed it.

Although the mare was now in her Derby year, Cutter worked her as much as the younger horses to maintain that high level of ability that she had shown early. He saddled her up and rode out into the pen. He gave her some warm up time which gave him the time to think. What was he going to say to Jesse? How was he going to deal with Aimee? It was already done, so should he put a stop to it now?

He set a program on the mechanical cow and the mare sunk low into position. Her senses took over when the cow zipped up the wire and she followed it. She was spot on with her timing and her footwork was quick. Every time Cutter rode the mare, it impressed him, and he used the colt and the mare as a guide to compare all the other horses he had in training.

Her focus was in sync with her willingness to lower herself in the sand and keep up with the cow. Every stop was impressive and every turn was accurate, and Cutter ran her up and down the wire, giving him time to process everything else except for cutting. He was on autopilot.

When Jesse showed up a short while later, he took the remaining horses out of the barn and got to work in the stalls, cleaning them out. He avoided Cutter in the pen and kept busy by making up the feeds when he was done. He had no idea how much Aimee had told her brother, and he didn't know if he was going home or not.

In the kitchen, Raylee was making her morning coffee when Aimee wandered down, still in her clothes from the night before.

"Good morning," Raylee said, trying to be cheerful.

"Is it?" Aimee replied, and she took a seat at the table.

"Well I don't know. You tell me." Raylee hadn't talked to Cutter so was still unsure how things went down the previous night. She poured Aimee a juice and sat at the table with her.

"Is he still mad?"

"Who, Cutter?" Raylee asked. "I don't know. I didn't hear him come back to bed last night and I haven't seen him this morning."

"Have you seen Jesse?"

"I haven't seen anyone... Do you want to tell me what happened last night?"

Aimee gave Raylee a rundown on how the events of last night played out. While Aimee did all the talking, Raylee just listened. She was close to Aimee and she understood how Aimee was feeling. It was also replaying in her mind the events from last year when her father walked in on her first time in bed with Cutter. Her father was mad too. It was history repeating itself.

While Cutter was furious at both Jesse and Aimee for their inappropriate behavior under his roof, his approach to Jesse was going to be slightly awkward, since it was Jesse who was standing at the end of the bed when Cutter got caught with Raylee by Allan Tremayne. What could he possibly point out to Jesse that he hadn't already done himself?

It was driving him crazy that he really had no argument to run with.

When Cutter finished with the mare, he walked her in circles. He had worked her into a healthy sweat and she was hot. The sun had just broken and lit up their world, giving out an instant warmth and adding to his need to give the mare a well deserved rest. It was going to be another warm day.

Jesse cautiously came out of the barn with both the pally and the roan, saddled and ready to ride. Cutter gave Jesse the reins of the mare and they exchanged horses.

"Let her cool down. I want you in the pen," Cutter instructed him.

Jesse didn't question it, just doing exactly as he was asked. He tied the mare up in the shade and unsaddled her, ready for Aimee to give her a wash. He went to the pen and threw his leg over the blue roan. Giving the two young horses time to warm up, both Jesse and Cutter rode around in circles chasing one another, not saying a word.

When the horses were warm, Cutter called Jesse over. "I'm setting a new program," Cutter said of the mechanical cow. "I want you to ride her so I can see how she looks."

Jesse hadn't spoken one word yet and was relieved that nothing had been mentioned about the night before. Maybe Aimee had talked her way out of it and there was nothing more to discuss and therefore, nothing to worry about.

He lined the horse up in front of the cow and Cutter started the program. It zipped up the wire and Jesse and the filly followed it until it stopped, with Cutter giving him instructions from the side. Fine tuning his techniques, Cutter was breaking down each move and Jesse was listening, focusing on the horse's movements and the cow.

When he was done, Cutter took to the mechanical cow while Jesse sat to the side and watched. They were worlds apart and Jesse knew that he could learn a lot from Cutter, if he ever wanted to take on this sport professionally, and if he had any kind of future there on the ranch.

After they were both done, they tied the horses up and unsaddled them, throwing their saddles over the colt and the gelding.

"It doesn't look like we're getting any help today," Cutter noted. "So it looks like it's you and me."

It gave Jesse a nervy feeling. He'd much rather have gone on the ride with Aimee alone, as he was desperate to spend time with her and find out exactly what happened after she left the barn. He was hoping that she wasn't upstairs packing her bags, or worse still, she may have already gone. That could be the reason she hadn't shown up for work. His head was running wild with every possibility and while he was wanting to know what the outcome was, he couldn't ask.

They rode out the gate and over the first rolling hill, the sun already feeling steamy as it hit them on the back.

"Do you like my sister?" Cutter asked.

Jesse had been expecting it sooner or later, not thinking that he'd actually got away with it. "Yeah. What's not to like? She's funny and smart and she's got a killer smile." Jesse's compliments were a little young, and Cutter had to remember that Jesse was only twenty-two. Though Cutter never thought of his sister like that. He always thought she was sweet and innocent, but mostly naive. Little did he know the real Aimee, until last night.

"What did she tell you?" Jesse asked. Since Cutter had brought it up, he was now desperate to know the details.

"Everything... and more."

Jesse hesitated. "And you're not sending me home?"

Cutter didn't look at him and he kept his eyes from showing his real feelings. "I need you here. And I need Aimee here too."

It gave Jesse some peace of mind, that Aimee hadn't gone home and was still at the ranch. "And you're okay with it?" he asked, feeling hopeful.

"No. I'm not okay with it," Cutter said abruptly. "But I can't change it. I just need to know that you like her enough not to hurt her."

"I get that. And we're still getting to know each other. But I really do like her," Jesse assured him.

"So if you really like her, then there's something I need you to do for me."

"Anything. What is it?" Jesse was willing to do anything to please Cutter right now.

"I need you to cool things down. I want you to back right off and take it steady. If you're meant to be together then it will work out. But you need to be friends first."

Jesse didn't like the idea, except that he had no choice but to respect Cutter's request and he agreed. After all, he could have been on a plane going home early that morning and instead, he was training a young horse on the mechanical cow and riding over the ranch.

The mood in the kitchen was still flat. Aimee was still sitting at the table with her chin resting in the palm of her hand, staring at her empty glass and feeling that there was nothing to be happy about.

"You know what you need to do?" Raylee asked, trying to give Aimee the encouragement that she needed.

"What?"

"You need to pull yourself together and get to that barn. You need to show Cutter that you want to be here and that he needs you. Because if you mope around all day and don't put in, then he'll have no choice but to send you home."

"Do you think he'd do that?"

"I don't know what he's thinking at the moment, but if you and Jesse back off each other for a while, and you keep up with your work at the barn, then he'll have no reason to send you home."

Raylee's advice was spot on and Aimee knew it. She dragged herself upstairs to get changed and came back down, ready for work.

"And don't forget to smile," Raylee added, just as Aimee left the house.

Although she had to force herself, Aimee picked up her shoulders along with her smile when she arrived at the barn. The boys were nowhere to be seen and she looked around, finding three horses tied up, and she took them one at a time into the wash bay. She gave them a good scrub, making them clean up like new. She knew the routine, only this time she put in extra effort and gave extra detail to each horse, cleaning out their hooves and platting their tails. Aimee threw their summer rugs on and gave them their feeds before leading them out to their yards.

When she finished with the last horse, the boys arrived back at the barn. Aimee felt sick with uncertainty about the response coming her way, but when

Jesse gave her the reins of the gelding, he gave her a sneaky wink to let her know that everything was alright.

"Do you want me to unsaddle your horse?" she asked Cutter.

"Yes ma'am," he said, and he tied the colt up to the rail. "We're going to town. If you need help, just ask Raylee to give you a hand." Cutter was friendly enough, although he didn't give her any sign of what he was really thinking.

It was news to Jesse. He didn't know they were going to town and he had no idea what for.

They asked Raylee if she needed anything from town before they jumped into the truck and drove out the front gate. Raylee was instantly jealous, that she had to stay at home and do the housework while Jesse got to leave the ranch and go out for a couple of hours. She figured it was Cutter's way of keeping Jesse and Aimee apart, and she wondered how long he needed to keep it up for.

When they sat in the diner and ordered a late breakfast, Jesse was still feeling the guilt and even more so now that Cutter was being so nice to him. He didn't deserve this, but Jesse wasn't going to argue about it either. While they avoided talking about Aimee, her name was dropped a couple of times when Cutter talked about his family.

On the inside of the window, there was an advertisement stuck to the glass panel of the booth they were sitting in, and Jesse was trying to read it from the inside out.

"Is there gonna be a rodeo here?" he asked, and he gently pulled the flyer off the window so he could read the details.

"Sure is. It's on at the same time every year but it's still a few weeks away," Cutter explained. "Everyone in the town turns up and it draws a big crowd from all over."

Jesse was instantly interested. "Are we going?"

"If you want."

"Hey, maybe we could enter?"

Cutter was adamant. "Except that I promised Raylee there'd be no more bulls."

Jesse thought about it then tried another angle. "So maybe she wouldn't mind if you entered with me in the team roping?"

"I don't know... She'd probably think it was the same thing."

"But it's not and you know it. Look," he said, while he was reading down the page. "There's steer wrestling and roping... And I could go in the saddle bronc."

"You're supposed to be here cutting, not riding at rodeos."

"It's just this one. And come on, I'm sure your sister would love to see us both ride."

Cutter was sure of that. Aimee would love to watch her brother ride in a rodeo and see Jesse ride a bucking horse. The townspeople that knew Cutter well would love to see him ride too. It had been many years since he'd last ridden there. "I'll think about it. But you know who the biggest hurdle is gonna be, don't you?"

"Leave that to me," Jesse said, very sure of his ability to turn Raylee around.

They went to the stock supplies and picked up some horse feed, loading it into the back of the truck then drove back to the ranch...

"No way," Raylee said severely. She was sweeping out the feed room while the boys brought the bags of chaff and grains in, placing them on the ground in front of the feed bins.

"Come on, Raylee. It will be good for him... For all of us." Jesse was doing his best to convince her that they should enter in the rodeo. "We promise you... no bulls."

Raylee knew that roping and wrestling were tame compared to bull riding, yet she was still not convinced that it was a good idea and she stayed firm on her decision.

Over dinner, Jesse was still going on about it, with Aimee showing more interest than Raylee would have liked, leaving her the only one who was against it.

"You know Cutter could rodeo with his eyes closed," Jesse said, praising Cutter's ability, coming from every direction he could think of. "There's no way he'd get hurt like he did last year."

"Just so that you know, it was Cutter who made the conditions that you were here to be cutting and there was to be no bronc riding," Raylee stated, to pass the blame onto someone else.

"Hey, don't look at me," Cutter said in defense. "I'd never tell a cowboy he couldn't rodeo."

It seemed that with Raylee digging her heels in, everybody backed off. At least for now. With two against one, and the other sitting on the rails, they were sure to wear her down eventually.

That night when they went to bed, Cutter and Raylee made sure that Jesse was confined to the barn and the front door of the house was locked, leaving Aimee on strict instructions not to leave her room before five a.m.

It was the first time that Cutter and Raylee had been together alone that day and he filled her in on what happened the night before. Raylee had heard most of it from Aimee, but it was still worth hearing again from Cutter's perspective. Raylee's suspicions were right when she figured that Cutter was doing everything he could to keep them apart for the day, including taking Jesse into town instead of her.

"You know you can't keep them apart forever. It's keeping us apart too," she said.

He sat up on his elbow and looked down into her face. "I'm sorry. I know this is not a great honeymoon time for you, and I promise you that after the show, we'll take some time out. Just you and me. On our own."

Raylee was looking noticeably sad. It was in her eyes.

"Are you alright?" he asked, but she didn't answer. "Raylee, what is it? Is it Jesse and Aimee? Is it too crowded here?"

"No. It's not them."

"Well then, what is it?"

She was tired and had so much on her mind, but she never wanted to bother Cutter with her problems, especially with his training and workload, and the issues he had with Jesse and Aimee now.

"It's nothing," she said, dismissing it quickly and she rolled over.

Cutter was confused and now worried. "It's not nothing. What is it?" he asked again, and he pulled himself in close behind her.

"You've got enough to worry about. Don't worry about me. I'll be fine."

He didn't believe her. He rolled her back over so that he could look into her eyes. "You don't sound fine. And you are my first priority. You come before my training and all the other bullshit I have to deal with."

"It really is nothing. Honestly."

"Raylee, if you don't tell me what it is... then I might have to tickle it out of you." He ran his fingers down her side and she began to squirm, wriggling and giggling from his touch. She was sensitive there and he knew it. They wrestled on the bed and he sat over her, pinning her arms down. He gave her gentle kisses on her neck and she laughed from his games. When he nibbled on her ear and kissed around her cheek, it made her skin prickle from the warm sensation.

Her mood changed and instead of being sad, she was loving the attention and was wanting more. His playfulness turned serious when he bit her on the neck in a moment that turned into a passionate gesture. They were totally in love with each other and that night, there was not another thought in the world as he gave her everything she wanted. Everything she needed.

"I've got a surprise for you," Cutter said to lift Raylee's spirits, when she wandered into the barn the next morning. Cutter had trouble sleeping and was awake most of the night, trying to figure out what her problem was. She had arrived in Texas on a high and within weeks, she was hitting a low point. He made it his mission to fix it, and fast.

"What is it?" she asked curiously.

"I'm not telling you just yet."

"Hey, that's not fair."

"Yes it is. Isn't that what you did to me? Tell me and then not tell me."

When Raylee surprised Cutter by bringing the colt back to the ranch from Australia, she'd done the same thing, playing that same cat and mouse game. Cutter thought that it was only fair that she got a taste of what that was like.

"How long do I have to wait?" she asked.

"Long enough for me to have some fun with it." Although Cutter was never going to hold out for that long.

"Now that's really not fair."

"Well I could tell you... but then it wouldn't be a surprise, would it?"

Raylee loved that he was returning the gesture, although she had no idea what the surprise could be. A million ideas ran through her mind, starting with a new puppy. Cooper was gone now and there was always room on the ranch for a dog or two, especially since they had already established that a family was not on the immediate agenda. Maybe it was a dishwasher. Since Marnie was away and there were more mouths to feed, Raylee thought that a dishwasher was something that would be extremely useful and give her more time away from the kitchen.

While they saddled the horses together, they talked endlessly about everything that was going on with the training, while visions of what the surprise could be kept popping up in Raylee's head. She dreamed of a real honeymoon, a new car, her own saddle. It could have been one of a thousand things that Cutter could surprise her with and he wasn't giving anything away to let her get even close to guessing what it was. Perhaps he was thinking of getting her name tattooed across his arm.

Raylee kept looking at him with curiosity. He threw his leg over the horse and rode out into the pen, before he really fell for those soft green eyes and she got her way.

# Chapter Six

Cutter knew exactly what the problem was with Raylee. He was sure that their intimate nights together weren't going to resolve it, as her downward spiral had hit rock bottom by the end of the week. He was feeling confident now that he had come up with the perfect solution. As he ripped up the sand in front of a cow, his mind kept going back to his wife and the surprise. The horse sunk low and was switched on, yet Cutter's focus was elsewhere.

Aimee sat in the corner and helped keep the small mob together while Jesse pushed them back when needed. Raylee rode into the pen to give a hand in one of the corners and that immediately picked up Cutter's mood, allowing him to concentrate again. He loved having Raylee there, and he knew just how much she'd missed out on since she'd arrived back in Texas, with the house and office work weighing her down. She was still young and had grown up with everything at her beck and call, and now she was struggling to keep up with the duties of a housewife when really, all she wanted was to be at the barn and in that yard.

After a dozen times of checking his watch, Cutter called an end to the session. He had relaxed about Jesse and Aimee spending time alone again, after he made it quite clear that they both understood the new rules put in place and wouldn't cross those lines for fear of both going home. It gave Cutter more time to spend with Raylee, since he was certain that his lack of attention to her was contributing to her problem.

True to his commitment of making her a priority, they headed to town for lunch, leaving Jesse and Aimee to deal with the horses and ride over the ranch. When they sat in the diner, Cutter kept checking the time and Raylee was becoming suspicious that her surprise might be closer than she thought. She was on a high from anticipation.

She had covered just about everything she could think of from a new foal to some hand picked flowers. Her mind was doing overtime and she was sure that out of the thousand things she came up with, it was bound to be somewhere on her list.

Much to her disappointment, they drove away from town with no mention of it and she felt slightly let down to her deflated state again. Back to domestic bliss. Oh joy for me, she thought.

Cutter pulled the truck up at the side of the house and they carried the grocery bags up the steps, taking their boots off and leaving them outside on the porch. As they walked in the door, Raylee was still forcing out a slight laugh at the silly flirting games they'd often play, when she came face to face with her mother standing in the kitchen.

Raylee froze, unsure of what was going on. Her mother was in Texas. Was she there to convince her to go home? She wasn't sure if she should put up her guard or let it down completely. She half smiled, pleased to see her but still trying to figure out what was going on and why she was there. Had something happened to her father that her mother could only tell her in person?

Evelyn returned the smile. Raylee was so shocked to see her mother that she couldn't think straight. She turned around and looked at Cutter, wanting to see his reaction.

"Surprise," he said.

Raylee looked back at her mother then back to Cutter. "Did you know?" she asked.

"Of course he knew," Evelyn answered on his behalf. "Cutter called me and invited me over to see you."

Raylee put the grocery bag down and threw her arms around Cutter's neck and kissed him on the cheek. "Thank you." She raced over to her mother and did the same, holding her and giving her a squeeze. She pulled back. "I can't believe you're here," Raylee exclaimed.

"I couldn't say no. As soon as I got the call, I started packing my bag and booked my ticket. I wanted to come and see where you're living and what you're doing. But mostly, I just wanted to see you."

Raylee became teary all of a sudden as the shock had just worn off and the reality of seeing her mother in her house was setting in. She needed this more than she realized. Her eyes were showing her emotions and she couldn't stop looking at her, and Raylee hugged her again when she couldn't contain her happiness. While Raylee was tucked in under her mother's wing, Evelyn called Cutter over too. He was more than happy to greet his mother-in-law with a hug, as their conversation over the phone had been pleasant enough and the beginning of a relationship had already been formed. Evelyn seemed willing to put everything that had happened in the past far behind her and Cutter felt an acceptance that he'd not experienced before.

While they all stood around the kitchen counter close together, talking about the shock Raylee just received, Allan Tremayne walked in from the sitting room. It took Cutter back a step, as the tables had just turned and it was now Cutter who was surprised.

He stood up straight. "What the hell do you think you're doing here?" Cutter asked abruptly.

Evelyn grabbed Cutter by the arm. "I asked him to come," she said.

"Well why would you do that?"

The tightness in Cutter's hands released slowly when he watched Raylee rush to her father and throw her arms around him too. He shouldn't have reacted like that. It just poured out of his mouth with a lot of good reason but without any thought.

"That is why," Evelyn said, as the two of them stood next to each other watching Allan with his daughter. She was trying calmly to reach him. "Raylee needs this. You both do. So I asked him to come with me so we can sort this out once and for all." Evelyn made no apologies as she explained.

"Well I don't know if it's a good idea," Cutter said more to himself than to anyone else.

Allan was still holding his daughter and when Cutter looked at Raylee, he could see the love there. He kept silent for fear of blurting out any more than he should.

"We've got a lot to talk about," Allan said. "Starting with an apology."

That was enough to instantly ignite Cutter's anger for a second time and his fist became tight again. "An apology?" he said rudely. "If you think that I'm gonna apologize to you again, then you've got me confused with someone else who gives a flying…"

"Stop it," Raylee said quickly to silence him in front of her parents, although he was fired up and was not going to give in to Allan's expectations.

"Actually, it's me that needs to apologize," Allan said hesitantly.

Cutter was stunned and confused, and was left wondering what on earth was going on. It wasn't what he was expecting to hear, and while he tried to get his head around the idea of Raylee's father standing in his kitchen, he remained unsure of what to say next.

Raylee went to Cutter and gave him a hug. She looked up at him. "Thank you," she said. "You've made me the happiest wife in the world."

That said, Cutter knew that was the end of the confrontation... for now.

"Why don't you get your mom settled in. I'm going for a ride," he said quietly to Raylee.

"I'll come with you," Allan said forcefully, and had already made his way to the door.

"It's alright... I think I know my way around my own ranch, thank you," Cutter replied. Raylee looked at him with pleading eyes. She didn't need to speak. "Alright," he gave in. "Just don't talk to me," he said dramatically and he strutted to the front door.

Cutter was still fuming as he walked to the barn. He could feel Allan a few paces behind and it totally annoyed him. Jesse and Aimee were nowhere to be seen and they were the last thing on his mind when he brought the gelding in for Allan to ride.

"Find a saddle in the tack room," Cutter said abruptly. "But not mine," he added quickly.

Allan didn't speak. He went into the tack room and found an old stock saddle. "And not that one either. That's my dad's," Cutter said with a sharpness that had already been toned down a notch. "You can use that one," he said, and he directed him to another saddle that looked like it hadn't been used for quite some time.

It was tense in the barn while both men saddled the horses in silence. The tension was thick and the air could have been cut with a knife. Mostly from Cutter's side, while Allan seemed more relaxed than ever, taking it all in his stride.

As they rode up the first rolling hill, Cutter didn't look back. Allan was lagging behind and was taking in the view, with the house and the barn disappearing when they rode down the other side. The feed was coming through nicely and the cattle were in great shape. This had been Allan's life while he was growing up and then raising a young family, but since the family had sold the cattle station and downsized to the vineyard, he hadn't been on a ride like this. So far, he was impressed.

He caught up to Cutter who was soldiering on and not waiting for him. There was no eye contact, no conversation and no connection at all. It was like they were two riders on two horses on two completely different rides. They rode on.

The most insane thoughts were going through Cutter's mind while he was riding towards the back pasture. Every encounter they'd had so far was either an argument or a fight, with the first time involving a rifle which resulted in Cutter nearly being shot. He thought of Raylee and how sad she'd been the last few weeks. Maybe she was missing her family and having her parents around would help. They rode on some more.

How long would they stay? Not too long, he silently hoped. Long enough to spend some time with Raylee and make her happy, then leave. Yes... a couple of days should do it. They rode on in silence.

What was Allan thinking just turning up at his house like that? He could have stayed in town and surprised Raylee there instead. He didn't need to come to the ranch. The more Cutter was loading his mind with these crazy thoughts, the more it was winding him up and making his blood boil, until he stopped.

Hey, what am I doing here, he asked himself. He was sitting on the mare looking at the graves in the yard. The afternoon sun was on its way down and the breeze was cooling the day to a lower temperature that was a welcome relief.

He got off the mare and tied her to the wrought iron fence. He didn't care what Allan did. He could have ridden home for all Cutter cared, but since he was there, he opened the gate and went in, kneeling in front of his mom and dad's headstones. He read them again, taking the time to remember his parents fondly.

"Is this your family?" Allan asked quietly.

"Yes sir, and now Raylee's the start of my new family," Cutter replied, not adding any more that would open up old wounds and start a conversation.

For Cutter, Macca was the greatest man he ever knew and he was grateful that he had the opportunity to be a part of his family. He thanked Macca in his mind for everything he'd taught him and he shared his thoughts with the headstone on how well the ranch was running now. Macca would have been more than pleased, Cutter was sure.

His mom would have loved Raylee. He was sure of that too. Mary-Ann was a beautiful mom with a gentle soul and because of both his parents, he'd had the best, most decent and respectful upbringing a child could ever have had. Then why couldn't he get his head around this situation? Why couldn't he be forgiving of Allan, like Allan seemed to be forgiving of him? If he had his father there now, he'd ask for his opinion. His thoughts ran quickly through his head, searching for the answers. He didn't need his father there to ask him. He knew exactly what Macca would say and what he would expect Cutter to do... and nothing less.

"It's a shame you missed the wedding," Cutter said, still sitting in front of the headstones and not looking at Allan.

"I have many regrets in my life," Allan said. "But that will always be at the top of the list."

"You know, you'll never have the opportunity to walk her down the aisle again... I'll make sure of that. I'm gonna love her 'til the day I die."

"And I believe you." Allan was sincere. He wasn't just saying it to bridge the gap. Cutter genuinely believed him.

Cutter stood up, still staring at the graves. He needed to go there, he just wasn't sure how he got there. He felt Allan's presence behind him, close by. "Well you could always take a leaf out of my book," Cutter said, and he turned around to look at him. "Live life with no regrets."

"You're a good man, Cutter... I was wrong about you and I want you to know that I apologize." Cutter could tell that those words were not easy for Allan Tremayne to get out. "And I'm pleased that Raylee went with her heart and came here to be with you."

"Not as pleased as I am," Cutter replied.

It was a strange moment and one that needed finalizing before they went back to the house. Cutter wanted to show Allan that he was a good man, that he was decent and respectful, and was going to make a good husband for his daughter. He held out his hand like he had done before. This time, Allan grabbed it and pulled him in close to his shoulder in a show of acceptance. It was brief, then he pulled away.

"And if you ever try to shoot me again..." Cutter said.

"If you look after my little girl, then I'll never have a reason to," Allan replied.

They took to the saddles and made their way to the back pasture where the cows were grazing. Tiny calves popped out from behind their moms, as the calving process had started overnight. It was a sight that would soften even the toughest of cowboys.

On the way back to the house, Cutter gave Allan a rundown on the way the program worked and Allan took it all in like it was second nature to him. He was a natural on a horse and Cutter could see that Raylee's father really was a cowboy from way back. When they arrived back at the barn, they were greeted by Jesse, who hesitated slightly when he came face to face with his old boss.

"I'm sorry I just left you like that, Allan," Jesse said. "But I had a better offer." Jesse's way of dealing with Allan Tremayne was to add a little humor. He'd worked for him long enough to be part of the family.

"Well, it looks like we didn't lose you completely," Allan said.

"Where's Aimee?" Cutter asked, just to satisfy his curiosity as to what they had been doing all afternoon.

"She's at the house. Helping with the dinner." Jesse looked Cutter in the eye and he returned it. He knew from that look that Jesse had been respectful to his sister.

They unsaddled the horses and finished feeding for the night. The three of them walked side by side to the house and when they reached the porch, they could smell something amazing coming from the kitchen.

With the table set, dinner finalized and Aimee and Allan receiving their first introduction, they all sat around the kitchen table when it was served. Cutter sat at one end opposite Allan, and when he looked around, it made him think fondly of the table. He'd shared every meal at it with his mom and dad while he was growing up, and it was not very often that it was this full. As they passed the meat and potatoes around between them and filled their plates, the conversation flowed easily.

It was good to have Jesse there, filling in the few silent moments as he gave Allan and Evelyn an update on everything that had happened since he'd left Australia. Well, almost everything. They talked about the vineyard and what the boys were doing with the horses, and where Randall was going to take the program next.

Evelyn was a good cook, and Cutter felt that having her there was exactly what Raylee needed. There were some serious discussions about cutting, breeding and ranching, while there was also some laughter from everyone about Aimee's first day on the ranch, when her secret encounter with a certain mouse accidentally escaped from Raylee's lips.

At the end of the meal after the fun had died down, Evelyn put her elbow on the table and pointed her fork towards Jesse and Aimee in a casual way. "You know, you two make a really nice couple," she stated.

Aimee smiled from the compliment.

"Oh, trust me. They're not a couple," Cutter said quickly to squash any hopes of a reunion.

"Well, maybe you should be. You look really nice together." Evelyn didn't understand the situation so was more than happy to pursue it further.

"Well we would. But we're not allowed," Aimee said, then she looked at Cutter with a stare that could only be described as I told you so. She redirected her eyes to the other end of the table, looking for more support. "What do you think, Allan?" Aimee asked.

The table fell silent when everyone looked at him. Allan was now under the spotlight and had to be careful about what to say. Everyone knew the history except for Aimee, and she innocently put him under pressure without knowing it.

"Well," Allan began to say, then paused, choosing his words carefully. "I'd have to say... that a man's house is his home, and whoever is under his roof needs to respect that." He looked down, picked up his fork and began digging around his plate. Cutter was torn between knowing that it was a shallow dig at him, and that it was also Allan's way of telling Jesse to be considerate of the rules.

"But there's one thing I do know," Allan went on to say, and everyone hung on to his next words. "If it's true love, then nothing will stand in the way," Allan stated, and he gave Cutter a friendly wink across the table that no one else caught sight of.

It gave Aimee the pick-me-up that she needed, giving Cutter a loving smile while she touched Jesse on the leg under the table.

"Hey, hands above the table," Cutter said, like the overprotective brother he was, and everyone laughed at him before he thought about how it sounded.

The clean up was huge, but with three girls all sharing the load, it made it so much easier. Raylee was nearly bouncing out of her skin with excitement that she not only had both her parents back together in the same room again, but that they were both in Texas.

She had taken her mother's bags upstairs earlier and had given her Macca and Mary-Ann's room. While it seemed strange for Cutter to offer, it was the right thing to do. Allan took Marnie's room downstairs and Raylee helped him to settle in, leaving Jesse and Aimee with the job of making the tea and coffee.

Cutter took Evelyn out to the porch and they sat on the swing. "You didn't tell me Allan was coming," Cutter said. It was a question and a statement rolled into one.

"I'm sorry. But it was all so last minute and there was no time to let you know, and besides, I was sure you wouldn't have liked the idea." Cutter could tell that Evelyn was an honest woman. "It even surprised me when he agreed," she added.

"Well maybe it was a good thing," Cutter admitted, after sharing the afternoon with him.

"There's something else I need to tell you," she continued.

Cutter looked worried, as if he was expecting an announcement that was not going to be good. He hesitated to ask what it was, yet he knew that he had to. "What is it? Is everything alright? Has something happened at home?"

"I'm sorry. I didn't mean to worry you," she said, seeing that concern in his eyes. "Everything is fine. But I may have hinted to Allan that there might be a second chance for us." Evelyn was confiding to Cutter her deepest feelings.

"Really? There's a chance you might get back together?"

"I don't know. But when I asked Allan for a divorce, it was because he'd become this controlling, irrational and arrogant man that I didn't marry some thirty years ago," she explained. "He changed when he sold the cattle station and went into business. It was like all this money and power had gone to his head, and I wasn't about to put up with his arrogance any longer."

Woah, Cutter thought. Maybe Raylee's mom was a down to earth, tough cookie after all. He didn't know that she was the one who had called it quits after all those years together, that she had asked for the divorce and moved out of the house, leaving Allan alone to wallow in his own misery. When they had arrived back from Europe, it seemed that Allan had turned his anger onto Cutter. By doing this, Allan used the situation to bond them together in their marriage as well as their roles as parents. They were to fight the good fight together.

"But don't get me wrong," Evelyn said to interrupt his thoughts. "Allan was most upset with you and Raylee when he found you together," she added, not to let him think that under the circumstances, it really was okay to take Raylee to his bed.

"So is he here for you or for us?" Cutter asked.

"Both," she said with clear definition. "I told him that the unreasonable way he handled the situation was only an example of the man he'd become... Being on his own has really given him some time to put everything back into perspective."

"Does Raylee know any of this?"

"No. And I don't see any point in building up her hopes just yet. She'll just be pleased that you and her father are at least on talking terms, and if that's all that's accomplished from our visit, then she'll be satisfied with that."

"Well, for what it's worth, Evelyn, I think that you're a strong woman. And I hope that everything works out the way you want it."

The porch door swung open and out came the tea and coffee. Cutter stood up to let Allan sit next to Evelyn. Really, it was so that he could sit next to Raylee on the low bench under the office window, while Jesse and Aimee leaned against the rail.

They all talked some more. Mostly about the ranch and the show coming up. Cutter sat back taking it all in. Here he was, sharing a late night cup of coffee with Raylee's family on his porch. He almost had to pinch himself that this was happening, yet he was pleased for Raylee and could see the excitement in her. When he touched her on the leg, her hand gently touched his and their hands locked together in a warm hold.

It was getting late for everyone. Raylee could see her parents fading after the long day of travel and her father's ride over the ranch. Aimee gave a huge yawn that seemed to be contagious and it gave everyone that same feeling.

When Raylee snuggled into bed behind Cutter that night, she was still on a high. "That was the best surprise ever," she said, and she squeezed him tight. "And here I was, thinking you were getting a tattoo."

"What?" he exclaimed, and he rolled onto his back to look at her. "Are you serious? You thought I was getting a tattoo?"

"Why not?" She touched him on the arm. "I'd love to see you branded with my name splashed all over you," she said, then she giggled.

"I am not getting branded," he said with certainty, which made her giggle even more.

"Well, branded or not, I thought of everything there was, but never did I think in a million years that you had called my mom and asked her to come over."

"I love you, Raylee Jones," he said, and he pulled her in by the back of the neck to kiss her.

"And I love you too, cowboy."

# Chapter Seven

It was a late start to the day. Cutter didn't make it to the barn until after six o'clock and as soon as he arrived, it was straight into it again, taking the horses into the cutting pen and bringing a few head of cattle in. The training program was underway.

Raylee went to the barn only a half hour later with her father. They saddled up and met Jesse and Aimee in the corners. Cutter let more cattle into the pen and by seven o'clock, there was a full blown cutting event going on.

The two girls sat in the corners on the back wall, while Jesse and Allan sat out in front to apply the pressure. Everyone was in position. It was exhausting for Cutter to be talking at the same time as he was cutting, yet he was explaining everything to Jesse from a trainer's perspective while everyone else just listened.

With Allan wanting to be part of the action, there were more hands to help and they ran through the morning ahead of schedule. Evelyn took over the kitchen to give Raylee the well deserved break that she needed, and everyone was getting along just fine. Allan even sat on the horse and silently admired Cutter's skills through the training process, and he could see how the colt came to be a champion.

During the evening, there was only one strained moment when Evelyn asked if there was a bottle of wine to have with dinner. There was an instant silence when Cutter, Raylee and Aimee all looked at each other. It was such a foreign word in the house as the ranch had never seen a drop of alcohol since Mary-Ann had arrived some twenty-six years ago. Cutter and Aimee, between them, gave a quick and simple explanation of the events that went back to well before Aimee was born. Their father had an addiction to the bottle, which in the end led to the painful marriage breakdown of Pete and Mary-Ann.

"I'm so sorry," Evelyn apologized. "I had no idea."

"You've got nothing to be sorry about," Cutter said, and he tried to soften the awkward moment for her. "After all, you own a vineyard. It's just that it's not for everyone."

Jesse was learning more about their lives every time they sat down together for a meal and was starting to see where Cutter and Aimee had come from.

From his overview of the table, Cutter was intent on watching the connection between Raylee's parents. He was looking for signs that they were starting to bond together and reconnect. There were some noticeable moments that looked like there was a slight spark on the horizon, although Allan would unintentionally put it out before letting the fire burn.

"I think now would be a great time to discuss the rodeo," Jesse said, when everyone finished dinner.

"I told you, there's nothing to talk about," Raylee said firmly.

Cutter sat back, relaxed in his chair and shrugged his shoulders at Jesse as if to say he wasn't getting involved.

Allan, however, would deeply involve himself. "What rodeo?" he asked.

"Dad, Jesse's not here to ride broncs, he's here to help Cutter with the training. The show's only a month away and they need to be focussed on that," Raylee said, to put a sudden end to the topic.

"I'd like to see him ride," Aimee weighed in, thinking that it sounded like fun.

"No," Raylee said abruptly.

Cutter watched the debate unfold, not saying a word.

"Well it's alright for you," Aimee said to Raylee. "You've grown up around it all. I've never been to a rodeo before."

"Well I didn't say we couldn't go... I just said they couldn't ride," Raylee said smartly.

They all sat around the table in silence. Raylee thought that it was put to rest until her father brought it up again. "It's a shame," Allan commented, since he was finding it difficult to let it go. "I could come out of retirement and show these young boys how it's done."

While Cutter, Raylee and Evelyn all laughed at the suggestion, Jesse and Aimee thought it was a great idea and jumped onboard with him straight away.

"Yes... And you could team up with Cutter in the team roping," Jesse said. "I've already offered him my services, but you know... the wife pulled on the brakes... But maybe she'd let her old man ride with him."

The table had come alive again with fun and laughter at the thought of seeing Allan swinging a rope from a horse at high speed. Both Jesse and Aimee were wanting to see team Jones ride at the rodeo, but not Raylee, while Cutter was neither one way or the other. He'd competed so much over the years that it wasn't such a big deal to him.

"You've probably forgotten how it's done, Allan," Evelyn pointed out.

Allan was making it light-hearted for everyone. "Trust me, Evelyn... You never forget. It's like..."

"Alright, Allan. Not in front of the kids. We all get the idea," she said to quieten him down.

Everyone laughed some more. Cutter sat back and was just thinking. Maybe it was exactly what Raylee's parents needed to reignite that spark again. Evelyn would have to be impressed if her husband - ex husband - competed at the rodeo. They'd ridden over the ranch together and Cutter knew that he was an experienced rider. He may be a little bit rusty in the pen, but with a few more weeks and some practice, Cutter could certainly get him up to speed, to where he needed to be.

It was another late night when everyone went to bed. Cutter was so sure that Aimee was beyond tired, that she'd not even think about slipping out of the house and sneaking over to the barn for a bit of fun. It may have still been on her mind, and that's why Cutter made sure that she was exhausted by the end of each day.

The house was quiet and as Cutter lay in bed next to Raylee, he could tell that whatever had been weighing her down was now gone. He didn't bring it up, but he touched her in a way that gave her every reason to feel loved.

After a full training session in the cutting pen, Raylee went to the house to see her mom. They both came back to the barn in the truck, ready to drive out.

"Where're you going?" Cutter asked, while he was pushing the last steer back into the yards then he closed the gate.

"We're going over to see Emma. She's been house bound and is feeling like she wants some company," Raylee explained.

"Good idea. Give her a kiss for me," Cutter said, and he watched as she climbed back into the truck and drove away. He leaned on the rail and waited for her to reach the top of the driveway before he turned around to find Allan, Jesse and Aimee all looking at him.

"What?" he asked, skeptical of their look.

"Now that Raylee's gone, we could have a practice for the rodeo," Aimee suggested. She was the spokeswoman for the other two, since they felt she would be able to reach her brother where they couldn't.

"I knew you were all up to something," he said.

"It's only practice," Jesse pointed out.

"Yeah. And what Raylee doesn't know, won't hurt her," Allan added. "You know what they say... What happens on the ranch, stays on the ranch."

"Please..." Aimee was throwing Cutter her pleading eyes.

He looked at the three of them standing there and could see that they were going to do their best to wear him down and drive him crazy in the process.

Cutter reluctantly gave in, not wanting them to hound him every day until the rodeo. "But I'm just letting you know, that if we get caught, I'm denying everything," he informed them forcefully.

Allan and Aimee took the horses into the barn and unsaddled them, while Jesse brought the gelding in and threw a roping saddle on. Cutter had quit the gelding from the cutting pen years ago when he showed more potential on the ranch and in the roping arena. Cutter led the colt in and saddled him up. The colt could do anything on the ranch and he was fast.

When they all went back into the sand yard, Cutter noticed how the chutes were all greased up and in good working order. He looked at Jesse.

"What? I knew you'd say yes," Jesse replied to that look he was given.

"And just for the record," Cutter said. "I didn't say yes."

Before they brought a young steer into the chute, they gave Allan some practice swinging the rope from the ground. His co-ordination wasn't too bad for someone who hadn't been to a rodeo for many years. With a couple of weeks up his sleeve, he'd get the hang of it. Although, accurately aiming it at the calf would be a whole different challenge.

When they got their co-ordination working, Aimee went to the barn and came out with a practice dummy and placed it in the middle of the yard. That was when the real fun began. The three boys each had a practice from the chute, throwing the rope at the metal frame with the plastic head that sort of resembled a calf.

While there were many stuff-ups, there was also a lot of laughing.

Cutter was dishing out the instructions, mostly to Allan, who was taking one step backwards for every two steps forward. But at least he was making progress. It was his first attempt in years and he wasn't doing such a bad job for an old retired cowboy. When he fluked the rope around the calf dummy's head, he pulled the rope tight and gave a victorious shout, much to the amusement of everyone.

Even though there was still a lot of work to be done on the timing and the accuracy of the rope's aim, Cutter decided to bring in the smallest steer from the yard and put it in the chute for Jesse to have a run at bulldogging. Aimee was intrigued and she sat on the top rail and watched, not understanding what was going to happen next.

Cutter lined himself up next to the calf and when Allan pulled the chute open, the steer ran into the pen at full speed with Jesse giving chase and Cutter keeping the steer straight. Aimee thought it was exciting, until Jesse launched himself off the horse and tackled it by the short horns. He twisted the head and wrestled it to the ground, much to the shock of Aimee, who was all of a sudden aware of the danger and could see why Raylee didn't want any of them entering in the rodeo.

When he stood up and dusted himself off, Jesse picked up his hat out of the sand and walked back to his horse. Aimee's relief turned to admiration when she thought that this was the best thing she'd ever seen. There was something about this cowboy and that moment, that made her want to immediately disregard the new house rules and take him up to the loft to give him his reward.

Before they were all caught out, they decided to end the practice session and go on a roundup to bring in a mob of smaller calves that were more suitable to roping and wrestling. When Cutter rode behind everyone, he was taking in the new view. Looking at his sister, at Jesse and at Allan, never did he imagine that this would ever be happening on his ranch, and it was only because of Raylee that this moment was taking place.

They worked well together. Aimee was growing in her ability and confidence every time they went out, while Allan looked like he was having the time of his life, rounding up the calves and heading them towards the gate.

They walked them steadily back to the yards and gave them some hay while Jesse and Aimee took the horses in and untacked them, before feeding up for the night. It had been a great afternoon and when they all arrived on the porch, Raylee and Evelyn were surprised by the spark between them all. They carried on with their bantering and the friendly bond was almost questionable to Raylee, who was wondering what had happened to make everyone so happy and get along so well.

"How's Emma?" Cutter asked, when he took his hat off at the basin to the side of the kitchen and washed his face and hands.

"She's good. She's feeling much better now that she's been resting," Raylee said. "But she's bored. If she feels up to it, she might come with us to the rodeo."

Cutter immediately felt guilty at the mention of the rodeo and when they all took their seats and sat down for dinner, it was noticeably quiet. Raylee felt like she had to say something to get the conversation flowing. "So, how was the training today?" she asked.

Nobody answered and she looked at Cutter.

"Oh sorry... I didn't know you were asking me... Yeah, it was good," he said, and Raylee was now sure that something had happened.

"What did you bring the calves in for?" she asked innocently, just to make small talk.

"Umm..." Cutter was put on the spot and wasn't very good at lying. He'd always been taught to be truthful and the lie wasn't sitting well with him. "Your dad wants to have a go in the cutting pen and I thought it would be better if he had the smaller calves to work with." Cutter wasn't sure where he pulled that one from but he hoped it sounded believable.

It must have. "Well I'm glad you're looking after him," Raylee said, thankful, and she looked down the table at her father who was looking at his plate. "Better to be in the cutting pen than the rodeo arena. Right Dad?"

"Can you pass me the potatoes, Aimee?" Allan said.

It was silent again. Nobody was saying much and nothing came from Jesse and Aimee at all. Had something happened between them that Raylee should know about, but the dinner table was not the right place to ask? This was a far different dinner than the night before and Raylee was curious to know what was going on.

It was driving Cutter round the bend not to tell Raylee about the practice. While everyone was well pleased with keeping it a secret, Cutter knew that it was resting on his shoulders if they got caught. He was responsible for everyone and was feeling quite uncomfortable about it.

"I can't do this," Cutter said to Allan and Jesse when they sat on the porch after dinner, waiting on the girls to come out.

"Just give us a couple more days... When they see how good we are, they'll think it's a great idea," Allan pleaded, and Cutter was more entertained by Allan's confidence in his own ability than anything else.

When the six of them sat on the porch in the soft light, the long day and the quietness made everyone feel tired.

"My shoulder's aching," Allan said, and he started to move it around to stop it from locking up. "Evelyn, can you rub my shoulder?" he asked.

"It's your doing. You shouldn't be on that horse," she said, unsympathetic to his pain. She put her hand on his shoulder anyway and gave it a light rub, while he closed his eyes and purred like a kitten.

"I think you need to slow it down a bit, Dad," Raylee suggested. "Maybe you need to have a day off tomorrow. You're not getting any younger."

"I'm good. And Cutter needs the help," Allan replied, still with his eyes closed while he was enjoying Evelyn's touch.

"But that's what Jesse is here for," she pointed out.

"I'm alright. I'm just finding muscles that I haven't used in years... A couple more days of this and I'll be fit and young again."

Evelyn laughed. "I think those days are long behind you, Allan. You need to start acting your age. Your cowboy days are so far in the distant past, you should leave it to the younger boys."

Before Evelyn totally humiliated and crushed Allan in front of everyone, Cutter came to his defense. "Actually, he's doing a damn good job out there, and I need him in the cutting pen." It was Cutter's way of getting Evelyn to see that her husband still had some appeal to offer her, and Allan looked silently thankful.

Raylee had to pinch herself. Was Cutter giving her father a compliment? Never did she imagine that this could happen. She looked at her parents sitting on the swing. Her mother was touching her father, still rubbing his shoulder. Oh my goodness, she thought. What is happening here? While she buried her thoughts and feelings, she was secretly pleased with what she was hearing and seeing.

Cutter gave Jesse a signal, to tell him that it was time he headed to the barn.

"I think I'll say goodnight," Jesse said, before he handed his empty cup to Aimee and gave her a quick peck on the cheek.

"Hey, that's enough," Cutter said. "Now get outta here." He gave Aimee the same look.

"And that's my cue to leave," Aimee said, catching on quickly. "Goodnight everyone," she added, before she went inside the house.

"Well, I've got an early start in the morning," Cutter informed everyone else and he stood up. "Come on, Raylee. You look tired too."

"I'm alright," she said. Cutter gave her that same look he gave Jesse and Aimee, to tell her that it was not only time to go to bed, but that it was to give her mom and dad some time alone. "But an early night wouldn't hurt," she added as an afterthought, even though it was now past ten o'clock and she didn't realize it was so late.

She gave both her parents a kiss and said goodnight, leaving them on the swing in the quietness of the porch.

When Raylee pulled the covers back and climbed into bed, Cutter was sitting up, propped up on a pillow, waiting for her. He had one arm supporting his head while he ran his hand over his bare chest. Raylee was wide awake.

"I've got something I need to tell you, Raylee," Cutter said. His guilt was playing hard against his honesty and had been getting the better of him as the night went on.

Raylee, however, was not listening and was fully excited. "Did you see my mom and dad?" she asked.

"Yes ma'am, I did. They seem to be getting along really well," he noted.

"They haven't got along this well for years," she said, hopeful there was something more growing between them. She ran her hand over his skin, feeling the natural ripples on his stomach from working on the ranch. Cutter didn't exercise or work-out at all. He didn't need to. Between lifting bales of hay and working with the horses, his fitness came from his daily routine and workload.

"Maybe it was a good thing your dad came over too," he admitted.

"It was a great thing. And I can't believe you're both getting along too. Whatever you're doing, keep doing it. Whatever it takes, you need to keep working with him," she insisted. "Now, what is it you need to tell me?"

Cutter looked at her. She was on a high and he loved that. Raylee was feeling happy again and he didn't have the heart to take that away. He had missed that smile. He reached up and touched her cheek. "I just needed to tell you that I love you," he said.

Raylee looked ready to explode. "You have no idea just how happy I am right now."

Cutter had to make a difficult decision. Tell Raylee about the rodeo, or not tell her. She had insisted that he keep doing whatever he was doing to build the relationship between himself and her father, and it was noticeably helping the relationship between her mother and father too. Allan was so consumed with entering in the rodeo, that he was already making plans for his next practice. He wanted that one last chance to ride in an event again and perhaps impress Evelyn, whom he was desperate to reconnect with.

In the barn, Cutter already had the pally saddled up ready for a session while Jesse was in the sand yard with the roan. He made some final adjustments to the saddle and was about to get on when Allan came in.

"How's your shoulder?" Cutter asked.

Allan gave it some movement to loosen it up. "It's pretty good... I think Evelyn did the trick last night."

Cutter was amused more than he was letting on. "I'm sure she did."

"Hey, do you think you could send Raylee to town today? We need to get them out of the way for a while."

Cutter didn't need to think long and hard about it. "I've got a better idea," he said, and he took to the saddle and rode out of the barn, leaving Allan to wonder what the game plan was.

He met up with Jesse and they went through the routine. First the pally, then the roan. Cutter could see Jesse getting better every time he was in the pen and if he was more focused on cutting than bronc riding, then Cutter could see a career ahead of him, especially as he was still quite young. What amateur cutter wouldn't want the best teacher in the business to get them to pro level? For Jesse, he was in the dream position.

Both the horses were coming along nicely. Since Jesse arrived at the ranch, he'd become quite fond of the roan and would often take her out over the ranch for a ride. His connection with her was plain to see and he favored riding her over the pally. The young horses he'd been working with were now returned to their yards for a time and wouldn't come back in for further handling until after the show.

With the show closing in, it should have been the first thing on everyone's mind, yet the rodeo seemed to take their interest.

After a long, drawn out breakfast, everyone was keen to get back to the barn. Cutter went to the office to make a phone call. He sat in the old leather chair and spun around to look up at the photos on the wall of his family while he waited on Johnny to answer.

"Hey, bro. What's up?"

Cutter could ask Johnny for anything. His plan didn't take any convincing or pleading, and Johnny was right onboard the moment he was asked to help put it into action.

"Everyone ready?" Cutter asked, when he stepped out of the office and met them all on the porch.

Just as Raylee pulled her boots on, the phone rang. She went inside to answer it and came back out after only a quick minute. "That was Johnny," Raylee said. "He needs me to go over to the house to sit with Emma while he goes to town," she added, half disappointed.

Evelyn was being supportive. "I'll come with you," she said without any hesitation.

It had worked. With the girls gone for a couple of hours, everyone had a chance to set up the pen for another practice session. While Jesse and Aimee saddled the horses, Cutter and Allan picked out a reasonably sized calf and prepared the chutes. Everyone was quick on the job to give them as much practice time as possible.

When everything was set up, Johnny arrived at the yard.

"Hey, I thought you had to go to town?" Cutter called out.

If Johnny was going to be part of the plan, then he was not going to miss out. "Yeah right. And let you have all the fun?" He joined in on the practice and even had a run on the calf, pulling it to the ground in an impressively quick time. While they both hadn't competed in a rodeo since Cutter pulled out years ago and went cutting, they certainly had not lost their touch. It was like old times again.

Roping calves needed a little more technique, and Johnny was there to give Allan some help where he needed it. Aimee was busy running around and releasing the rope from the plastic dummy when his aim was good and resetting it in position for the next run, and when it wasn't, she'd call out encouragement.

Allan's rope swinging was coming along and he managed to get it around the dummy's head more often than he missed. Except that a calf on the run was going to test his ability and his accuracy.

They loaded the calf in the chute while Allan got the horse in position.

"We've only got a half hour left, so let's get on the job," Cutter announced.

Allan chose to take the head of the calf leaving Cutter to take the heel. Together they had to get their aim and their timing right to at least get a score on the board. As far as the quickest time, Cutter was sure they were out of their league.

They managed to squeeze in a dozen runs with half of them failures and the other half more entertaining than serious. When Cutter looked at the time, he called it in.

"It's time," he said loudly so that everyone could hear. "You'd better get back," he said to Johnny, in case Raylee arrived home early and found out what was really going on.

They spent the afternoon in the cattle yards, preparing the older calves to go back out to pasture. Allan stood on one side of the crush, opening and closing it when each calf was pushed through. Jesse worked at the front and when the calf was in position, he gave it a drench, while Cutter stood to the side with the hot iron and branded it. It left Aimee to stand on the rails and help push them forward each time another one was released.

Allan had done this thousands of times before on his cattle station, although not for many years. He was loving every minute of it and was reliving those good old days when he worked alongside his brother. Allan never had the opportunity to share this experience with his two sons. They never showed any interest in working on the land and when they grew up, they were more focussed on going off to study law and accountancy, and wreaking havoc in their mother's wine cellar when her back was turned.

What Allan never expected, was that it would be his daughter who would be living the life that he loved.

With four of them on the job, it was done quickly and they kept them in the yards for the night. By the end of the day, Cutter noticed that Allan was slowing down, and not wanting to push him any harder, he let Allan clock off early. Allan headed to the house, leaving Aimee and Jesse to wash the horses and prepare them for the night in the barn, throwing their rugs on and checking their water. Cutter finished with the night feeds and cleaned out the tack and feed rooms.

After another long and tiring day, dinner was on everyone's mind.

"How's Emma feeling?" Cutter asked Raylee, after he cuddled her from behind and kissed her on the neck while she stood at the kitchen sink.

She turned around. "She's good, but wow is she big. I don't ever want to be that big having a baby," she said.

"Like I said... Better you than me."

She smacked him in the stomach with the back of her hand in a playful gesture. They were standing alone in the kitchen and he pulled her in close by the waist and kissed her.

Allan walked into the room. "Oops. Sorry," he said, and he went to back out again.

"That's okay, Allan. Come in. I'm going up for a shower anyway," Cutter informed him. He grabbed an apple from the fruit bowl and took a bite as he headed towards the stairs. He stopped next to Allan. He'd just had a shower also and was a little dressed up for such an ordinary evening. "You trying to impress someone, Allan?" Cutter asked rather sarcastically.

Allan looked down at his clothes. "Do you think it's a bit over the top?" he asked quietly.

Cutter took another bite of his apple and looked him up and down. "Nah... But you might wanna tone down that aftershave," he said. "It's gonna clash with my dinner." He gave Allan a taunting smile and he went upstairs.

Raylee stood in the kitchen and held back a grin. She was still unsure how this was all happening. Her husband was now closer to her father than her brothers were, and she would never have believed it, if it wasn't happening before her eyes.

Every day on the ranch and every night at dinner was a repeat of the previous day. Conversations flowed, experience was gained and broken relationships were being healed. With the lie becoming bigger each day, the unsuspecting victims, Raylee and Evelyn, were unaware of the devious plans to get them out of the way.

They would spend a couple of hours with Emma each afternoon to give Johnny the opportunity to go out to work on the ranch or go to town for supplies. Raylee couldn't say no to Emma. She loved spending time with her and it was nice to be needed by such a close friend, especially under the circumstances. Really, Johnny was turning up at practice and had decided that he'd enter in the rodeo as well.

Cutter had been asked to supply the cattle for the event, and the team brought them into the yards with only one day left. Everyone was feeling nervous. Even Cutter. Not from the thought of competing again, since that didn't faze him one little bit. He just wasn't sure how Raylee was going to react when she found out they had all been scheming behind her back.

She was on top of the world though, and if it meant sneaking around to create a positive atmosphere among everyone, then Cutter was prepared to keep at it.

"I think my dad's up to something," she said, lying in bed.

Cutter felt a surge of guilt. "What makes you think that?" he asked.

"I don't know. But he's different. Like he's changing or hiding something. He's so much more relaxed about us and he's being so... nice."

"Maybe he just likes spending time with us here."

"Or maybe you know what he's up to and you're not telling me," she said, and she sat up on her elbow and looked down into his face, trying to read him.

They were so close now and it made Cutter feel uncomfortable that he was part of the lie. "What makes you think that I know anything?" he asked.

"Because you've been spending all day, every day with him, and I think that you know."

"And if I did know, would you expect me to tell you?"

"Yes. Of course I would."

"And if it was a surprise, would you expect me to tell you?"

"So it is a surprise?" she asked.

He toned it back down again. "I never said I knew anything." Cutter tried every angle to get out of the discussion. "Anyway, why don't you ask him?"

"Maybe I will."

Cutter changed the course of questioning to steer Raylee away from the truth. "Has your mom said anything about your dad?"

"I've asked her, but she says nothing... I don't think she has any need to get back together with him. I think this trip for her was all about me and has nothing to do with them." Raylee sounded disappointed, even though she was still pleased that everyone was getting along so well. After everything that had happened since her parent's trip to Europe, that was as much as Raylee could ever hope for. "I'm just so thankful that you made that phone call to her."

Cutter was too, and when she tucked back in under the covers, he snuggled in close behind her. With one day to go, Cutter didn't have to live with the lie and hold onto the truth for much longer and he couldn't wait until it was out in the open. He decided right there and then, that he'd never get himself into that compromising situation again.

Not for anyone.

# Chapter Eight

From the time the house woke up, the rodeo was on everyone's mind, even though the discussions over lunch in front of Raylee were mostly about the afternoon program at the barn. They all wanted to finish work early so they could make their way to town and get the best view of the arena, before the crowd arrived. The cattle truck was arriving soon to pick up a load for the event and the horses were all washed, fed and either put out into their yards or stabled for the night. Except for the few they had to sneak out.

Cutter convinced Raylee to leave early and follow the cattle truck in, which was just an excuse to give Jesse and Allan a chance to load the horses and drive to town unseen. When they arrived at the grounds, Raylee and Evelyn set up the blanket on the grass, marking out their boundary before the gates were opened to the crowd, while Cutter helped unload the cattle.

Everything was going smoothly. The plans were unfolding and the girls were none the wiser. Johnny had Emma settled with Raylee and set her up with everything a pregnant woman would need for one night out. As the people flowed in through the gates, any available patch of grass was soon covered up and it became a tight squeeze closer to the start time.

Aimee found the girls sitting back and enjoying the late afternoon sun. She began to feel nervous, for the secret was about to be revealed. Aimee was doing well not to let the cat out of the bag, but then again, Raylee was not suspicious of her and therefore had no reason to question Aimee in that way.

Just as it was about to start, the music died down and the announcer came over the speakers to welcome everyone to the 31st Annual Summer Rodeo. Raylee was sure that everyone from the entire town and neighboring surrounds had turned out for it, as there was standing room only left around the top of the embankment.

Raylee looked over at her mom. Evelyn was laid back on the blanket with her sunglasses on and was looking relaxed. She looked younger than she was, and Raylee could tell that she was enjoying herself like a person should when they are on holidays.

LINDA ELLISON

Evelyn hadn't been to a rodeo for many years, even though Tremayne Industries was a regular sponsor at different events back home. In fact, the last time she went to a rodeo was before they sold the cattle station, and that was the last time that Allan rode in one. It looked like she didn't have a care in the world and was being thoroughly entertained by the Texan spirit, with the red, white, and blue flags hanging overhead and the smell of cotton candy and popcorn filling the air. There were pony rides for the children and market stalls selling everything from professional bull riding vests to kids' toys. Everyone was well catered for. It was like a mini carnival.

As the sun sank low, Raylee sat with her legs crossed in front of her, diving into a box of freshly popped buttered popcorn, when the announcer introduced the first event of the night... The steer wrestling. She looked around for the boys.

When the first cowboy was introduced, everyone looked towards the chute. It took a few seconds for the calf and the horse to settle, and when the cowboy was ready, he gave a nervous nod to the officials. He was quite young and from the neighboring town, and it was only his second rodeo event.

The chute was pulled open and he chased the calf out. His timing was a little off when he left the saddle and landed on the calf, and tried to wrestle it to the ground in what was a disaster from the start. The calf was slick and before he had it flipped over, it twisted out of his grip. It was a no score. It was enough to get the crowd fired up though, and they cheered him on when he stood up out of the dirt and brushed himself off.

"Where are those boys?" Raylee said out loud to no one in particular.

"I don't know," Aimee lied. "But if they don't hurry up soon, they're going to miss it."

Aimee was doing a good job of lying with purpose.

After several riders had taken a run, the leader board was turning over, placing everyone in order according to the fastest times. Raylee didn't know any of these cowboys, but was enjoying being there for a good night out, away from the ranch with her family and best friends. Her only wish was that Cutter would hurry back soon so they could share the night together. With the cattle being his, she presumed he'd got caught up at the back of the chutes and wouldn't be much longer.

They loaded the chute again. And again. It didn't take long between runs and the program was running through fast with only three cowboys left to take their turn.

"I can't believe I'm introducing this next cowboy here tonight," the announcer said with excitement to wind up the crowd. "Not only is he the best horse trainer in the country, but he's a local hero and a legend in this very arena. It's been too many years since you've seen him ride here, so please give a very big welcome back to... Cutter Jonessss..."

"What?" Raylee said, as she choked on a popcorn and spat it out onto the blanket in front of her. Her mother gave her a pat on the back and a swig of her drink. "What's going on?" she asked anyone who would give her an answer. It was too late. The chute was pulled open and Cutter and the colt accelerated at full speed from the jump while Jesse and the gelding ran alongside the steer to keep it straight. Cutter launched himself off the horse and wrestled the young steer to the ground in what could only be described as an unbelievable and impressive fast run.

From his introduction in the chutes to picking himself up out of the dirt, it all happened so fast that Raylee was stunned, and she stood up alongside everyone else who was standing to applaud him. Mostly, it was so that she could see. While she should have been absolutely furious, she found herself to be proud, and therefore she wasn't sure what to say. The crowd were going wild for him.

Cutter dusted off his jeans and picked up his hat, and he ran over to the announcer who was standing on the arena floor holding the microphone. He grabbed it and his voice filled the arena. "That was for my wife," Cutter said loudly, totally pumped up by the response he was receiving from the crowd. "That one was for you, Raylee Jones," he added, as he looked and pointed in her direction. He gave the microphone back to the announcer and ran towards the chutes.

Raylee stood there with tears starting to build. It was the most special, public display of a loving gesture that anyone had ever given her. Evelyn put her arm around her daughter and Emma came in from the other side and they both gave her a squeeze, making her smile. They all sat down again and when his name went to the top of the leader board, it gave the crowd another reason to make some more noise.

The announcer came on again, introducing Jesse as the next cowboy. Raylee put her head down in her hands and looked up in enough time to see Jesse take his run. It was a far better run than he had at the rodeo back home last year, and it was clear that his skills had come a long way from having a great trainer by his side. While Jesse's time put him three places behind Cutter on the leader board, Raylee was still pleased for him and she looked at Aimee who was just as excited.

"Did you know about this?" Raylee thought to ask at that very moment.

"Yes ma'am," Aimee replied.

"Well why didn't you tell me?"

"Because you never asked."

Raylee was pleased now that she hadn't known. Her heart began to settle before the announcer introduced Johnny as the last cowboy to challenge the leader board. Everyone looked at Emma.

"It's alright. Johnny told me," Emma said. "He didn't want to shock me into labor."

Cutter kept the steer straight for Johnny as he too was quick to throw himself at it and take it to the ground, rolling it over in one motion. Just like Cutter, Johnny was a natural, and Raylee could only imagine the two of them at home on the ranch, taking down any unsuspecting young steers that were just leisurely grazing when Macca wasn't watching.

The night was just starting to get interesting.

When the announcer introduced the saddle bronc as the next event, Raylee looked at Aimee. "Please tell me Jesse's not going to ride," she said, expecting that there would be more common sense between them all than authentic cowboy spirit.

"You said yourself he's good." Aimee sounded impressed even though she had never seen him ride a bronc before.

Hmmm, Raylee thought. Wait until she sees what this is all about.

It didn't take Aimee long to find out. When the first bronc rider was thrown to the ground, she started to see Raylee's point of view. The cowboy got to his feet and stumbled, then limped to the rails and collapsed by the gate. The officials helped him up and all but carried him out the back and out of sight. It had shocked Aimee just how dangerous this event was and she immediately wished that Jesse wouldn't ride now. There was nothing she could do, and she held her breath for every rider who took to the saddle and rode the good ride.

Aimee's heart rushed when the announcer called out Jesse's name as the next cowboy to make his way to the chute. He was wearing an old pair of chaps from Cutter's rodeo days, and Aimee thought that he looked pretty damn hot.

Jesse was in his element when the chute was pulled open and he found a good rhythm with the horse from the jump. He made good ground around the pen and with his spurs digging into the sides of the horse, he was lifted higher from the saddle with every buck. He held on tight, with his free arm thrown behind him in the air for balance.

Raylee looked at Aimee again, who could barely see through her fingers, her hands covering both her eyes. She looked back at the clock. "Come on, Jesse," Raylee said loudly, as the timer was running away but not fast enough. She held her breath too, when he lost his hat and nearly his balance as he rode out the buzzer, much to the relief of all the girls. He was the first cowboy to ride out the full eight seconds and the crowd let him know it.

Jesse was timing his get-off strategy when the pickup men came in to help. He was clear of the horse when he lost his feet and stumbled to the ground.

"That was awesome," Aimee exclaimed, and Raylee could do nothing but agree.

Before Jesse could pick himself up out of the dirt, the horse twisted in full swing and came back around, bucking directly towards him. He curled up into a ball, keeping his legs in close and his arms shielding his head.

The crowd got to their feet and were responding with shouts to get the horse away from him quickly, and the girls stood up too so they wouldn't miss what was going on. Jesse was nearly trampled before the pickup men came in and separated him from the horse, releasing the flank strap and diverting it back towards the gate and when Jesse stood up, he received a cheer from every spectator in the arena.

He dusted off his hat, gave a brief wave to the crowd, and headed to the gate where Cutter met him on the arena floor to see if he was alright. Jesse had just made a good first impression with the locals. Especially the girls.

As soon as he was safely behind the chutes, Aimee ran down to the fence to see him. He caught sight of her and was making his way over when he was stopped by a group of six young girls dressed in their short shorts and cowgirl boots. They had him blocked and he couldn't get through, wanting to talk to him to find out who he was and where he was from. Aimee stood there feeling instantly jealous, until he excused himself politely and pushed his way forward, and he made his way over to the fence to see her.

"Are you alright?" she asked.

He didn't answer straight away. He pulled her face into his and kissed her. "I am now," he said, when he looked closely at her. "I hope that didn't scare you."

"Are you kidding? That was the sexiest thing I think I've ever seen," she stated, making him smile. "And I was a little bit scared," she admitted. He kissed her again before he left her at the fence and she watched him walk back through the people to the yards.

The four girls were having the best night, although Raylee was still expecting a damn good explanation when she got home. From everyone.

Jesse's name sat high on top of the leader board. He'd just made a name for himself in the rodeo world, especially when a couple of reporters from a national magazine wanted an interview and photo. Who was this young bronc rider from Down Under, Australia, who was training horses with Cutter Jones and keeping his talent limited to this small town event? Well, they soon found out, when he answered their questions and stood by the chutes for a photograph.

As the events changed and rolled out one after the other, they were well into the second half of the program when Raylee suddenly felt sick. She looked at Aimee. "Cutter's not riding a bull tonight, is he?" she asked.

"No ma'am. Definitely not. He'd never do that to you again." Aimee gave Raylee the reassurance that she was looking for, although she still felt sickly from the thought of it.

Evelyn was still enjoying herself. Jesse was like a son to her and she felt as proud of his achievements as any mother would. As for her new son-in-law, he was in a league of his own and she could see that he was loved by everyone in the arena. Most of all, he was loved by her daughter and that was something special.

Emma and Aimee felt anxious when the team roping was about to begin. Raylee, thinking that the boys' events were over, got the surprise of her life when the announcer called out Cutter and Allan Tremayne to the chutes.

"What the..." Raylee said.

Evelyn sat bolt upright. "Did they just say Allan's name?" she asked. "There must be some kind of mistake," she said, and Aimee laughed at them both.

As in practice, Allan took the head while Cutter took the heel. It happened so fast that Evelyn didn't have time to blink, when the chute opened and her husband was chasing the calf with the rope swinging above his head. Cutter had the heel rope in motion and when Allan accurately threw the rope over the calf's head and held the tension, Cutter aimed for the heel and looped it around its leg, then pulled it tight also.

Over the noise of the crowd, Evelyn could hear Allan celebrating, as he rode up to Cutter and gave him a high five and a big Aussie smile. He had done it. They had done it together, and he was sure now that Evelyn wouldn't think that it was such a crazy idea. Allan was convinced that she would be impressed that there was still some cowboy left in him. It wasn't the fastest time of the night, but they at least got a score on the board. Allan hadn't been expecting any miracles and was just happy they'd had a successful run.

Jesse and Johnny teamed up also. They had a few practice runs together at the ranch and thought they'd throw their luck into the mix and see what happened on the night. It was worth the try, for with a good aim and a good time, they managed to steal the night and take the first prize, much to the absolute shock and surprise of Aimee and Emma, who could do nothing but stand up and hug each other, celebrating their victory.

Raylee couldn't believe it. It really was one of the best, most memorable nights of her life. It was right up there with her wedding, her first buckle and even her first time together with Cutter, although it was memorable for different reasons. She couldn't let go of her smile as she looked around at everyone. Everyone there was her family. She had a best friend in Emma, a great sister in Aimee, and her mother was someone she aspired to be like. Her father was her hero, Jesse and Johnny were like brothers, and in Cutter, she had everything in a man that she would ever need and more. He was her cowboy.

Raylee was not so unhappy now that she hadn't known about the rodeo. While there were still so many questions to ask, at the end of it all, they were irrelevant compared to the outcome.

When everyone sat on the porch that night after the cattle were unloaded and the horses were put away, they retold the night over and over again. Raylee sipped her coffee, making it stretch out longer than she'd have liked. She loved listening to everyone's laughter and being at the center of their jokes, that she and Evelyn had no clue as to the secret practice sessions that took place and all the sneaking around that went on behind her back. While she was slowly winding down from the high she was on, she felt the warm touch of Cutter's hand behind her neck and it made her feel sleepy. Her yawn showed everyone that she was tired and she was the first to stand up.

"I'm going to say goodnight," Raylee said, and Cutter repeated her words to everyone and led her by the hand to the door.

"Oh, and everyone's got the morning off," Cutter added, before he went inside the house and chased her up the stairs.

Five minutes later, Allan and Evelyn made their way inside also. It had been a long day and morning was going to come around fast, even though they had Cutter's permission to sleep-in.

It left Jesse and Aimee on the porch alone. They made their way to the swing and when Jesse stretched his arm out across the top, Aimee took it as an open invitation and dived right in and kissed him, not wanting to waste any time. She was all over him and he took it, like any respectable cowboy would. She threw her leg over his and faced him, sitting on his lap and began to unbutton his shirt.

"Hey," Jesse said, and he stopped her by grabbing her hands. "We can't do this." He pushed his hat back slightly and looked at her closely.

"I don't care," Aimee said honestly.

She started kissing him again and he nearly got caught up in the moment.

"Wait..." he interrupted again. "You know the house rules," he said as a subtle reminder.

"I don't care," she replied, and it was obvious that she really didn't.

She leaned down and kissed him again. Jesse was wanting this as much as Aimee and he needed to be strong to resist her advances.

"Your brother is gonna kill me," he stated. He pulled her away and lifted her off him. Buttoning up his shirt, he walked to the rail. Aimee didn't speak, but followed him over and leaned into him, finding his buckle and she tried to release it.

"Don't you want me?" she asked.

"Of course I want you... I'm desperate for you," he admitted.

Telling Aimee that was a big mistake. She wouldn't give up and did her best to wear him down. He pulled away and looked at her.

"I'm going to the barn," he said, leaving her heart to break in two.

She couldn't believe he'd say that after he'd openly confessed his need for her. He gave her a quick peck on the cheek and walked off. When he reached the bottom of the steps, he turned around.

"Oh, and it's dark out here... So be careful on the way over," he added, leaving her to pick up her smile as she leaned against the rail, watching him walk into the darkness.

It would be a rare occasion for Cutter to sleep past daybreak. The early morning light was like an instant alarm clock if he ever missed his regular five a.m. wake time. He was not aware of how late it was when he rolled over in bed and found the other side empty. As he stretched out his arm and touched Raylee's pillow, the thoughts of last night came flooding back to him. It wasn't the rodeo that put the smile on his face that morning. It was the way his wife had gently and lovingly tended to every one of his needs.

He sat on the side of the bed and took a much needed stretch, then pulled out a clean pair of jeans and made his way to the bathroom. The sunlight was beginning to shine through the window and the last thing on his mind was the horses. He trusted that Jesse would have everything under control at the barn and had fed up already.

When he arrived downstairs in the kitchen, Raylee had the table set for six, with the coffee brewing and the bacon and eggs ready to put on. All she needed now was the family to turn up. They sat around, just the two of them and had their first coffee of the morning, sharing their thoughts on the night before.

Raylee thought that the rodeo was great. She was amazed that her father still had it in him and she knew her mother was impressed too. Raylee also knew that he couldn't have done it without Cutter's help and she thanked him for that.

With the morning moving on, Raylee was wanting to get breakfast started before it was lunch time. "I'm just going upstairs to see if Mom's awake," she said. She came back downstairs only a minute later. "That's funny," she said, totally confused. "She's already up and gone."

"Gone where?" Cutter asked.

"I don't know. But her bed's already made."

Cutter couldn't help himself and he began to tease her. "Or maybe she never slept in it last night."

Raylee looked at him with hopeful eyes. "Do you think so?" she asked, and she dropped everything in the kitchen and headed for Marnie's room.

"Wait," Cutter called out as he chased her down the hall. "Don't go in there," he insisted.

Raylee wouldn't listen. She gave a single knock on the door and burst into the room with Cutter standing on her heels. She gave a shriek. A happy shriek. Her parents were buried deep under the sheets and were fooling around.

"Damn it, Raylee," Cutter said loudly, looking embarrassed. "Ah, I'm sorry Allan," he said, and he grabbed Raylee by the arm and pulled her back towards the door.

Raylee slipped out of his grip and went further into the room, standing right next to the bed. She couldn't have got any closer to them if she tried.

"Raylee, get out," her mother said with only half a breath.

Raylee was beaming. "Are you back together?" she asked with excitement, even though it was hardly the right time or place to be asking that question.

"You heard your mother. Out," her father demanded.

She didn't move. There was a hesitation before Cutter rushed over and grabbed her from behind. He picked her up by the waist and carried her out the door. He put her down so that he could close the door, but not before he took one last look at what he couldn't believe was happening.

They stood on the other side of the closed door in the hallway and stared at each other, then Raylee jumped up and landed in Cutter's arms.

"They're back together," she exclaimed.

"Now you don't know that," Cutter said, to bring her down a level in case they only got lost in the moment. "That doesn't mean it's official."

"Well it sure looked official," she said.

"We can hear you," Allan shouted out so that Cutter and Raylee could both hear. Cutter grabbed Raylee by the hand and led her back to the kitchen. She was beside herself and didn't know what to say next. The thought of her parents getting back together was floating around in her head, and she knew that if she opened her mouth to speak, it would all spill out at once.

She fussed around in the kitchen, occasionally giving Cutter a look from the corner of her eye and making them both smile. She was still celebrating the night before and the morning only added to her happiness.

There was so much love going on at the ranch.

When the front porch door swung open, Aimee walked in, still dressed in her clothes from the night before and her hair was all messed up. She rushed through the kitchen with no intention of stopping. "I'm sorry, I slept in," she mumbled under her breath.

"Hold it," Cutter called out and he stood up. Aimee reluctantly turned around to look at him. She could see a strange look in his eyes and before he could ask any questions, she turned around and ran up the stairs.

He looked at Raylee who shrugged her shoulders. "Did she stay in the barn last night?" he asked, although he was looking more for Raylee's opinion rather than an answer.

"It looks that way," she replied, still distracted by her parents.

Cutter looked angry. "I'll kill him," he said, and he charged towards the door where his boots were waiting for him.

"Wait," Raylee called out, and she caught him by the time he reached the porch. He already had one boot on. "Let's think about this first before you go and do something you might regret," she said, trying to be realistic as well as reasonable. "Please..."

As it turned out, there was a little bit too much love going on at the ranch, and Cutter instantly blamed the rodeo for everyone hooking up under his roof last night.

They walked back into the kitchen. Raylee straightened out his seat at the table and he sat down. He put his elbow on the table and rubbed his face while Raylee stood behind him and squeezed his shoulders to help calm him down. He was fuming.

"What are they thinking?" he said more to himself than to Raylee.

She answered anyway. "You don't need to jump to any conclusions... You don't want to react like my father did. Do you?"

Raylee tactfully made Cutter see that the way he handled this situation could be a defining moment, rather than an irrational response that could take months, or even years to repair.

When Evelyn slipped upstairs unnoticed, Allan walked into the kitchen. He had his chest puffed out so far it was making his back arch.

"Well you look pleased with yourself," Raylee giggled.

Allan grabbed a small bunch of grapes from the fruit bowl. "Looks like being a cowboy has its advantages," he said, with a sense of pride about more than just his ride last night.

Cutter was only slightly amused by his comments. He still had visions of Jesse and Aimee running around in his head. "Allan... Can I talk to you in the other room please?"

They walked together to the sitting room, leaving Raylee in the kitchen to start the breakfast, since everyone was slowly turning up. Cutter closed the door behind him and Allan felt a big talk coming on.

Before Cutter could begin, Allan took the opportunity to get in first. "Look, I'm sorry for what happened. I didn't mean to..."

Cutter wasn't listening. "I can't believe she did that," he said, thinking out loud to himself.

"I know," Allan agreed. "I couldn't believe it either. But you know it's been a long time coming."

"But I thought I made it quite clear. This is my house," Cutter said firmly.

"But I thought you were all for it. I thought you were encouraging it to happen."

Cutter began pacing around the room while Allan sat on the couch. "What the hell would I encourage that for?" Cutter asked.

"Because it's what she wanted. She just didn't realize it until last night when she saw the real man... A real cowboy in action."

"Well I'm starting to think that maybe the rodeo was a big mistake."

"Well I'm sorry you feel that way, but I have to disagree with you there," Allan said.

"I should have listened to Raylee."

"But I don't think she even saw it coming." Allan was very calm while he sat there defending himself.

While Cutter was running his hands roughly through his hair, he was pacing in front of the cold fireplace, not looking in Allan's direction at all.

"Do you wanna talk about it? Let's get it out in the open right now." Allan was prepared to go into full detail with Cutter and lay it all out, to clear the air.

"Yes. I think it definitely needs to be talked about. I wanna know how. I wanna know when. And I wanna know why," he said abruptly, still not looking at Allan. He put his hands to the back of his head. "On second thoughts, I already know the how and the when is obvious... And the why doesn't need too much explaining either... But what I don't know, is what I should do about it." Cutter took a seat on the opposite couch and looked at Allan for the first time, wanting some advice.

"Well," Allan began to say. "Why do you have to do anything at all?" he asked. "Just let it be. Let's see where it goes first."

"I have to do something. This is my house and my ranch, and I'm not having this bullshit of bed hopping going on under my roof when I thought I made it clear," Cutter said arrogantly and he stood up.

Allan jumped to his feet also and threw it back at him. "Oh. So it's okay for you to come into my house and find your way into Raylee's bed, but it's not okay for anyone else in your house?" Allan approached Cutter. "How is that fair?"

"Look. I've already apologized to you for that. Several times," Cutter said defensively. "But you just can't let it go, can you?"

Both Cutter and Allan were riled up and the tension was instant. They both tried to get in first and grabbed each other by the shirt and pulled their faces close, giving each other the look of death.

"You of all people should know what I'm going through," Cutter said aggressively. "You should be the first to understand. That's why I called you in here."

They were only inches away from each other when Allan had a light bulb moment. "Wait a minute... Who are we talking about?" he asked.

"Jesse," Cutter spat out, while he still had a firm grip on Allan's shirt and his teeth clenched, ready for a fight.

Allan released his grip instantly and pulled Cutter in for a fatherly hug. He slapped him on the back and began to laugh. He pulled back to look at him. "Jesse?" Allan asked.

"Yes. Jesse... Who did you think I was talking about?"

Allan kept laughing. "I'm sorry. I thought we were talking about Evelyn and me," he explained.

"No... Jesse and my sister spent the night in the barn."

Allan leaned forward, still laughing. "I'm sorry. It's really not funny. You have every right to be pissed with him. I'm just so thankful that it's not me you're annoyed with." Allan couldn't help it and he laughed some more.

Cutter was beginning to see the funny side of their discussion and how it could have easily got mixed up like it did, and he started to laugh too. "I'm sorry I grabbed your shirt," he apologized.

"And I'm sorry I brought up the past," Allan replied. "But to be completely honest, I'm not at all sorry for what happened last night with Evelyn."

They looked at each other and kept on laughing. Jesse and Aimee's night in the barn was now overshadowed by a near serious misunderstanding, and it took some time before they were able to walk out of the sitting room to the kitchen, where the smell of bacon frying was filling the house.

"And just for the record, I'm really happy that you and Evelyn didn't listen to the house rules... And so is Raylee," Cutter said truthfully.

When they reached the kitchen, it was awkward. Jesse and Aimee were sitting in their usual seats at the table opposite Raylee and her mother. Cutter didn't speak and Allan didn't look at anyone, and they both sat down at either end in silence. When they caught each other's eye, the laughter built up again and they couldn't hold it in, leaving everyone to wonder what had happened in the sitting room.

"I'm sorry, but do you want to share with everyone what's so funny?" Evelyn asked her husband.

"I'd rather not," he replied quickly, and he started to butter his toast while he was trying to control himself. The more he was trying, the more intense it became.

Raylee looked at Cutter. He had gone into the sitting room ready to kill Jesse and had come out not the way she imagined he would. Luckily for Jesse.

"And just so it's clear," Cutter began to say, and he had to take a deep breath before he could continue. "You pair are not off the hook, no matter what this looks like." He pointed to both Jesse and his sister as he spoke, while he avoided looking in Allan's direction for fear of losing it again.

The rest of the breakfast was friendly enough while the accusations and allegations were put on hold. They talked about the rodeo, and how impressed all the girls were with their cowboys. While they had already explained to Raylee and Evelyn how their practice sessions took place, they now gave them the details of Johnny and Emma's involvement, which surprised them both all over again.

"I knew Dad was up to something," Raylee said with confidence. "I just didn't know he had everyone else in on it too."

Her father was looking pleased with himself and so was Cutter. Not from his own results, but because he had been responsible for getting Allan back in the arena, having a successful run, and giving Johnny one last chance to prove he still had it in him before he retired for good and became a father.

After everyone had finished their breakfast, Allan was still sitting at the table when he changed the subject. "What's the plan for the next couple of days? You know we're leaving on Tuesday," he announced.

It wasn't news to anyone. With the last few weeks spent training the horses and practicing for the rodeo, the time had just flown by. Cutter looked at Raylee. He was good at reading her mind. She was nowhere near ready for her parents to go home just yet and she'd have liked it if they could stay a while longer.

"Why do you need to go home?" Cutter asked both Allan and Evelyn. "You could stay and help me get ready for the show."

The show was only a couple of weeks away and those last two weeks were going to be spent full time in the cutting pen. With the cows still calving out and the general running of the ranch still a priority, Cutter was genuine when he asked. He could easily use the extra hands and Raylee still needed help with the house.

Evelyn looked at her husband. "I know the boys will have everything in order on the vineyard, and you can call the girls at the office and tell them to reschedule any meetings you've got lined up until you return," she said, to let him know that she was all for it.

"We don't want to intrude any more than we already have," Allan said.

"Are you kidding?" Raylee intervened. "You're not intruding. You're helping. And it would be so good for you to see Cutter ride at the show."

"And you ride," Cutter added to Raylee.

"What?" she asked.

"I thought you'd just know. I entered you to ride the colt again. I wanted to see if you could get one better on last year."

Raylee only looked half surprised.

"That's awesome," Aimee said. "Can Jesse ride too?"

Cutter let her down gently. "I'm sorry, Aims, but the colt only gets one ride in the Non Pro and it's Raylee's horse," he explained. "Besides, Jesse got to ride last night and did a damn good job of it," he added, while he looked at Jesse.

They all stood up to get ready for a day of work. "Oh, and by the way," Cutter said. "I hear that summer rain is on the way, and we could be in for a few wild storms over the next bit of time."

When they hit the porch and pulled their boots on, the sun was shining without a cloud in the sky. It was a perfect summer day and not a whisper of a breeze could be felt. While no one could imagine the storms coming, Cutter knew this land better than anyone else and he knew how quickly the weather could turn. He'd have to be prepared and have everything in order on the ranch and for the show, so that it didn't hold him up in any way.

Cutter went to walk down the steps of the porch. He turned to look at Raylee. "Hey, are you coming?" he asked.

Raylee looked at her mom who was standing by her side. "Go," Evelyn said quickly.

Raylee's excitement was clear when she gave her mother a kiss on the cheek and grabbed her boots. Cutter took her by the hand and they walked to the barn together.

Allan, Jesse and Aimee all tended to the horses and the barn, while Cutter took Raylee for a ride over the ranch. Just the two of them. They needed the time together and he needed it as much as she did.

They rode out through the gate, stopping to look back at the barn and the house.

"I don't know what to do, Raylee," Cutter said without explanation.

"About what?" she asked.

"About Jesse and Aimee. I don't know what to do or what to say to them." Cutter was totally confused. He didn't want to be the grouch that Allan was when he caught them in bed together.

"Do you want to know what I think?"

Of course he did. That was part of the reason he wanted her on the ride. Raylee was the one person who he could pour out his deepest thoughts and concerns to and he always valued her opinions, even if he didn't always take them onboard.

"I think that you need to stop being the parent and start being a brother," she said.

He could only pull his concentration away from the view to look at her for a fuller explanation.

"You see, Aimee already has a mom and a dad, but what she really wants from you, is a brother. A brother who understands and wants to listen. She wants to be able to tell you things that she can't tell her parents, and ask you for advice when she needs it." Raylee could see exactly what Aimee needed. Perhaps it was because she had been in that same position herself. "It doesn't mean that you'll always agree with her choices, or that she'll make the right decisions. But if you try to be both, you'll push her away."

Cutter looked back at the barn. He stared at it for the longest while and he thought of Pete and Beth. The last thing he wanted was to push his sister away, yet he didn't want to let her parents down either.

They rode through each pasture, talking about the rodeo and how great it was to see Johnny ride again. With Johnny's parents away, Raylee had been a big comfort and good friend to Emma over the last while, and she was pleased that she had been tricked into spending so much time with her.

They rode through the mob of steers, checking the numbers and looking at everything as they made their way further out the back. Raylee loved riding the colt. It was good to be back on him and in two weeks' time, she would be going to the show and riding him at the highest level of competition. She felt those butterflies in her tummy again, even though her experience last year told her there was no need to worry.

When they reached the cows in the back pasture, Cutter did a quick head count. There were a few more calves than yesterday and he was hoping that by the time they were packed up and going to the show, they would all be on the ground. He really wanted to ask Johnny to go to Dallas as well, just to give him one last chance to be on the team again. If Johnny said yes, and with Marnie still away, the ranch needed to be locked down with everything taken care of, and there was still a lot of work to do to get organized.

Before they headed home, Cutter wanted to stop by the resting place. They hadn't been there together since everyone arrived at the ranch and it was the first opportunity on their own.

After placing the flowers on the graves, Cutter stood behind Raylee who was still kneeling on the ground. She could feel the rays of the sun striking the bare skin on her arms and it gave her a tingling warmth.

She stood up and looked at Cutter. Here she was, standing in front of the man she loved while they were standing in front of his parents, and she felt the need to share her heart with him. "I know my parents will never replace your mom and dad. I mean, how could they? But I want you to know that they are as much your family as I am."

He didn't reply. He just took her hat off and pulled her in close to his chest and kissed her head. They stood in the yard as close as two people could get and stared at the graves, only breaking away for him to put her hat back on and leave. They untied the horses and rode home side by side, flirting and teasing each other all the way, and laughing at the irony of catching her parents in bed together.

When they rode through the last gate, it was time to head straight into the cutting pen. Everyone was there waiting, and the session began as soon as Cutter threw his leg over the palomino filly and tuned her up. The mob was settled at the back of the pen and everyone took up their positions in the corners, ready for Cutter to walk into the mob for his first cow.

# Chapter Nine

The training took up the best part of each day. With every horse and every session being a priority, Cutter was getting through the workload with the help from his new team. Everyone was onboard and was putting in just as much as Cutter was. Especially Jesse, who was doing everything he could to keep busy and stay out of Cutter's way, for fear of having a run-in with him over the disregarded house rules.

When the weather started to change for the worse, it made the conditions much more difficult, though the pace never slowed down. The horses never missed a beat and everyone seemed to lift their efforts to ensure that everything ran smoothly.

The few thunderstorms that did come through gave everyone a taste of the powerful forces of nature that Cutter had seen many times before. The sudden blasts of high winds and rain, followed by thunder and lightning, got everyone used to the routine of securing everything down quickly and taking cover in the barn until the storm had passed.

The forecast was not looking good leading up to the show, but they all continued on, taking turns visiting the cows and calves with Cutter insisting that three go instead of the usual two. When Allan took the girls on the ride over the ranch, it left Cutter with Jesse in the pen.

They had not talked about the night of the rodeo, and Jesse was very uncomfortable being left with Cutter on his own. They both rode into the barn to change horses, and when Cutter went to the tack room looking to change the cutting bit on his bridle, he passed Jesse in the feed room. It was now or never. Cutter knew that he couldn't let things pass by without having a discussion, and he could tell that Jesse had been purposely avoiding him altogether.

"Hey, can I talk to you?" Cutter asked.

Jesse knew. He knew what was coming and he was feeling the guilt all over again. He didn't answer. He didn't need to, when Cutter came into the room and sat on a bale of hay.

"Do you like my sister?" he asked again, as he had done a few weeks ago.

"Yeah. She's great," Jesse said.

"No. I mean, do you really like her?" he asked in a different tone.

"Are you asking me if I love her?"

Cutter gave him a look to confirm the question.

"I think I do," Jesse said cautiously. "But how do you really know?" he asked.

Jesse was still young and Cutter had to turn back the clock quite a few years to be able to put himself in Jesse's boots right now. He remembered being twenty-two and reckless, hooking up with girls after a show and never seeing them again. At least Jesse wasn't sharing himself around. He could at least be thankful for that.

"You'll just know," Cutter said. "When the right one comes along at the right time, you just know it."

"Did you know Raylee was right for you?"

"No sir. I thought she was the most spoilt rotten, stuck up and bossy little upstart I'd ever met," he said and Jesse laughed, totally agreeing with him. She had not been any different at school and Jesse knew exactly where Cutter was coming from. "But when she let that guard down, I came to know her in a way that changed my opinion of her. I was wanting to know the real Raylee and to do that, I needed to get close to her. And I did, before we crossed that next line... I didn't wanna go there and do that to her if I wasn't sure... and by then, I just knew."

Cutter was making it clear that when he first met Raylee, he liked her enough to be respectful to her. They came to be friends first and lovers second, building the foundations of friendship and trust before quickly turning their relationship into a romance.

He stood up and walked over to Jesse and placed his hand on his shoulder. "All I ask, is that you do everything right by her."

"I will," Jesse promised.

Cutter walked out of the feed room, but not before he stood at the door and gave Jesse an afterthought. "But that doesn't mean I'm giving you the green light," he said. "You can sneak around all you like... I just don't wanna know about it," he added, and he left to change the bit on his bridle.

Every day was a repeat of the day before. The strong winds blew, the showers of rain came down and the occasional hail storm interrupted the program. With the show so close, Cutter was keeping an eye on the weather for the next few days while the girls were preparing everything to go into the horse truck.

Raylee had all of Cutter's show shirts already hanging up and his chaps all cleaned and ready to wear. She had three pairs of boots put aside along with his black hat and his bags were almost packed.

With the last calf now on the ground and the horses placed in the right yards for the time they would be away, everything was falling into place. Raylee had the office up to date and the last day was spent catching up on anything that was left outstanding.

While sitting around the table for dinner, Cutter and Raylee gave everyone a rundown about the show. Between them, the two girls had to take care of the horses in the stables, making sure they were washed, rugged and fed. Jesse would deal with the preparation work with Raylee giving him any backup help he needed, while Allan and Aimee would take up their positions in the corners like they had practiced at home. That left Evelyn to make sure everyone was well taken care of for breakfast and lunch, with plenty of drinks throughout the long days. Cutter also wanted her to take time out to relax and enjoy the show.

He looked at everyone around the table. They were all talking and laughing at the silliest of things and were having the best time. He sat back silently and watched. This was his team, and they were now his family. Tomorrow he'd be going to the show with well prepared horses and a team that was so dedicated to him, that he couldn't have asked for anything more.

As he lay in bed that night, he pulled Raylee in close. "You know, I'm gonna be riding for you at the show," he said quietly. She sat up on her elbow and looked at him as she always did. "And I'm gonna be riding for the team," he added.

She loved that. She loved that he was starting to see everyone as having a place in his life. He pulled her face to his for a kiss. "And no matter what happens at the show, no matter how busy I get, you are my first priority and you always will be."

Morning came around faster than what everyone would have liked. Except for Cutter. He always had a good sleep no matter what the next day would bring, unlike everyone else, who was either excited about going to the show or had been sneaking around in the middle of the night and taking up valuable sleep time.

It turned out to be another wet morning when a dark and heavy cloud unloaded right over the barn and gave everything a good soak. The cool wind had a chill factor that was out of season and the rolling thunder gave a gloomy feel to the outlook. It was more than miserable.

Jesse had the float already connected to the back of Macca's truck. With a team of six and more horses to transport, they needed to take more than just the horse truck. Everyone went to the house for a late breakfast and to get organized, so they could be on the road before lunch. Evelyn came out of the sitting room and looked at how soaked they all were and she grabbed some towels, handing them one each. She had been watching the news and gave Cutter an update on the forecast.

"It's not looking good," Evelyn informed him. "It's been flooding up north from here and several roads have closed already."

"Then we don't wanna be too late getting out. If they close the bridge to town then we'll have to go the long way 'round and we don't wanna do that." Cutter didn't sound overly worried about it, as he sat down and had a quick bite to eat. He'd been cut off from town before, with forty-eight hours being the longest wait.

He kept checking the time and turned the radio on to the local station for the weather report. They didn't have time to sit around for long and after everyone finished breakfast, they scurried to get cleaned up and their bags to the porch.

While everyone headed to the truck to drive out, Raylee stood in front of the mirror, touching up her makeup, straightening out her shirt and fixing her hat. A flash of lightning filled the entire sky and cracked right above the house, making her feel like it had just struck her in the heart. The lights flickered and went out, and everything that was sourced by power instantly fell dead.

Cutter ran from the porch, up the stairs two at a time and rushed into the bedroom. "Are you alright?" he asked.

"I'm fine. I thought it hit the house," Raylee said, still feeling the panic.

"It's definitely knocked something out," he agreed, looking around the darkened room as they stood close together. "Come on. Everyone's left and we've gotta get on the road before they close it."

After locking up the house and pulling their boots on, they had to run for the horse truck in the mud. Allan was already on his way in Macca's truck with Evelyn by his side and Jesse and Aimee in the backseat.

Cutter took one last long look around. Everything was secured and tied down with the remaining horses let out into the well-sheltered pastures. There was nothing more he could do, except to call Johnny and let him know he was on his way and to give him a quick update.

As much as Johnny had wanted to go to Dallas for the week, he couldn't leave Emma for that length of time as she needed to stay close to her doctor. He disappointingly had to decline the offer and was staying at home to take care of her and watch over the two ranches. If Emma felt up to it, they would go to Dallas for the weekend of finals, although only if Cutter qualified.

It was a huge blow for Cutter, but he was more at ease now about driving away.

"I can't get Emma on the phone," Johnny said, sounding worried.

"Where the hell are you?" Cutter asked, though not to be angry.

Johnny could only explain in defense. "I figured that if we were cut off from town for a few days, then I'd come in and get some supplies."

"Well you'd better hurry up, or they'll be closing the bridge soon," Cutter informed him, as if he didn't already know.

"Bro," Johnny said. "It's too late. It's already closed and I can't get back."

Cutter threw his head back into the seat. He was thinking fast. They were cut off from town and he wondered if Allan had made it through in time or if they were on their way back to the ranch. Everything was processing in his head at the same time.

"Looks like I'll be taking the long way now," Cutter stated, although it was more to himself.

"Can you drop by the house first? Make sure Em's okay?" Johnny asked.

Cutter couldn't drive away knowing that Johnny was stuck in town and Emma was at the house on her own, without checking on her first. It would only take ten minutes and he now had to go the long way anyway.

"Keep your phone on," Cutter said. "We're on our way."

They drove the horse truck steadily up the long driveway. Cutter could feel the tires begin to sink in the mud from their fully loaded weight. That was all he was needing right now. With the truck slipping and the tires spinning all the way to the top, they only just made it to the sealed road and they were finally on their way. One last quick stop to check on Emma and they'd be heading to the show.

Luckily for Cutter, they were organized and left early enough, and had all afternoon and night to get there with the first go-round not until the next morning.

The house was in complete darkness as Cutter drove the truck in and parked as close as he could to the gate. He left the engine running.

"Wait here," Cutter instructed, since it would only take him a quick minute. It was just as wet at the O'Brien ranch with no ease to the rain. In fact, it seemed to be getting heavier and Raylee was more than happy to stay in the truck and keep dry.

He ran up the steps and knocked on the front door. Not waiting for an answer, he opened it and went inside, calling out loud enough to be heard from every room in the house over the noise of the rain.

"Emma... Are you here?"

There was no answer.

He walked around the kitchen. It was in darkness too. The power had been cut and all he could see was the flicker of a small candle she had lit on the kitchen counter.

"Where are you?" Again, his voice filled the room and bounced off the walls.

Maybe she was upstairs. He went to the stairs and was three steps up when he heard her voice. "Cutter?" Emma called out faintly, her voice sounding as if it was coming from the sitting room.

He ran down the hall and found her in the darkness of the room. She was standing up, leaning against the couch and was holding her tummy. He ran to her and held her, giving her support.

"What is it, are you alright?" he asked, before a big clap of thunder sounded over their heads and made them both duck for cover.

Emma looked at him. "I'm having this baby. I'm in labor," she announced.

"No," he said. "You can't be. Are you sure?" It was a silly question to ask, though he wasn't expecting it and it had totally caught him off guard.

"My water broke. And trust me, it's coming," she said, and she started to feel another contraction coming on.

The tone in Cutter's voice matched the look on his face. "This is so not happening," he said out loud to himself, not thinking that in that very moment she'd care what he said.

The thunder was rumbling and was in tune with Emma's distress. She was hunched over, letting her pain be heard and was breathing heavily. When she settled, he helped her walk to the kitchen where he pulled out a chair for her to sit on.

"Where's Johnny?" she asked.

"He's in town," he replied without detail, still holding her. "But he shouldn't be much longer," he blatantly lied.

Cutter knew that Johnny was stuck in town and there was no way home until the water reached its peak and went back down. He didn't know how long that would be, and he didn't know how long Emma would be in labor for. But what he did know, was that he had a truck load of horses out the front and a pregnant woman in his arms, and a show he had to be at in the morning.

Think, he said in his head. Think straight. What do I need to do?

"Are you alright here for a minute?" Cutter asked, and Emma could only nod her head slightly while she was trying to control her breathing. "I'll be back before you know it," he promised.

He kissed her head and ran for the front door, flying down the steps two at a time and reached the truck in only eight paces.

"Is she alright?" Raylee asked, totally relaxed, sitting in the front seat and holding her phone up high, looking for a signal. "My phone's not working."

"Raylee," Cutter said in a very deep and controlled manner that caught her attention. "Get the horses off and put them in the barn. We're not going anywhere," he announced, and he cut the engine of the truck dead.

She looked at him confused. "Is the road blocked the other way too?"

He ignored her question. "Have you ever delivered a baby before?" he asked seriously.

Raylee ran to the back of the truck and Cutter helped her with the first horse. She led it over to the barn and placed it in an empty stall. By the time she had all the horses unloaded, she was wet through.

She dived into their bags to find some dry clothes for them both, and made a mad dash out into the rain again and up the steps to the house. When she went into the kitchen, she saw Emma sitting on a chair with Cutter kneeling on the floor in front of her, holding her hands while she squeezed out the last inch of pain she was in, then she started to breathe heavily again.

"We've gotta get her upstairs," Cutter said to Raylee, who was dripping water all over the floor.

"It's alright, Emma," Raylee said, and she started to undress right there in the kitchen, throwing her wet clothes into a pile on the floor. "We're here... You've got nothing to worry about."

Cutter looked at Raylee. Of course there was something to worry about. A lot to worry about. Neither of them were experienced or qualified to deliver a baby, and being cut off from town, the doctor had no chance of reaching them to help.

Raylee pulled out some dry clothes and threw them on quickly. "I can't believe Johnny's going to miss this," Raylee stated.

"What?" Emma screamed.

"It's okay, Em," Cutter calmed her. "He'll be here soon." Cutter gave Raylee a look to say he'd already told the biggest lie of his life and to get onboard with it, quickly.

They helped her up the stairs to the bedroom and settled her onto the bed, giving her several pillows to lean back on and a towel to wipe her face. Raylee placed the candle on the side table next to the bed for some light. After Emma's next contraction was over, Cutter pulled Raylee aside to the corner of the room and they began to whisper.

"Don't look at me. I've never delivered a baby before," Raylee defended.

"But you're a girl. You'll know what to do," he said.

Raylee was scared and Cutter could see it in her eyes. "But you've delivered thousands of calves and foals before," she exaggerated. "It's the same thing."

"It's not the same thing," he said. "This is a baby. And it's... Emma."

"Which is all the more reason you need to get your shit together and do this." Raylee was trying to snap him into a positive frame of mind.

He looked at Emma lying on the bed. "I don't think you understand, Raylee."

"What's not to understand? Emma's having a baby and she needs you."

He looked back at Raylee. They were standing close together so that Emma couldn't hear. "But Emma's the first girl I ever kissed," he informed her.

"What?" Raylee laughed. "You and Emma?"

"We were only thirteen and she grabbed me behind the classroom at school one day. But don't worry, it was long before Johnny was ever interested."

Raylee was amused by the timing of his confession. "So what's that got to do with what's happening now?" she asked.

"Don't you get it? Emma was the first girl that I ever liked, and now I've gotta put my head up her dress and see where my best buddy's been going all these years."

His explanation couldn't have been any more to the point if he tried. When Emma started to build up an intolerance to the pain, she began to shoot out short bursts of breath while she was looking at them both still standing in the corner having a discussion... More than likely about her.

They went to the bed and stood on either side. "Okay," he said to Raylee over Emma's head. "We've gotta get a plan happening here."

Raylee agreed. The more prepared they were, the better the outcome was going to be.

"You need to get me some dry clothes," he said. He was soaked through and was quite uncomfortable. "And we need some old towels or something to lay on the bed underneath her." He was painting a mental picture for himself in his head, then was giving Raylee the list. "And we need a knife or scissors to cut the cord," he added.

When the contraction had settled, Raylee started to get on the job. "And what else?" she asked.

Cutter was thinking. "A peg, or something to clamp the cord after it's cut."

"And I'll boil some water," Raylee said, as if it was important.

"What do you need boiled water for?" he asked.

Raylee looked at him then shrugged her shoulders. "I don't know... But they always do it in the movies. It must be used for something," she added.

"And don't forget some candles... It's getting dark in here."

Raylee left the bedroom and went downstairs. The phone line to the house was down and she checked her phone again for a signal. It was still unresponsive. They had no contact with the outside world, adding to the pressure of the situation should something go terribly wrong.

She tried not to think about it, as she rummaged around in the cupboards for some towels and old sheets. She looked through the kitchen drawers for something sharp to cut the cord, and with the power still out and the pump not working, she found some bottled water and put a pot on the gas cooktop to boil.

She looked through every other cupboard until she found some candles that seemed to be more for decoration than for a blackout. Though in the current situation, she didn't think that Emma would mind.

While Raylee was out of the room, Cutter thought it was the best time to give Emma an examination. He felt strange, nervous, and guilty all at once. She was resting on the pillow with her knees already up and her feet pulled in close to her for comfort. She looked temporarily at peace.

"Emma," Cutter said quietly. "I need to see how far you are."

There was no hesitation. "Okay. But you'll need the candle so you can see," she said.

He rubbed his face... Hell, if it was that easy when I was in high school, I'd have really been in deep trouble, he thought.

He sat on the side of the bed near her feet. "And I'll need to take your knickers off," he said with complete respect as well as caution.

She was quick to reply. "I'm not wearing any," she informed him.

Right, he thought. This is awkward. A little resistance would have made it so much more acceptable in his own mind, except that Emma was cooperating and nothing that was taking place was fazing her in any way at all.

When he took the candle and placed it on the end of the bed, that end of town lit up quickly. Not wanting to pull her dress up any more than was necessary, he gently pulled her knees apart. Oh, I am so going to kill you Johnny when you get home. What on earth was so important that you had to go to town and leave me looking at your wife like this? His thoughts were completely messed up and were only interrupted by Raylee, who came back into the room holding a stack of towels, some dry clothes and two more candles, just like she'd been instructed.

"How does she look?" Raylee asked casually, as if she was asking for an opinion on how Emma was looking in a new pair of shoes.

"Well I'm no expert. But I'd say that it could be a long night," he replied, and he pulled her dress back over her knees. "Did you get everything?"

"Yes. But I'm just going back down to check on the water," she said, and she left the room again.

Cutter took the candle and his dry clothes to the bathroom and changed, instantly feeling better for the warmth. With both hands, he leaned on the basin and looked up into the mirror at his reflection, noticing that his face looked stressed. He wet his face with the little trickle of water to give his thoughts a clear view of what he had to do, and tried to wash his hands as best he could without the water flow. The wind and rain were lashing at the window and the flashes of lightning lit up the bathroom.

"Cutter..." Emma called out, and he rushed back into the room as the intensity of the contraction was reaching its peak. He sat on the bed and held her while she dug her fingers deep into his arm. She gave an almighty scream, followed by quick breaths for relief.

When she settled back down again, Cutter relaxed too. He pulled out his phone and checked for a signal. Nothing. He checked the time. It was getting late. He wondered if Allan had made it through to town or if they were all back at the ranch, with no Cutter and Raylee. If they had made it through, then it was only by a few minutes. Cutter had visions of them all arriving in Dallas at the show and unloading the horses into the stables, with no rider to ride them.

Aimee was the only one who had been there before, although she had never been beyond the cafeteria or the shops. They'd find their way around, he was sure, and the hotel was only across the road. Allan and Evelyn were seasoned travellers and Cutter only hoped that they were not too consumed with each other to remember they had a couple of kids to keep an eye on.

Why is this happening to me, he wondered. The countdown to the first go-round was now less than sixteen hours away. He looked at Emma. She could take more or less time than that. Either way, he couldn't leave her even if she had the baby right at that very minute, unless Johnny was there, and he knew neither of those two things were going to happen for him in time.

Emma's breaths were building up again and Cutter could tell that another contraction was coming on. There was less time in between and he knew that was a good sign.

The rain had eased slightly into the night, although the wind was starting to become destructive. The glass panes on the windows were rattling and Cutter ran over to the window to shut the blinds.

After another four hours, Emma was tired. Raylee kept wiping her face every time she lay back, but Emma had had enough and was starting to lose patience. With nothing to control the pain and her husband a no show, she was taking it out on Cutter. With every contraction, she gave him a deathly stare that he'd never seen before, while his arm was aching from her grip. She even tried to wrap her arm around his neck while the agony of her screams was breaking the sound barrier in his ear.

To be better prepared, Raylee found the diapers and some small baby clothes in the nursery, and a cotton wrap that Emma had insisted she bring into the room. Cutter looked at the small jumpsuit. He picked it up. It was soft, fluffy and white, but it was the size of it that made him feel a sudden rush of emotion coming on. He put it down quickly.

He looked at Raylee. There was no way he was wanting her to go through this, and after dealing with a teenage girl over the last while, he was sure that being a parent was now going to be the last thing on his to-do list.

Another two hours in and everyone was tired. Cutter had been pacing, while Raylee kept roaming the house looking for a phone signal. The strong wind had blown the rain away and the clouds had all but disappeared. It was well into the night when Emma announced that she was about to start pushing. She instantly got the attention of Cutter, who just got a shot of adrenalin, while Raylee was more concerned that they had everything on hand and ready.

"You ready for this?" he asked Raylee over Emma's head.

Raylee was more than ready. "Let's get this baby out," she said firmly, backing him all the way.

With every push, Emma grabbed Raylee around the neck and gave an unwomanly scream. They were certain she could be heard from town and therefore, they wouldn't be needing to make any announcement upon the baby's arrival.

Raylee gave her encouragement when she rested in between pushes. It was tough going, and every time Emma pushed, she was sure that she couldn't take any more.

"Come on, Em... You're gonna have a baby," Cutter said for extra encouragement. He was sitting on the bed between her legs. When she gave a drawn out scream of pain, Cutter got excited. "I can see the head," he informed them.

"I know, you idiot," Emma screamed. "Don't you think I can feel it," she yelled at him.

He was rubbing her legs for comfort. "You're doing good now." He was controlled and was ignoring the abuse she was throwing in his direction.

With every push came a tirade of words among screams of pain and suffering. Cutter gave them both a running commentary as to what was going on down there, and he placed another couple of towels under her ready for the baby to make its entrance.

When the baby's head was out, Cutter at least knew enough to check for the cord. It was free of the neck. When Emma gave that final push, the baby slipped out onto the towel and into Cutter's hands. He was completely stunned, amazed and overwhelmed at this tiny little thing he was holding and he looked at how perfect it was. This beautiful baby covered in muck had caused so much pain to its mother and caused him to miss the show.

"What is it?" Emma asked, still panting for breath but instantly relieved from the pain.

Cutter had never thought to look. He moved the cord out of the way and gave her a smile. "It's a boy," he announced, and Raylee gave Emma a squeeze in a congratulatory gesture, while tears began to flow freely from both girls.

Very carefully, Cutter placed the baby on Emma's tummy. He did everything right after that. From cutting the cord to cleaning the baby up and putting a diaper on. They wrapped him up and when Cutter handed him to Emma, his eyes filled up too.

"Thank you," Emma said. "You were both great and I couldn't have done it without you."

Cutter lay on the bed, holding her, while Raylee snapped a couple of photos from her phone.

"I can't believe Johnny missed it," Raylee said, while she was flicking through her phone and showing them the images she'd just taken.

"I can't believe it either," Cutter agreed.

Emma looked at him. "Cutter... Aren't you supposed to be at the show?" she asked. "Oh my goodness, Cutter... You missed the show."

He tried his best not to make a big deal out of it, although she knew that it was a huge deal. "I wouldn't have missed this for anything," he assured her.

Even if the road was re-opened, there was barely enough time to make it to Dallas and prepare the horses for the first go-round. He was sure that it would still be closed and that Johnny would be hours away, waiting for the water to go down. They couldn't leave Emma there alone with a baby, and now there was no need to rush. They would be lucky to make it back to the ranch by noon and to Dallas for round two.

There was no need to panic now about the show. Cutter had missed it and there was nothing he could do to change it.

Raylee helped Emma to the bathroom. With the power still cut and no shower, Emma found a good use for the boiled water. While he walked around the room, Cutter cradled the baby in his arms. He was wrapped up tight and Cutter looked at his little face and tiny hands. He was overwhelmed. Touching his skin and looking at the fine details of his nose and perfect lips, there was something special about holding this little bundle of trouble, that Cutter couldn't help but love. This night would bond him to this baby forever.

They cleaned up the room and when Emma was ready to lie back down to feed her baby, it was time for Cutter to disappear. He'd already seen enough of Emma and he didn't need to be around to see that. He decided to go to the barn and check on the horses.

It was dark when he opened the front door of the house and went outside. The wind hit him in the face and was enough to wake him out of his weary state. He checked the time. The night was just about gone. He could hear the squelch under his boots with every step, finding a couple of deep puddles and a fallen tree limb that had blown into his path as he nearly tripped over it.

Everything was settled inside the barn. The horses were dry and still picking at the remains of the hay and everything was in place after the strong winds. He needed to go there. He needed to stretch his legs and body, and give his head some space. He found a weak signal on his phone and called Johnny.

It didn't ring at Johnny's end, so he left a message. "Hey, bro. Everything here is good. Emma is fine. If you get this message, call me." He didn't want to break the news to Johnny in a phone message. It's not how he would want to find out that he'd just become a father.

He found a camp light and cleaned out the stalls before he went back to the house. It was still in darkness with the power still out. He knocked on the bedroom door before he went in. It would be daylight in another hour and everyone was exhausted, including the baby. Cutter propped up a pillow next to Emma, while Raylee found some comfort in the soft chair that Johnny had bought for Emma and the baby, and they all found the need to sleep.

They didn't hear the front door or the footsteps on the stairs, but they all heard the bedroom door open and woke to see a very tired and distressed looking Johnny standing in the doorway, taking in the scene.

Here was his wife, lying on the bed cuddled up with his best friend, holding a baby? Johnny was taking it all in. He knew there was a problem when he saw the horse truck out the front. But a baby? He rushed to Emma's side and gave her a kiss, before he looked into Cutter's eyes, then down at his child.

"You've got a son," Cutter informed him.

"A boy?" he asked Emma, and she nodded lovingly.

"And I would kill you right now if I wasn't so happy to see you," Cutter said.

Johnny pulled back the cotton wrap from the baby's face and looked at him. He was deeply moved and was just about to lose it when Cutter handed him his son.

Cutter stood up to let Johnny sit down next to Emma. Raylee came over and joined them and they all gave him an hour by hour description of the event, with Cutter leaving out the most intimate details that Johnny didn't need to know. That would be kept between the three of them.

With the road blocked from the rising water, Johnny had managed to talk his way across with the Emergency Services, although it still took him half the night to convince them that he needed to get home to his pregnant wife. They had to check out his story first and wait for the water flow to slow down. Emma explained how her water broke at the sound of the first loud clap of thunder. She still had three weeks to go before her due date, but had been feeling tense that morning as the storm had her on edge. She was now sure that's what brought it on so suddenly.

There was no use trying to get the truck to town and wait on the side of the road for the bridge to re-open, as it could still be a long wait and they would miss the first go-round anyway. Besides, Cutter was totally drained and cutting was the last thing on his mind right now. What he needed, was his own bed.

"I still don't know if Allan made it to Dallas," Cutter said. "But I guess I'll find out when I get home."

"Haven't you heard?" Johnny asked.

"Heard what?" Cutter and Raylee said at the same time. After the vicious storm, they were worried for the worst.

"When I couldn't get hold of anyone here, I called Jesse," he said. "They made it to Dallas and from what I hear, they're all having a really good time."

That was a load off Cutter's mind. At least the team had made it through.

"And that's not all," Johnny added. "With the bad weather and all the roads closed, they put the show back an extra day. They couldn't get the cattle in and only half the riders turned up."

Raylee looked at Cutter and was excited, while he was stunned, like so many times already that night.

"And if you can get outta here by the afternoon, you should easily make the first go-round with plenty of time to spare." Johnny was the bearer of good news.

They all sat around for the next half hour, looking at the baby and catching up on what had been a long and exhausting night, before Cutter started to yawn.

"Hey, bro, you look tired," Johnny noted. "I'll come and help you load the horses," he offered.

"Nah, that's okay. Em needs you and I've got the best help right here," Cutter said, and he touched Raylee on the leg. "Or maybe, I could leave everything in the barn and borrow your truck for a few hours," he added.

Johnny was only too happy to help. "You know where the keys are."

Cutter and Raylee left the bedroom and headed downstairs. It was now daylight, and the blue sky and puffy white clouds were reflecting in the puddles on the ground.

After feeding the horses in the barn, they found the keys to the old green truck and made their way out the front gate and drove home. They would be back there in only a few short hours after they'd caught up on some much needed sleep. But really, Cutter wanted to drop back in to see the new family again before he headed to Dallas for the show.

# Chapter Ten

The sun was shining in Dallas and the air had a steamy feel to it after the rain that was more than unpleasant. As they drove into the city, the cleanup was just beginning, as the strong winds had left debris and destruction everywhere. With the show being held back an extra day, Cutter and Raylee were right on time when they pulled the horse truck into the grounds late that afternoon, and picked up their passes at the gate.

It was as if Raylee was there only yesterday, as the events from last year came flooding back to her when she looked at the oversized trucks and goosenecks parked around the stable areas. They were not so insignificant this year in their new horse truck, and Cutter pulled it in next to the float outside C block, while Macca's truck was parked at the hotel.

The riders who had made it to Dallas before the roads were closed, had spent the long wait exercising their horses in the surrounding sand yards or riding around the grounds casually, while the mechanical cows were getting a good workout in the open pens once the rain had cleared. The cafeteria was doing a roaring trade and the shops were restocking continually as boots, jeans and hats were being unnecessarily bought up just to fill in the long day, mostly by Allan, who had shouted Jesse and Aimee to anything they wanted and had walked away unable to carry another bag.

Everyone was anxious for the show to start even though the car park was far from full. Riders were still making their way to Dallas, and would turn up through all hours of the night along with the cattle trucks, which were slowly arriving one at a time. Everything looked set to start at eight a.m. sharp the next morning. That gave Cutter and Raylee the chance to get settled in and get into the cutting mood again, after spending a restful morning at the ranch on their own, which they made the most of.

When they led the pally and the roan into the stable area and found their stalls, they were greeted by Jesse and Aimee, who were tending to the colt and the mare.

"Hey. It's about time you showed up," Jesse said to taunt them both.

"Why? I knew you'd have everything in hand," Cutter threw back at him, and by the look of it, he did. "And you could've ridden for me if you really had to," he added, although Cutter was only playing with Jesse.

"Don't worry. Aimee's mentioned it a hundred times already."

The horses had been out and ridden throughout the day and were now put away, looking in good show condition. Jesse and Aimee were taking the show seriously, and were focused on doing a professional job, taking control of the reins while Cutter wasn't there to oversee them. Although Cutter wouldn't underestimate the long night at the hotel, and he only hoped that whatever they were doing, it was for all the right reasons.

Jesse put the horses away while Cutter and Raylee went back to the truck to bring in the last two. Between the four of them, they unloaded the truck with everything they needed for the night and locked it up.

"Where's my mom and dad?" Raylee asked. "Don't tell me they haven't left the hotel room," she said jokingly, although it would have pleased her if it were true.

"No ma'am," Aimee said to burst her bubble. "They're upstairs having a coffee with my mom and dad," she explained.

"What?" Cutter and Raylee said at the same time.

"Can you believe it? They came to see me yesterday and I introduced them to your mom and dad. They got on so well that they came back to meet up again today." Aimee reeled the quick update off the top of her head and she seemed thankful that they were all preoccupied.

Cutter and Raylee couldn't believe it. Their family had gone from being just the two of them on their own a few months back, to a comfortable four, before it blew out to include Raylee's parents. Now with Pete and Beth in the mix of it, Cutter's family was expanding rapidly and it seemed now that he had a full blown support network, who were all there to watch him ride.

"Where's your sister?" he thought to ask.

"Oh, Cassie's here somewhere... She's probably upstairs buying a new hat so she can impress some of those cowboys," Aimee said, half meaning it.

"Well I'll be having a word to her about that." Cutter's thoughts poured out of his mouth and when everyone looked at him, he was suddenly aware that he had shared his thoughts out loud. "And did you introduce your mom and dad to your new boyfriend?" he asked as a diversion, to see how Aimee had dealt with Jesse.

"Of course I did." Aimee kept it simple, not giving any details away and leaving Cutter to wonder how that all went down.

With everything in order at the stables, they all headed to the cafeteria to meet up with the rest of the family. When they went inside the arena, Raylee felt that familiar feeling, the one she had when she was there last year. It was just as impressive as on her first visit and she looked down to the arena floor and could see herself riding the colt there all over again.

She touched her buckle, to silently re-live that moment.

"Are you nervous?" she asked Cutter, while they were walking to the other end. They were following Jesse and Aimee, who seemed to know their way around quite well now.

"About meeting up with all the parents?" he asked.

"No silly. About the show."

He shrugged his shoulders. "No more than usual," he answered truthfully. Cutter played it down and didn't make such a big deal out of it, to keep Raylee calm.

When Cutter was making his comeback into competition last year, he'd not competed for almost three full years. He went with only one Futurity horse and he was under pressure to perform. He had just one shot to make an impression and he did. This year, he had two Futurity entries and the mare, who he was confident would be a strong contender in the Derby. Though it was the colt that he was keen to show in the Open again, since everyone's expectations of him last year had been let down when he had a disastrous ride that resulted in a zero score. With that behind him, Cutter wanted to show the colt this year and remind everyone what a champion he was.

It wasn't too difficult to find all the parents and Cassie in the cafeteria. They were sitting around a table having a coffee and when the team walked in, everyone stood up and they exchanged greetings all round. Pete and Allan pulled a couple of tables together and when they were one chair short, Aimee positioned herself on Jesse's lap and wrapped her arms around his neck, holding him tight. They were as close as two people could get in public without being offensive, and Cutter sat there and wondered what her parents were thinking.

He looked at Beth. She didn't seem to mind at all, and she included Jesse into their discussions as if he had been part of the family forever. Maybe I've been a little overprotective, he thought. He looked at Pete. He was in a deep conversation with Allan and while it was obvious that Jesse had his hands all over Aimee's legs, touching her on the back and linking hands, Pete didn't seem to notice.

But Cutter noticed. He noticed their closeness and it seemed he was the only one who felt uncomfortable with their open display of affection and he decided right then and there, that he much preferred it when they were sneaking around behind his back.

After Raylee shared with everyone the details of Cutter delivering Emma's baby, it was immediately thrown straight back their way. "So you'll be next," Cassie said innocently.

It left the table silent and all eyes looking in Cutter and Raylee's direction.

Raylee felt the need to say something, especially in front of her parents. She couldn't find the right words. They had talked privately about it, yet this was the first time that it was thrown into the arena for family discussion.

"It's not the right time," Cutter said with a shortness to take the pressure off Raylee, and she was thankful.

With an early start to the morning, the team excused themselves from the table and headed back to the stables. With the last check on the horses and the feed done for the night, it was time to go to the hotel and settle in.

Tomorrow was the first go-round, and Cutter needed everyone to get an early night's sleep. He needed everyone to get on the job with him.

A fine layer of dust could be seen hovering around the lights of the covered sand yard, as a dozen or more riders were exercising their horses in the early morning freshness. When Cutter and Raylee arrived at the gate, they showed their passes and went straight to the stables, which were alive with activity.

Jesse already had the palomino saddled up ready to ride while Aimee was going about her business quietly, making sure all the other horses were fed and their stalls were all cleaned out. Music was playing softly on the speakers, since it was still relatively early. When the sun made its appearance, the night chill was suddenly gone, the temperature started to rise and the girls took off their jackets.

Cutter was impressed. Although he was there with more horses than last year, he still didn't have as many as the other trainers had, yet the team were all over it.

It gave him the time to relax, and carrying his chaps over his shoulder, he made his way up into the stands to watch the start of the first herd.

He watched silently, focusing on each cow in the mob and the breeding of each horse. Finding company with a few other riders who all had the same idea, he sat with them in a row, catching up and talking about cutting rather than anything personal. As each rider left to get geared up for their ride, the row slowly became empty and Cutter sat alone and watched each cowboy take to the pen.

It was going to be tough, with the scores surprisingly high for the first herd of the week. The cattle were controlled and many of the horses were outstanding. Cutter feared for the pally, that she may not be in the same league. Although he would ride by the game plan. Play it safe, and don't push her into taking unnecessary risks.

When Evelyn saw Cutter sitting in the stands on his own, she made her way through the levels of seating to reach him. This was where Evelyn would perch herself for the next week. If anyone needed her, they knew exactly where to find her.

During the change of the herd, Cutter went down to the loping area behind the judges' stand, where Jesse was riding in circles and the team were ready for their rider. After putting his chaps on and realigning his buckle, Cutter took to the saddle without a word to anyone. He needed to get the first ride out of the way before he could settle into this week long event.

When the second herd was introduced, the announcer came over the speakers giving a warm welcome to the next cowboy and his horse. Cutter was not distracted by the rider's two and a half minute run, as he took to the prep lane and gave the filly a tune up. It wasn't until he heard the buzzer that his nerves hit him in the gut, giving him an uncomfortable feeling. The team made their way out into the corners and he waited for them to get settled into their positions, while he was still making the filly respond to his commands. When the announcer introduced Cutter as the next rider to hit the arena floor, he was relieved that it was still quite early and the stands were barely scattered with people.

He took a deep breath. This was it. "Here we go," he said quietly to himself.

Walking out into the pen, Cutter held the reins high with one hand while he gripped the horn on the saddle with the other. The bell rang when he crossed the timeline and the clock on the back wall immediately started the countdown. Only two and a half minutes to go, he anxiously thought.

Raylee was more focused on the cattle when Cutter reached her in the corner and he began looking for the cow she had just pointed out. He brought it forward with a small mob of eight and he made his way through, disregarding one at a time as the pressure from Jesse and Allan helped push them back to the mob.

He was steady and controlled, and he found his position with the cow in the middle of the pen. As he placed his hand low, his heart gave an explosive rush that far surpassed what his head was thinking, then the cow sidetracked across the pen to find a way back to the mob. When the filly was slow to take off, a spur in her side got her moving and she caught up to the cow and she beat it to the stop. Predicting its next move ahead of the turn, she was now on the warpath.

The filly charged across the pen, keeping up with the pace of the cow then it stopped suddenly. The filly stopped too and they both gave a pause, keeping the focus fully connected. Head to head, nose to nose and eye to eye, there was a standoff, before the cow took off again and sped back across the pen at full noise.

When the cow darted quickly, it caught the filly out as her timing was a little off. She picked up the speed and chased it, stopping in her tracks when she intimidated the cow and was all over it again. While Cutter and the filly were not completely in sync with the cow, they finally got the break when it stopped still and turned away.

It was hard work, but it was time to breathe again.

Cutter picked up the reins. He looked up at the clock for the seconds remaining and walked back to the herd for his next cow. Raylee was already pointing out potential options for him and he had his eye fixed on it when he pushed it forward in a small mob. He was not so happy with the first cow, as the filly had performed better in training than she had just done. His second cow was now his chance to show the judges what she really could do.

Allan was following Jesse's lead when they came in towards the mob to pressure them back, leaving Cutter to single one out on its own. He felt all eyes in the arena drawn to him while all he could look at was the cow. He lowered the reins and held on.

The next thirty seconds were thrilling. Every time the cow ran, the filly ran too. Every time it stopped, the filly pulled up as well. Every pause, every turn, every electrifying run across the pen, the filly was mimicking it to perfection. She was low to the ground when she hotfooted from side to side, stirring the cow up to make a break, only to block off its attempt to get past. This was what Cutter expected of her. Her second cow was faultless.

The team were all on edge. It was the first time they had worked together outside practice and Raylee was sure that everyone would be impressed.

With little time left on the clock, Cutter pulled the first cow off the top of the mob. He chased it out as the last seconds were only there so that he could ride out the timer with his hand down. It sounded not a moment too soon and Cutter was relieved that it was over. What he would have really liked, was to take that first cow all over again. Yet it was done and whatever score came in next, was all he would have to work with towards the second go-round. It wasn't so much a bad choice of cow, as it was the filly who had been slow to get her head on the job.

The team headed out of the pen to make way for the next turn back riders to come in and replace their positions in the corners. Raylee caught up quickly and rode next to Cutter.

"Not her best," he said.

"She was alright. Her timing was a little off on that first cow, but after that she did pretty good." Raylee was trying to give Cutter the pick-me-up that he needed, although receiving a good score would do a better job of that. While the horses were being tied up to the rail, Cutter unbuckled his chaps.

"A two sixteen," the announcer called out, leaving Cutter slightly more pleased than he was when he left the pen.

"Well, it could've been worse," he stated.

"At least that gives you something to work with."

"Well she'll need to pull out something amazing in the second go-round if she's gonna make that final." Cutter was still not uplifted enough to put a smile on his face, although he was pleased that the first run was over. Now he could settle into the show.

As the team headed back to the stables, Cutter saw his rival, Tommy Parker, out the corner of his eye. He'd have seen that run and would be silently pleased.

That was all Cutter needed right now. To come face to face with Tommy, who would smile pleasantly while he was twisting the knife he had lodged in Cutter's back. Cutter ignored him, and he rode away from Tommy and his team, leaving the tension behind.

Aimee was still a little inexperienced in the cutting pen. She thought that Cutter's run on the filly was awesome. Without knowing exactly how the points system worked, she only saw her brother's ride as outstanding and thought that it was up there alongside Jesse's ride in the rodeo arena. She was impressed, and would flit around the stables without a worry in the world.

With the first ride out of the way and the points done, Cutter wasn't out on the blue roan until late in the afternoon. It made for a very long day and when the pally was washed and all the horses were back in their stalls, the next thing that was on everyone's mind, was breakfast.

The arena had started to pick up with a steady flow of spectators, who were anticipating an entertaining and action packed week of cutting. The sea of red and blue seats that looked down onto the arena floor, was slowly disappearing as the day progressed. People were taking up the rows and settling in to watch the biggest names in the game ride the best bred horses, and take on the unpredictable and sometimes erratic beasts that made this sport a good equalizer.

On the way back down to the stables, everyone was walking casually past the shops to fill in some extra time. While Cutter and Raylee were leisurely looking at everything as they walked past, Tommy Parker was heading their way. They didn't see him, until Raylee heard her name.

"Hey, Raylee,"Tommy said in an overly friendly tone that was almost forced, capturing her attention immediately. "Nice to see you again," he added, giving her a smile as he touched the front of his hat in a gentlemanly manner. They had just passed each other and by the time Cutter heard his voice and turned around, they were already walking away. Not to let the moment slip by, Cutter decided to tackle it, before it got out of hand as the week went on.

"Hey, Tommy," Cutter called out, and he relaxed his arm around Raylee's shoulder and pulled her in. "I believe you know my wife," he said, drawing tension between the two groups of cowboys. "So if you don't mind... It's Mrs Jones to you."

Cutter couldn't control the smirk on his face when Tommy was stunned into silence. Cutter stood his ground, surrounded by his family and he let Tommy walk away first before they headed back to the stables.

"I can't believe you just said that," Raylee laughed.

"Yeah," Jesse agreed. "And since we all have no idea what the hell that was all about, you're gonna need to give us a bloody good explanation."

Jesse, Aimee and Allan had all seen the stitches on Cutter's face last year when he had the fight at the show. What they didn't know, was who the fight was with and why. But they soon found out. Between them, Cutter and Raylee painted a picture for everyone as to why Tommy Parker had become Cutter's rival. They explained how the fight at last year's show played out and how it added more hatred to their already toxic conflict.

"Anyway, I can't afford to get another ban, so there's gonna be no more fighting this year," Cutter said, in case the boys were thinking differently.

It was a repeat of the morning routine at the stables, except that they were now in the heat of the afternoon and there was no relief in sight. Everyone knew their role in getting the horses out and ready to ride. Raylee took the roan into the loping area to get her ready. She wanted to be as much involved in the process as Jesse was, and to feel her input was needed and was not going unnoticed.

She rode in circles with the other riders, going through the motions like everyone else. When her eyes looked down, it made her feel dizzy and she began to overheat, until she quickly looked up, instantly making her feel better. As the herd was moving on, she listened to the announcer call out the scores at the end of each ride, with only a few outstanding results that were in complete contrast to the few disastrous ones. Everyone else was somewhere in between.

To get into that final, Cutter needed to get above those average scores and get a good solid result behind him. He met Raylee in the loping area and they exchanged horses and changed the length of the stirrups.

When he took to the saddle, he adjusted his hat into a more comfortable position and pulled at his collar, as the heat of the afternoon had only inten- sified, not settled down. He walked across the timeline and the bell rang to start the countdown. He held the reins at a height that was comfortable, while his other hand was loose on the horn as the sweat was annoying. His hairline was wet and when a drip of sweat ran down the back of his neck, it gave him a tickle that was more than irritating.

When he reached Raylee in the corner, she too was looking flushed, and she kept wiping her face and neck at the same time as she was standing up out of the saddle to point to a few options.

To make up for his first cow on the pally, he quietly disregarded Raylee's options and found one that he thought was a better choice. Completely surrounded by the herd, he had more cattle on the move than was necessary, leaving Jesse and Allan to apply the pressure gently to the mob, so as not to cause a stampede. With the last three cows locked together in the middle of the pen, it was now up to Cutter to separate them. The horse launched forward when she felt the spurs in her sides, and three cows became one when Cutter had successfully driven them apart. It was time to put his hand down.

The reins fell to the horse and Cutter relaxed in the saddle, into position. The filly was switched on and she kicked up the sand to chase the breakaway cow and she overpowered it at the stop. Woah, Cutter thought, this filly is shit hot. She was mimicking every twisted swivel and turn in a heart-pumping and fearless performance.

There were no other words to describe it. She was downright cowy.

The noise and applause from the crowd echoed in Cutter's ears. He drew everyone in the arena to watch this unbeatable run while his focus on the cow was unbroken.

The cow quit in good time, turning and looking away, leaving Cutter to pick up the reins and head for the mob. The music was thumping, the crowd were applauding, and Raylee was smiling from the untouchable performance he'd just given the judges and everyone in the stands.

The filly was hot, just like everyone there, and a few more seconds wasted went unnoticed as he brought the mob forward cautiously and in control. One more cow like that, and she could break all records.

Cutter's strategy to play it safe was not on his agenda when he put the reins down on the second cow, as he felt the need to have that rush all over again. The filly gave it to him. With moves that were equal to the colt, she had the ability to reel the cow back into the center of the pen where she had it totally possessed. She owned that cow. The harder the cow tried to return to the mob, the harder the filly worked, and they danced in the middle of the pen only inches out of the sand to a rhythm that was consistent with Cutter's heartbeat.

With the clock ticking down, the filly was firing up. She controlled that beast and was stirring it on, driving it to distress. Finally it gave up on its need to return to the herd and looked away for another way out.

Cutter went back to the mob and finished with a cow off the side, riding out the last ten seconds on a winning note. He couldn't have been more pleased when he heard that buzzer, for the filly had done everything right and had not once put a foot wrong. Cutter was silently hoping she could repeat that same performance.

She could certainly be a champion if she were to continue at that level consistently.

The team were pleased too. Aimee could finally see the difference between Cutter's two rides and her expression said everything without adding unnecessary words. She was blown away at that ride and now had her brother at the top of the leader board along with the judges. A two twenty-six was no record breaker, but it was by far the best run of the day.

As for Allan and Jesse, they were pleased too. Yet they kept on with the job when they returned to the stables without feeling the need to re-dramatize the run all over again.

The girls took the filly into the wash bay while Cutter caught up with the owners and had a quiet talk about that ride. He was professional and would only talk up the filly and her ability, not his training methods or talent. It wasn't his way. They had flown in that morning from the other side of the country and were impressed with the ride and thrilled with the result. Cutter had some very happy clients.

With the last herd done, the arena was starting to wind down for the night. The cattle were pushed out of the pen and loaded onto the trucks, while the tractors came in to prepare the sand for the next morning. The teams were still busy in the stables with young girls and boys giving out the last feeds and final checks before darkness fell, while their trainers were back at their trucks keeping cool or up at the bar, thirsting for a beer or six before closing time.

As much as Allan and Jesse would have liked to join everyone at the bar for a drink, they kept the team together and made for the hotel. The long, soothing lukewarm showers took the sting out of the day and the air-conditioning was a welcome comfort.

Although the first day was now behind them, the team were still on a high when they met down at the restaurant for dinner. It may have been a tiring, hot and dusty day, but they all remained fired up. Cutter and Raylee knew how long the week ahead was going to be and they knew to conserve that energy. They all needed to make sure that by the end of the week, they had something left in reserve.

# Chapter Eleven

As another day ascended over the arena, the show was about to come alive again for the second day of competition. It was a day off for Cutter, who had shown his two horses on the same day in the first go-round. It meant a day to spend with everyone, relaxing and taking to the stands to watch the other competitors, while their breakfast, lunch and occasional coffee breaks in the cafeteria were a chance to catch up on the cutting and follow the leader board as it turned over the new placings after each run.

After an outstanding ride on the blue roan filly, Cutter was two points clear at the top and no one was coming close to his score, which pleased him even more. His ride on the pally, however, saw him outside the cut-off for the final and if she didn't give an exceptional performance in the second go-round, she would be out. She had one last chance to make an impression.

Through the day, the team took the horses out of their stalls and gave them some exercise around the available sand yards that surrounded the arena. They always kept together in groups of two or more, to stay clear of anyone who would like to stir up a bout of trouble.

When Cutter came back to the stables with a time slot for the mechanical cow, he saddled up the colt for Raylee.

"Aren't you going to ride him?" she asked.

"Aren't you riding him in the Non-Pro?" he replied, to let her know that it wasn't him that needed the practice.

She felt those butterflies again, fluttering around in her tummy and she was sure they were now doing double backflips, just to make her feel uneasy. Every time Raylee had gone to the barn to help Cutter with the training, it was to prepare a horse or sit in the corner. It had been a long time since she had cut a cow and put her hand down, and when she took to the saddle, she tried to control that feeling. She shouldn't be feeling nervous. She still had three more days before she had to compete, and a couple of runs on the mechanical cow would certainly sharpen her up, while the colt didn't need it at all.

To get the colt warm, Raylee rode around in the open yard just outside C block, with Cutter chasing her on the mare. She needed to be ridden too, as her Derby event was just as important as the others and he needed to keep her switched on.

In the practice pen, the colt knew exactly what to do as the cow zipped up and down the wire, and Raylee's nerves had all but disappeared as she concentrated hard and worked well with him. His timing was spot on and his brakes were working perfectly, while his instincts towards the cow were second nature to him.

Pleased with the colt's run, they rode back to the stables. It was a slow afternoon as they unsaddled the horses and prepared them for their stalls, and as they headed into the evening, that was their relaxing day all but gone. Tomorrow it was back to cutting, with the second go-round requiring all their attention.

"Why don't you stay in bed for a while longer before you come over," Cutter suggested to Raylee, as he wasn't out in the second go-round on both horses until after lunch.

There was no need to have everyone there at the crack of dawn. Cutter and Jesse could manage the feeds and take a few of the horses out for some exercise while Aimee cleaned out the stalls.

"I think the heat really got to me yesterday," she said, thankful for the morning off.

"Like I said. You're my first priority. And you can stay here as long as you need. You know where we'll be when you're ready." It was Cutter's way of taking care of his wife. He kissed her on the cheek and she rolled back over and cuddled herself up into a ball when he left the room.

She closed her eyes. Her thoughts were only of him. How much she loved him and how they had come to be together, and just how much had changed since the show last year. Cutter had a family again and that pleased her, as they were now both surrounded by people they loved. She felt sick. The uneasy feeling was back.

It struck her right then that there was a strong possibility that it wasn't just nerves. She had nothing to be nervous about. She tried to think of those happy thoughts again.

After she rolled onto her back to relieve the uncomfortable sensation in her tummy, her thoughts ran wild. No... I can't be, she thought, and she threw the quilt back and made a mad dash to the bathroom...

"You're late," Cutter said jokingly to Jesse, when the new loved up couple arrived at the stables a half hour later than was planned.

Jesse threw it straight back. "Well, I'd tell you that your sister had me tied up... But I don't think you wanna hear it," he said, with his twisted sense of humor that he pushed a little too far.

Cutter dropped what he was doing and stared at Jesse with a controlled dark look in his eyes. "You're right. I don't wanna hear it... And just for the record, I don't agree with it either," he said firmly.

Jesse laughed. "Relax. I'm only playin' with you. We just grabbed some breakfast before we came over and we didn't know the time," he explained.

Cutter knew that he had been baited, although he was still struggling to see the funny side. He did need to relax about Jesse and Aimee though, since nothing was going to slow it down now. Just like he didn't give up on Raylee, Jesse wasn't about to give up on his sister and in a way, he liked that.

They went through the morning routine and by the time Allan turned up, they were heading out for a ride. The sun was casting out shadows onto the ground and with the early morning warmth, they rode in them for some relief. It was going to be another blazing hot day, and it was just Cutter's luck that he drew both horses in the afternoon program.

It was still early when Evelyn arrived with a tray full of coffees for everyone. "Where's Raylee?" she asked, when she noticed she had one cup leftover.

"She's still in bed," Cutter said, and he checked the time. "I don't think she's been coping with the heat," he explained.

With the workload from the last three months catching up with her, Cutter was sure that Raylee was feeling the heat more than anyone else and was totally exhausted. After the long night by Emma's side, he knew that her body clock hadn't been rewound and it just needed to shut down for a while.

Cutter went back to the hotel room and silently opened the door. He didn't want to disturb Raylee in case she was still asleep. The bed was empty and the covers had been pulled up roughly, and although the curtains had been pulled back, the bedside lamp was still on, suggesting that she was still there.

Raylee came out of the bathroom, fully dressed and looking like a true cowgirl, with Cutter's eye drawn to the big belt buckle she had in place.

"Well good morning," he said cheerfully, even though it was almost gone. "Don't you look hot," he complimented.

Hot was not the word Raylee would have used to describe how she was feeling, but her sexy cowgirl look was bravely covering up her true feelings of sickness. She picked up her smile and they left the room to head back over to the stables.

It was back to work. Saddles were being thrown on and everyone was getting geared up for the run. Jesse already had the pally in the loping area, riding in circles together with Allan on the roan, as the two runs were fourth and sixth out in the next herd. Cutter went into the stands to watch and sat with Evelyn, who made sure he had everything he needed, fussing over him with food and drinks and a towel to wipe the sweat from his face. Together they calculated the minimum points needed for qualifying.

Raylee took over from her father, giving her the time to get back into the run of things. She was feeling slightly better for the extra sleep, yet she started to feel dehydrated, followed by a bout of motion sickness that made her feel flushed when she didn't keep her head up and looking forward.

With two riders to go, Cutter made his way down to the team. He stood with Raylee at the fence and put his chaps on while she made some final adjustments to the saddle. She felt the need to say something. Anything. She wanted to tell him how she had been feeling that morning, except that he was so focussed on taking to the saddle and the timing wasn't right. They both rode away in different directions.

When the buzzer rang in Raylee's ears, the team made their way out to the corners. The herd was settled and when Cutter started the countdown as he rode across the timeline, everyone was tense for him and the roan.

He drew an audience. After the filly finished the first go-round on top of the leader board, everyone was lured to their seats to see if she was a fluke or the real thing. And they weren't disappointed. Her first cow instantly gave her points on the board when she graciously ripped up the sand in what was an ultimate showdown between her and the cow.

As for Cutter, he was having the ride of his life. With perfect technique and show-stopping style, the filly was clueless as to the performance she was wooing the crowd with. She was just doing her job. She was just doing what she was trained to do, and Cutter was only half the reason behind her talent. Together, their timing was spot on.

She was showing courage on her second cow. Pressuring it to sprint, blocking it to stop. Facing it square on and provoking a reaction. She had the cow so stirred up that it didn't take the time to pause, as it was pushed to its limits and was determined to join up with the mob any which way it recklessly could.

The rest of the ride was just as thrilling and when the last seconds came off the clock to finalize his ride, Cutter pulled up the reins when he heard the buzzer. Totally confident of his run, he reached down the filly's neck and felt the steam coming off her. He heard the crowd raise the roof and when he turned and looked for Raylee, she was riding over to him, so excited that he'd done it again. They both knew he'd just guaranteed his position in the final, even without knowing the score.

There was no time to start celebrating and Cutter took the pally into the prep lane to give her a quick workout while the next cowboy was taking his run. She would respond to his pressure the same way as the roan, going through the same motions and routine, yet Cutter was aware that she did not have the same grit that his other champion cutting horses had.

With the team taking up their positions in the corners, Cutter could only hope that the filly had enough in her to at least qualify for the final. He would like to accomplish that for her owners, who had high hopes and had thrown a lot of money her way. Cutter needed to push her harder than the roan, without pushing her beyond her ability.

Her timing was better when Cutter put his hand down on the first cow, as she made a break for it across the pen. Not to be overpowered in the turns, the filly kept up the speed and was a true reflection of the cow when she sprinted back to the middle. Her swiftness and surge of highly spirited energy had the cow fearful and wanting to return to the mob. Every breakaway run from the cow was hunted down and reeled back in for a blast of short sharp moves that were pleasing to the crowd and scoring valuable points with the judges.

It had pleased Cutter too, and with only thirteen seconds left on the clock, he was looking for his third and final cow, driving it out from the mob. All he needed now, was to finish with a memorable run. But when he put his hand down, the cow kicked up and was running in circles, madly shunting its way through, while Cutter and the filly had to control the uncontrollable. It was a mess, and all that hard work she had done down low at eye level in the sand, was now a recovery for points as they went into damage control before the sound of the buzzer.

What had been a superb performance through most of the run, finished with a completely screwed up ending. Whatever points she gained from her first and second cow, she had just lost in the dying seconds.

It was devastating to finish that way. Cutter was so certain he'd done enough, until one rank cow ambushed his dream run and crushed the filly's chances of making the final. He was not happy. As they walked off the arena floor, the announcer filled in time on the speakers while the scores were coming in. Cutter had done everything he could and now all he could hope for was that the score reflected her undeniable talent. She had pulled out some big moves and proved herself. It was no disgrace.

A two seventeen was a fair result. Not a point less, and possibly a point or two more would have been acceptable, if Cutter were judging his own ride.

At least she had a score on the board, and although it was nowhere near the top, it was still respectable. The pressure was now off. When they all headed back to the stables, the girls once again took both the horses into the wash bay. The last thing on Raylee's mind was her dizzy spells and feeling unwell, as the thought of her husband sitting on top of the leader board gave her something to be happy about.

If nothing else, he had everyone talking about the blue roan filly and had just made a name for her in the cutting world. If they'd never heard of Blue Jean Baby Girl before now, then they were sure to know her name by the end of the week.

It was another morning off for the team, while the last day of the second go-round was taking place, before they squeezed the Open into the late afternoon program. Allan and Evelyn took up the offer to leave the venue for the morning when Pete and Beth invited them out for a tour of the city. It left Jesse and Aimee to take care of everything at the stables, and Cutter and Raylee to stay in the hotel room and laze around, just catching up on some rest.

At daybreak, Cutter woke up and stood silently on the balcony. He watched the arena come alive again with a flow of riders arriving, busily getting back to work. While he was enjoying the morning off, it was more for Raylee's sake than his own. He gave a weary stretch and watched the sun come up, lighting up the rooftops of the arena and stables before it quickly hit the ground and spread over the sand yards. He took it all in. He loved this sight, and he loved his life. He owed it all to two people, and everything that had happened since his mother brought him to the ranch to live with Macca, was only a long path to discovering his true self.

The good and the bad that had come about were only lessons in life that would define his character and shape him into the man he had become. He couldn't change it even if he wanted to, and when he thought of Raylee, he was convinced that he would never change any of it.

He turned his thoughts to his sisters. They had grown up here. If his mother had stayed together with Pete, then Cutter's life would have been in the city too, doing exactly what city kids do. His life of ranching, horses and cutting would never have existed, and he was unashamedly thankful at how things worked out.

His life flashed before him as he thought of his family of old and his family of new. It still shocked him every time he thought about them. The loss of his parents and finding out he had sisters, while Raylee was that one in a million chance encounter. But never did he imagine that he would have two sets of parents now, who were kind and caring, and supportive of everything he did.

He wondered where Marnie and Doug were, and if they would turn up in Dallas for the finals. He missed Marnie, and he knew that Raylee had missed her too. With Marnie on vacation, they had both come to realize just how much work she did in the house and how much they needed her.

When Cutter slid the door behind him, he went back to Raylee and lay down, going over all those fond memories from the comfort of bed. Raylee was using the time to catch up on more sleep. The air-conditioning was keeping the temperature down so low, that she had the covers pulled up to her face.

He reached over and tickled her arm underneath all the layers, as he lay on top and was enjoying the coolness on his skin. He pulled the quilt back slightly to look into her face. She was sound asleep, totally out of it, but he wouldn't stop touching her out of habit that they were so close. He rolled over again and closed his eyes, drifting back to a place that was far away from his family, the ranch, and from cutting.

A bang on the door lifted him out of bed at the speed of light, and he tried to adjust his eyes to the room at the same time as he was scouring around for his jeans. He found them and pulled them on. Damn it, where's my shirt, he thought. He was stumbling around the room finding nothing fast.

"Hang on," he called out. Who the hell was knocking on his door at this time of morning? He ran his hands through his hair then checked the time. What? Eleven o'clock, are you kidding me? He looked through the peep hole.

"Who is it?" Raylee asked, while she was still hiding under the covers.

"It's Jesse and Aims," he announced, then opened the door.

"Well, look at you two," Jesse said happily, and they marched into the room before being invited in. "Nothing like having a sleep-in, is there Aimee?"

"I wouldn't know," Aimee snapped back, playing along. "I'm not getting much sleep these days, being up so early and working hard all day."

"Oh yeah?" Cutter said smartly. "Well you may wanna try going to bed early for some actual sleep and not going there to…"

"Alright," she agreed, laughing at the same time. "I get it. You don't need to spell it out for me. Now, you wouldn't want a coffee by any chance, would you?" she asked.

"Nah," Jesse carried on. "It looks like they haven't earned one yet."

"Give me that," Cutter said aggressively, and he took the cup from the tray and gave them both a friendly smile. "What're you doing here anyway?" he asked, and he headed back to his pillow and propped it up behind him.

Jesse had everything under control at the stables. The horses had been out, ridden and fed while Aimee had cleaned the stalls.

"We thought you'd want an update." While they were at the arena working, Aimee had been keeping an eye on the leader board and she couldn't wait to let her brother know. "You're still sitting on top," she said with pride. "But the pally is out, sorry Cutter… But everyone's been talking about her. Said she'd make a good Derby horse next year."

Cutter could breathe a little easier now. There was nothing he could do that would change the result and the waiting game for the pally was now over. He took a sip of his coffee. It was exactly what Cutter needed to alert himself to the fact that it was nearly lunch time.

"What you got there?" Raylee asked when she saw Aimee holding a magazine. She sat up against the bedhead and was thoroughly enjoying the way the fresh coffee was bringing her senses alive.

"This is what we've really come over for," Aimee replied, taking a long last sip of her coffee before she reached over and put the empty cup on the side table. She fell onto the bed and flicked through the pages. Jesse took his hat off and sat down on the edge of the bed, then spread across the end, feeling the sudden need to unwind.

"I think she's read it like five times already," Jesse stated, looking at the ceiling while she was still finding the page.

"Here it is," Aimee announced, and everyone sat on the bed together and listened. She started reading mid sentence. "...but the surprise packet of the night was when Australian rodeo star, Jesse McCallister, entertained the crowd with his impressive eight second ride in the saddle bronc. On further investigation from our team, we discovered that his rodeo talents are taking a backseat to legendary cutting horse trainer, Cutter Jones, who also won the steer wrestling after nine long years away from the rodeo arena. At 22 years of age, McCallister is sure to have a long career ahead of him, although it's not clear yet if it will be in the rodeo arena or in the cutting pen alongside Jones, who has taken the youngster under his wing for training. If his win in the team roping with Johnny O'Brien is anything to go by, then we know which discipline he should be following. Watch out for this young cowboy. He's likely to pop up anywhere, and if he does, then he's sure to be taking home a buckle or two." Aimee was smiling as she finished reading. She looked up when she put the magazine down, expecting the same response from everyone.

Raylee threw the covers back in a hurry and ran quickly for the bathroom and everyone wondered what on earth was going on. She closed the door behind her.

Cutter followed at a lesser speed. "Hey, are you alright in there?" he asked, from the room side of the bathroom door.

"I'm fine," he faintly heard her say over the flushing of the toilet.

"She doesn't sound fine," Jesse added.

Aimee agreed. "Yeah. When I'm fine, I don't sound like that." Although Aimee was only trying to be funny, Jesse hit her with a pillow to shut her up. "Or maybe she didn't like your story," she said to Jesse, to wind him up some more.

Cutter knocked on the door. "Do you need me to get you anything?" he asked.

"No, I'm okay... I'll be out in a minute," she replied weakly.

Cutter needed to clear the room before Raylee came back out. "Maybe it's best you go for lunch. Have some time out and I'll be over later," he said nicely, to direct Jesse and Aimee to the door, and that was their invitation to leave.

After they said their goodbyes, Cutter went back to the bathroom just as Raylee opened the door to come out.

"I'm alright," she said, looking quite pale. "I don't think that coffee agreed with me very much." She crashed back into the bed and pulled the covers up again as the cool air was giving her an unsettling shiver.

Cutter sat next to her on the bed. "Do you want anything?" he asked.

She didn't.

He touched her forehead. She was hot. He found a face towel in the bathroom and wet it, giving it a tight squeeze to get the last drop of water out and he placed it across her eyes.

"That feels better," she said, thankful for his concern. "I'm alright. Really. I'm starting to feel better already."

"I can always get Jesse to do the afternoon shift at the stables and let you rest up for the day."

"No. Honestly. I need to get out of this room and I want to come over. Just give me twenty minutes and I'll get ready."

After ten minutes longer than she'd requested, Raylee felt the need to get up and have a shower, whether she was going to the stables or not. She came out of the bathroom dressed ready to go, like nothing had happened. She looked at the bed. Cutter had pulled the quilt up and had tidied the room for her.

"I'm ready," she announced.

"Are you sure you're feeling alright?" he asked.

"Nothing wrong," she said to take the worry away. "Just a bad coffee I'd say."

While it was weighing on Raylee's mind for the rest of the afternoon, Cutter put it behind him and went to work in the stalls, cleaning them out again and looking each horse over thoroughly. Raylee tended to their manes and tails, taking pride in her work and care in how they looked. They took a couple of horses out for a walk, riding around the grounds casually, while her thoughts were drifting away with all the possibilities.

Cowboys and cowgirls were coming up to them, catching up on the best rides of the go-rounds and the results that were constantly shifting and rearranging the top twenty on the leader board. Cutter was still sitting on top, and no one had come close to his score let alone knocking him down a placing or two.

Overall, the pally had really struggled at this show, more than Cutter expected. While he was disappointed with the result, he was more than happy to take her on for extra training and ride her in her Derby year, where he was confident she would shine. Everyone was right. She had shown her potential and with more time working on the ranch, she had the makings of becoming a good solid cutting horse at the top level of competition.

On their way back to C block, they passed Tommy and the rat pack. Their unintentional closeness caused a tense feeling from both sides. Cutter knew that Tommy and his team despised him, although he was sure that it wasn't as much as it was returned.

Their hate for each other grew from what should have been a blameless incident over a girl, to a major falling out which had also secretly divided many of the riders. With two good horses in the event, Tommy was safely into the final along with his team, without the need to see the end of day results. But hey... what kind of final would it be without their rivalry to add some spark to the event? As long as they kept Raylee out of their war, then Cutter could deal with Tommy Parker on his own, in and out of the cutting pen.

As the second go-round was finishing up, the loping area was full of riders who were preparing the horses for the Open. The stakes were higher than ever, as this elite group of thirty horses were what everyone came to see.

The Open would give Cutter the chance to make up for his disastrous zero score from last year, when he walked out of the pen with only seven seconds left on the clock. His fight with Tommy had left him injured, and his tolerance to the pain fell short in the dying seconds of his run.

The draw was now out and it was the first time this week that he and Tommy had back to back rides. But he didn't let it bother him so much. As far as he was concerned, the colt was guaranteed to be unbeatable.

When Raylee and Aimee went to the stables to saddle their horses, Jesse was already loping the colt. Allan was back from his outing and was rubbing shoulders with other riders while watching the cattle. Mostly it was to keep out of the sun, though he was also enjoying the company and was totally wrapped up in the event, loving every minute of it.

Allan wished that he could turn back the clock and try his luck in the cowboy arena all over again, instead of downsizing to the vineyard and going into business. While it had been profitable for him to do so, it was also the end of his life on the land and as he looked at Cutter in this competition, he could only be satisfied with being there on his team.

With the humidity causing Raylee to dehydrate, her dizzy spells were only coming under control when she steadied herself against the stable door or the horse.

"I'll be there soon," Raylee said to Aimee, not letting her know how she was really feeling. "You go ahead and I'll meet you in there."

Aimee checked the time. "Don't be long, we're up soon," she said, and she left Raylee behind and rode towards the arena.

Raylee wiped her face and took some quick short breaths to steady herself. She knew she had to pull herself together and fast. After replacing the halter with a bridle, it was time to head to the arena whether she was ready or not. The show would go ahead and not wait for Raylee Jones.

Aimee rode in ahead of Raylee and saw Jesse riding in circles. She was immediately distracted by him, before she found Allan sitting at the fence. She rode over to him and started to watch the cattle also. She was more than impressed with the horses in this event, as their performances were without a doubt unmissable. It was the best of the best, and there was not a horse that didn't live up to its high profile name.

As each rider was taking their turn, it was getting close and Cutter needed to head down for his ride. Jesse pulled the colt up at the rail, ready for the handover.

Just as Raylee was on her way in, she felt the sudden need to stop outside the arena when she saw a tap. Not wanting to go into the arena without washing her face first and taking a drink of water, she tied the horse up to the rail and crouched down in front of the tap, letting the cool water pool in her hands to take a sip.

Tommy Parker was on his way in for his ride. He was up next and was in a hurry. Noticing Raylee by the tap, he thought he should stop. He looked around. There was no one from the Jones team anywhere and he decided to ask politely if she was okay.

He leaned on the horn on his saddle. "Excuse me, Mrs Jones," he said to get her attention, although it was more to taunt her in case stopping was a bad idea. "Are you alright?" he asked.

Raylee splashed the water over her face and stood up to see who was talking to her. The sun struck her in the eyes and she looked for the shade of his hat, so she could see who it was. It made her feel dizzy again and she crouched back down.

Tommy landed on the grass next to her and could tell that she wasn't looking her best. He tied his horse to the rail next to hers and leaned over, placing his hand on her shoulder.

"Are you okay?" he asked again. "Raylee, you don't look so good."

She didn't reply. She stood up fast and felt the world spin around her when she stumbled and took a fall. Tommy put his arms out to catch her, but not before she hit her head on the fence rail as she went down.

# Chapter Twelve

Standing outside the arena in the burning sun, there was panic. Tommy didn't know what to do as Raylee lay in his arms completely out of it, and when he looked around, there was no one to help. He reached for her hat and placed it on the horn on the saddle when he stood up, holding her close to him and wondering what he should do.

He instantly began to sweat. Not from the heat of the day, but from his close encounter with Raylee Jones in the most twisted and unexpected of circumstances.

The medical team. He needed to get her to the small building behind the chutes straight away. He swept her up in his arms and without running, he walked as fast as he could to the medical rooms that were wedged underneath the arena seating, tucked away from all the action. Tommy was greeted at the door by a nurse, who led him to the examination room and gave him instructions to lay Raylee on the bed...

Jesse gave Cutter a stern slap on the back to get him revved up before he mounted the colt ready for his ride in the Open. He was up soon and he looked around for Raylee.

The official called Cutter to the arena floor. "You've jumped the queue. You're up now," he informed him.

"What happened to Tommy?" Cutter asked, although Tommy could have dropped off the face of the earth for all he cared.

The official gave no sign of knowing any details. "Don't know. But he didn't turn up so you're on next. You've got an extra minute to get ready."

Cutter let the team know. He kept looking around. "Where's Raylee?" he asked them all.

No one knew where she was.

"She was at the stables when I came in," Aimee explained, being the last one to see her. "She was right behind me."

The team rode out into the pen with Jesse taking Raylee's place in the back corner, while the official sent someone in quickly to fill the missing turn back position.

Cutter took the colt into the prep lane and began to get him ready. Where was Raylee, he wondered. If she wasn't feeling well again, she may have gone to the stands to sit with her mom. Coming to his own conclusion was his only reassurance and he dug his spurs in and ran the horse through the routine...

"What happened?" the nurse asked Tommy, while he stood next to the bed and looked into Raylee's face. Her cheeks were flushed and she was overheating.

"I think she fainted... She hit her head when she went down," Tommy informed her, while he was still catching his breath. "But I caught her just before she hit the ground."

The woman was busy, preparing the room and arranging everything that was needed for an examination while not looking at Tommy. When she touched Raylee's skin, she noticed her ring.

"Is this your wife?" the woman asked.

Tommy stumbled over the question and before he could answer, another question was thrown at him.

"What's her name?" she asked.

"Raylee," he answered quickly.

She asked more questions about how long Raylee had been knocked out, had she drunk enough water for the day and was she feeling unwell before she fell.

Tommy could only fumble his way through the questions. He pulled up a chair and sat next to the bed. Damn it, he thought, I missed my ride. He'd not even given it a second thought while Raylee was weighing his arms down, and his ride would be all but over by now.

The woman was most concerned about Raylee's temperature. "Unbutton her shirt," she said.

"What?" Tommy asked. He was surprised by her instructions and his reaction was abrupt.

"I'll get something to cool her down, but you need to unbutton her shirt so that we can get her temperature down fast." She went into the joining room leaving Tommy to stand up over the bed and look into her face again. His hands were shaking, knowing that this was the most awkward situation to be in.

Starting at the top, he popped each stud on Raylee's shirt one at a time until he reached her jeans. He felt a hot flush when he looked at her buckle. It was the buckle she won last year at the show when she'd beaten his horse, and he tilted it his way to read it. Not to get sidetracked, he pulled her shirt open and lay it back on the table. Raylee was now lying bare on the table with only her black bra coming between her and his curiosity.

The woman handed him a wet towel. "Cool her down with this," she said, while she placed another wet towel over her eyes and forehead.

Raylee began to stir. She was waking up.

"It's alright, Raylee... You've just taken a bump to the head. You're in the medical room and you're here with your husband." The woman was talking firmly as she was well experienced in this kind of situation. "Keep her cool... I'll get some more towels and some ice," she said to Tommy, and she left the room again.

Tommy took the wet towel and began to wipe Raylee's skin, down her neck and around her shoulders. Everywhere he was told. She stirred again and went to take the wet towel off her face, when he grabbed her hand away. "Shhh..." Tommy tried to keep her calm, yet he felt that same hot flush again when her hand found his and she held it for comfort...

As Cutter rode across the timeline, he looked up into the stands for Evelyn. He found her easily enough, as that seat was hers for the entire show and he knew exactly where to find her. There was no sign of Raylee.

Jesse pointed out a few options for Cutter and as he started to get the herd moving, he was losing focus. While the team were taking this run seriously, Cutter would have rather gone back to the stables to look for his wife. It would be the longest two and a half minutes of his life and he wished it over before it had even begun.

He looked controlled and professional as he made a clean, clear cut, driving any cow out from the mob and he put his hand down. That was about the best part of his ride. His placement and footwork were not in sync with the horse and the cow, and every stop and turn had the worst timing.

Every rider, spectator and trader had turned to the arena floor to watch this ride. Expectations were high and no one could have predicted the disastrous run he was having. Cutter's head was everywhere except on cutting. He was just going through the motions. What had happened to Raylee, he wondered. Where was she, he thought. As the seconds were coming off the clock, the colt should have been wooing the crowd with Cutter in the driver's seat taking control. Instead, he was having a wrack and ruined run by driving himself crazy.

If his first cow wasn't bad enough, his second cow would make any rider walk out of the pen. It drove the colt to the far side of the arena, leaving him to sprint back across the pen to the other side. The cow charged at the colt, trying to blast its way through. The colt was strong enough to force it back, although this messed up ride was only showing everyone in the stands how not to cut. Cutter and the colt were being slaughtered by the cow and the run was a complete wreck.

With Raylee missing and Tommy a no show for the second most important ride of the week, Cutter was starting to overthink, tangling up the two separate issues and trying to find a connection. He was almost convinced there was more to their disappearances and he wanted to know what. No... That's impossible, he thought. There's nothing to connect Raylee to Tommy. She hates him as much as I do.

Cutter looked at the clock when he turned for the final cow. Still another twenty seconds to go. Hurry up. He'd had enough and wanted this ride over. He could have easily picked up the reins and walked out, except that his zero score had played on his mind for the whole of last year and he may have been reading more into Raylee's disappearance than was needed. When the buzzer sounded, it was a relief. For the first time he heard the crowd, who encouraged him all the way off the arena floor while he was surprised by their response. It seemed that he was the only person in the arena who missed the entire ride.

The team met in the loping area behind the pen and tied up their horses.

"What happened?" Aimee asked. "That was the worst ride ever," she stated, showing him how disappointed she was.

"Shut up, Aimee," Jesse interrupted.

Allan's face said just as much, and when they all looked to Cutter for his explanation, he gave them a sense that something was very wrong.

"What is it?" Allan asked curiously, while they were still trying to figure out what had just happened in the pen.

"It's Raylee," he said seriously. "Something's wrong with Raylee and I need to find her."

"She's probably gone back to the room if she wasn't feeling well," Aimee said, trying to add calm to the situation.

Cutter tried to convince himself that it was a possibility, until he pointed out the obvious. "But she would've called someone to let me know."

"Maybe she called Evelyn?" Allan added, to ease the panic that was now on the rise with everyone.

They split up. Allan went to the stands to see Evelyn, to ask if she had seen or heard from Raylee. Aimee went to the hotel, expecting to find her tucked up in bed. Jesse took some of the horses back to the stable block where she may have been, although he highly doubted, leaving Cutter to wander around the different sand yards while his thoughts were running wild.

He looked everywhere. He asked a few people that he knew. Raylee was nowhere to be found and had not left a hint of a clue. Then he noticed two horses tied up with no riders and he made his way over to them. It was his horse. It was her hat. What the...? It was confusing. Is that Tommy's horse, he wondered.

There must be a good explanation for this. There must be a very good reason why his rival and his wife had both disappeared and had just left two horses tied to the rail. He looked around some more. They can't be together, and if they were, then they couldn't be far away.

His phone rang. Fully expecting to see Raylee's name, he pulled it out of his pocket to answer it. It was Allan. Evelyn didn't know that Raylee was missing, except for her not taking up her position in the corner, and they began to make their way down.

While he had his phone out, he called Jesse. "No sign of her here," Jesse said.

"I found her horse," Cutter informed him, and he explained to Jesse where he was.

He wandered around some more...

"How long have you been married?" the nurse asked Tommy.

Raylee was still on the bed with the wet towel over her eyes, holding Tommy's hand. She was still feeling drowsy and her head was pounding, although she found the need to answer for him. "A little under three months," she said, and she gave Tommy's hand a gentle squeeze.

The woman left the room again to get some more ice. Tommy sat there looking at Raylee and was concerned for her. Should he leave? Should he stay? Just the thought of having his hands all over her body was wrong to him on every level yet for some reason, he didn't put a stop to it. In the back of his mind, there was almost a need for revenge. It was crossing his mind that this could even the score. Raylee felt his closeness and while she wasn't thinking straight, her thoughts poured out of her mouth.

"Cutter, I think that I might be pregnant," she announced.

It hit Tommy at that moment that this had been a very bad idea. He should have taken her to the medical room and gone straight back to his horse and gone cutting. The outcome would have been so much more favorable, and even without a score on the board, he'd have been in a much better position than where he was right now.

He didn't know what to do next. His heart was pounding out of control and his head was racing fast. He looked around the empty room. They were alone. Looking at Raylee stretched out on the bed, barely dressed, he reached out slowly and placed his hand on her tummy, and when she felt his warmth, she was quick to touch it...

When Cutter saw the medical rooms under the arena seating, it struck him that it could be a strong possibility and he raced over.

"Excuse me," he said to the woman, while standing in the doorway. "I'm looking for my wife. Has she been brought in by any chance?"

The woman looked up at him. "We had a young lady come in a little while ago," she started to say, and that was enough for Cutter to walk in and head towards the examination room. "Wait," she called out. "She already has her husband in there."

That didn't stop Cutter. He had to look for himself. It was the closest, most logical explanation that he could come up with and if it wasn't Raylee, then he didn't know where to look next. When he slid the door open slightly to look inside, his relief and fears were realized at the same time. He couldn't see her face, but he knew those boots and those jeans, and he'd recognize that buckle anywhere. But that shirt? That shirt that was open and her body exposed for everyone to see.

When Tommy saw him, he dropped Raylee's hand and he stood up. Cutter looked confused. What was going on, he wondered. He was relieved that he'd just found her... but with Tommy Parker? Why was he in the medical room holding his wife's hand? He couldn't get his head around what his eyes were telling him.

Hell has no fury like Cutter Jones watching another man comforting his wife. Especially this man. He threw his angry eyes in Tommy's direction and lost control. Whatever level of calm and relief he was feeling that he'd found her, was instantly gone. Without words, he launched himself at Tommy and grabbed him by the shirt, reefing him away from her bedside. There was a scuffle in the small room and the nurse ran in behind them to control the situation.

They were all but going to kill each other, as the rage in both their eyes was deadly. She ordered them both out, standing over her patient and protecting her from their wrangle, as Raylee had drifted into a state of unawareness again.

Keeping a firm grip, neither cowboy was going to let the other go, yet they managed to leave the room still tangled up with each other.

The first swing was thrown by Tommy when they reached the door and they both fell out the doorway of the medical rooms and onto the dirt. Cutter stood up and felt the sting on his lip and he touched it, then wiped the small smear of blood away. He ran for him, driving his shoulder into Tommy's gut and the two of them hit the ground and wrestled fiercely among punches. The repeat of their fight last year was back on.

When Cutter had Tommy pinned down and was about to lay all his fury into him, he was grabbed from behind. He was pulled to his feet and he turned around quickly to defend himself from whoever was going to attack him. It was Jesse and Allan standing there, holding back the aggression that he was just about to unleash on Tommy. His breathing was heavy as he stood looking down on him, while Allan restrained all of Cutter's anger and Jesse stepped in between them.

"Let it go. He's not worth it," Jesse said to Cutter, before he looked at Tommy lying back on his elbows on the ground. He was roughed up and covered in dust. "Get outta here," Jesse warned him quickly, before they released Cutter for a second go-round.

Tommy stood up. He was alone, without his pack around him, while Cutter was surrounded by his team. Tommy had a scrape on the side of his eye and he picked up his hat and looked at them all. "You're welcome," he said sarcastically, to let them know that he had only been there to help Raylee, not hurt her, and he walked away. He thought about telling Cutter more than it was his place to, but if he could do it to Cutter, he certainly couldn't do it to Raylee. It wasn't his news to break and he was decent enough to know it. What he would do, however, was have the last say. "And by the way," Tommy said, while he was still fully charged up and showing his evil eye. "I missed my ride for her... Did you?" He didn't need to add anymore and he turned and walked away.

Cutter felt those words hit him in the heart. It was true. Cutter knew that Tommy had missed his ride and that he'd stepped up and took Tommy's place.

He had a sense of deep regret now. Whatever had happened, Tommy was there for Raylee and he wasn't.

Cutter ran back inside, where the nurse drilled him over what had just happened, although he wasn't listening. All he wanted, was to see if Raylee was alright.

She was still resting on the bed, dazed but awake. Her temperature had gone down and her words were a little unclear at times. She mumbled something softly, and Cutter sat on the side of the bed and picked up her hand and touched her face with the other. She seemed unaware of the drama going on around her.

"How do you feel?" he asked.

"I don't know," she said, rubbing the back of her head and feeling the bump that was causing her pain. "I think I might have fainted," she guessed.

"We should probably get you to the hospital."

Raylee didn't like the sound of that. She was alert enough to know that she didn't want to go to the hospital. "No. I'm not going. I just want to go back to the room and lie down," she said.

"Well they might let you do that after you've rested here for a while." Cutter touched her bare shoulder and she could feel the warmth of his hand on her cool skin. The ice and wet towel had reduced her temperature and she was now back to normal. Raylee took his hand and slowly moved it down her body where she rested it on her tummy. She was wanting Cutter to say something. Anything.

"What was Tommy doing here?" he asked.

Say anything but that, she thought. "Tommy was here?" she questioned him. "What for?"

Cutter didn't want to alarm her. "I don't know. But don't you worry about it. I'm here now and that's all that matters."

The bump on Raylee's head had gone down considerably and her throbbing headache had subsided by the time she was back in her bed at the hotel room. It had been getting late into the afternoon before the doctor arrived at the grounds, and after a thorough examination and a lot of persuasion, she avoided a trip to the hospital and was able to leave with strict instructions put in place.

Just like Cutter's run-in with the bull at the rodeo last year, Raylee's knockout had the same forty-eight hour surveillance applied to her. She was to be monitored for further dizzy spells and ongoing sickness, although she was certain of the reason for the way she was feeling. With Cutter not responding to her the way she would have liked when she broke the news to him in the medical room, she was unsure how he was feeling about it and it played on her mind. Cutter, on the other hand, was making a fuss, constantly asking if she was alright and refilling her glass with water, so that she didn't dehydrate. He kept propping up her pillow and was making her comfortable, in between his affectionate touches and tickles to soothe her needs.

"I'm alright," she said. "I'm not the first person who's fainted on a hot day." Raylee tried to ease Cutter's mind, yet she really wanted to discuss her thoughts and the possibilities as to why she was feeling so unwell.

"You fainted because your temperature was up. You might be coming down with something," he said with care to show his concern, and again, he touched her face as he had done so many times already. Just to make sure.

Coming down with something, she thought. He can't be serious?

"I can't believe I missed your ride." It had just come to mind that Cutter had ridden the colt in the Open while she was laid up in the medical room.

"You didn't miss much," he said, still kicking himself over the result, yet he knew it was for all the right reasons.

"Well, how did you go?" Raylee was all of a sudden enthusiastic to hear all about the colt's ride. She was starting to feel better and her eyes were sparkling again when their discussion went back to cutting, although he didn't give her that winning smile that she was expecting. "You did ride him, didn't you?"

"Yeah, I rode him."

"And?"

"And what?" he asked.

Raylee wouldn't give up. "And how did you go?" she asked again.

"Better than last year." Cutter was avoiding her questions. Any result was going to be better than his zero score from last year, and while it was one ride he'd rather forget, Raylee wasn't going to allow it.

She touched his arm. "You know I'll find out tomorrow when I ask my mom," she said, to give him one last chance to hear it from him.

"I got a score on the board this year," he said, still dancing around her question and not sounding too pleased. She looked at him and didn't speak. Her eyes were sending him the right message and he hesitantly continued. "And I totally screwed it up," he added.

"What happened?"

"You're what happened." Cutter was making it quite clear that she was the only reason behind his poor result. "Aimee left you at the stables and you were fine. When we were called up to the pen, no one knew where you were and I panicked. But they sent me out anyway and what I should've done was pulled out and gone looking for you. I can't believe I didn't do that," he said, totally down on himself.

Raylee tried to recall the afternoon. "I remember feeling dizzy and stopping for some water before I went in. Then I woke up on the bed with a sore head and feeling like I'd been hit by a truck." At the mention of it, she rubbed her head again, feeling the small bump that was still tender. She smiled at him. "But I knew you were there with me. You're always there for me."

No he wasn't. Cutter wasn't there for her and he knew it. He was now feeling the guilt of walking into that cutting pen, and another surge of anger that Tommy had been there holding her hand in his place. She was none the wiser and at this stage, he wasn't going to make her aware of it either.

"So, you haven't said... What did you score?" she asked.

Cutter spoke under his breath. "A ninety-five," he managed to force out with great difficulty.

"What?" Raylee blurted out, deeply surprised. "As in a one ninety-five?" she asked loudly.

"And I don't wanna talk about it." The score was the last thing Cutter wanted to talk about that night. He'd not had a score as low as that, ever. Well, not since he'd turned pro. The score was irrelevant to him compared to the health of his wife and the blame he was loading on himself. He found a diversion. "And now you won't be riding the colt tomorrow," he said, to let her know that under no circumstances was he allowing her back on a horse, even if she wanted to. "But you don't need to worry about that... I've got the perfect plan."

# Chapter Thirteen

It was another day and another event. Today was the mare's chance to shine in the Derby. She would have two go-rounds to qualify for the final, just like the other horses, while the Open Non-Pro would fill in the last three herds of the afternoon.

The mare had stolen the show last year and was the reason Cutter was back on top of his game again. She was outstanding in every way and had interest from all over the country as to when her first line of progeny would be available for sale. Cutter even had a couple of serious offers to buy her after the show, with one interested party prepared to give him a blank check. While the money would have been nice to add to his bank account, Cutter couldn't part with her no matter how much money was being thrown his way. Her bloodlines were first rate and her strength was enhanced by her athletic build. Add in her cow smarts and huge heart, she was the complete package. A horse that good was not something a trainer wanted to let slip out of their hands, and Cutter declined every offer that was thrown at him. Crossed with the right stallion, her foals would be valuable and Cutter would be in control of the bloodlines that followed.

When Evelyn spent the morning with Raylee in the room, it was to enable Cutter to go to the stables to get geared up for his ride. Being under strict instructions from the doctor, Raylee was not to be left alone, and Cutter's commitment to the mare was only enforced when she all but pushed him out the door to leave. After a disastrous ride on the colt, Cutter needed to save face and do a good job on the mare, without Raylee taking his full attention.

Evelyn fussed around Raylee the same way that Cutter did, making sure she had everything on hand and was feeling on the mend. Evelyn sat on the side of the bed and they took the time to talk. They caught up on everything that had happened since Allan and Evelyn arrived in Texas, and how Raylee had only hoped that things would turn out the way they did. She let her mother know exactly how happy she was, until she felt the sudden need to race to the bathroom... again.

"That's it... You're going to the hospital," Evelyn demanded, and she reached into her bag for her phone.

"No. Mom, I'm okay. Really," Raylee said when she walked out of the bathroom, to reassure her mother there was nothing to worry about.

"Raylee, you're sick. You need to get checked out," Evelyn insisted.

She grabbed her mother on the arm when she lay back down. "I'm not sick... But there's a chance that I might be pregnant," she announced.

"What? Are you sure?"

"No, I'm not sure. But I've been feeling like this for a few days now and I think that's why I fainted," Raylee explained. "I didn't throw up because of my head. I threw up because I feel sick and I think I know why."

There was a certain level of excitement from Evelyn although Raylee wasn't showing her mother the same in return. "What's the matter? Aren't you happy?" she asked, and she touched her daughter on the forehead to check her temperature.

Raylee was holding back. "I don't know. I'm not sure what to think. I know that Cutter isn't ready because he said that he wasn't... And when I told him yesterday in the medical room that I thought I might be pregnant, he didn't say anything."

"Maybe he's in shock."

"Or maybe he doesn't want it. We only just got married and I think it might be too soon for him." Raylee was feeling let down by Cutter's lack of excitement, yet she was feeling the same way. "I know it's too soon for me," she admitted.

"Well, either way, you need to find out first and know for sure." Evelyn would make that happen, since there was no point in assuming something that may not be true.

"I'm scared," Raylee confided. She started to build up a river of tears and held them back until they peaked, then flowed down her face, running over her cheeks and touching the corners of her mouth. She gave a sniffle.

Evelyn looked into Raylee's eyes and knew that feeling. She could only speak from the heart as any mother would do. She wiped her daughter's face. "You know, Raylee, when I had your brothers, our family was complete. Your father had his two sons to follow in his footsteps and take over the cattle station one day, and I didn't want any more children."

This was news to Raylee. She never knew that she was the unwanted baby in the family.

"When I found out I was having another baby, I cried for weeks. It was the last thing I wanted when I was trying to cope with two little boys and was thinking about going back to work on Dad's vineyard. But when you came along, your father and I couldn't have been happier... You loved the horses and the land when your brothers didn't, and you followed your father around in his shadow, always wanting to help but always getting under his feet and in his way."

It made Raylee laugh. She remembered strutting around the property in her oversized boots and hat, and asking lots of questions to her father who was trying to go about his work quietly. When he put her on a horse, she loved it. That was the connection to her father that would make them inseparable from that day on.

"You see, Raylee, the most beautiful baby will come into your life at exactly the right time whether you're ready or not... And when it does, you'll wonder what on earth all these tears were for."

Raylee didn't know she was the unexpected surprise of her parents' life. She reached up and hugged her mom.

"And now you can see why your father didn't like it when another man came into your life. All those years ago we weren't ready for your arrival, but you soon made a special place in your father's heart and you were his little girl. He just wasn't ready for you to grow up... He knew it would happen one day, but you gave him quite a shock in more ways than one."

Raylee needed her mom. She needed to hear just how much she was loved by her family, and she cheered up after a few more tears and one final let go. After a long, in depth, heart to heart about her brothers, her nieces and nephews, and her growing up on the cattle station, she decided that it was time to get up and face the day. She went for a shower and came out dressed ready for the arena, although there would be no riding within the forty-eight hours, and certainly none if she returned a positive test.

The bump on her head was all but gone, yet when she pulled her hat into position, she could feel the remains of yesterday's crash landing. She still wasn't sure how she came to wake up in the medical room and she never thought to ask. There were more important things on her mind that morning, as Evelyn made sure that they would know by the end of the day...

When they arrived at the arena, Jesse had the mare in the loping area, working her into a sweat, which wasn't too difficult under the conditions. When Cutter took her into the prep lane for her fine tuning, everyone else was waiting to take up their positions in the corners. It was the first time that Raylee had seen Cutter ride from the stands and she got a bird's eye view when they sat only three rows back from the rail.

When he walked across the timeline, Raylee felt that fluttering rush in her tummy again, and she was trying to decipher if it was cutting nerves or something else. She could hear Jesse clearly talking to Cutter about the cattle as he made his way through, nudging each one out of the way to push his selected cow forward.

Raylee tuned into the discussions that were taking place two rows back, when she overheard more details about Cutter's ride on the colt and just how bad it was.

They would not give him an inch of respect and played down his talent, saying that he'd lost whatever ability he had years ago and had only fluked his triumphant results in the go-rounds. It was enough to wind Raylee up into a spin and it was only because she didn't want to miss any part of his ride, that she didn't turn her back on Cutter to give them a piece of her mind.

Her only hope was that Cutter could repeat that same magic from last year and leave them to eat their own words.

And he did. The mare's gutsy blast across the pen had everyone on the thrill ride from the first move. She wooed the crowd and burned up the sand for the full two and a half minutes as the cows she cut were provoked by her extraordinary ability to work them into a complete frenzy.

She was throwing her weight around that pen and was skillfully afflicting those cows with fear. Every cow had her switched on. Every run had her on the move. Every burst of energy was magic. When she lowered herself into position in the sand and found that groove, it was scoring her points on the board. She was turning it on for everyone and was having a winning ride.

Raylee didn't need to turn around to tell Cutter's critics what she really thought. As the buzzer sounded they had changed their tune as to what a remarkable trainer he was. Huh, she thought... and that's not all he's good at. It put a smile on her face, especially when the judges thought that it was right up there with the best of them, giving him a whopping two twenty-six to take with him into the second go-round.

That was the last herd before they changed for the Open Non-Pro. Raylee and Evelyn made their way to the cafeteria for something to eat. She felt the need to have something light to add some comfort to her tummy, and to control the headache that was coming on fast.

She expected to see the team after they were done in the stables, as her ride on the colt was not going to happen and the mare was now their last ride for the day. When they took a seat under the window and Raylee bit into her sandwich, Beth arrived and pulled up a seat. The two moms had greeted each other with a hug while Raylee received a kiss on her bulging cheek as she was trying to down her mouthful quickly.

Beth discreetly pulled a small wrapped up package out of her bag and gave it to Evelyn over the table. Raylee knew what that package was.

"Please don't say anything," Raylee begged, and Beth could see that the look in her eyes was more fearful than anything else.

The mercury was still rising into the late afternoon and even though the sun had started to sink towards the west, it was still intense. The three women took their cool bottles of water and made their way back to their seats to catch the start of the next event, the Open Non-Pro.

It was Raylee's one and only chance to ride in the cutting pen that week and show everyone that the colt really was up to the job. She couldn't believe that she had come all this way with one shot at winning another buckle and she'd had to withdraw. When they all sat back down in the stands, Cassie found them and joined the end of the row. She was dressed from head to toe in her new cowgirl clothes and was proudly sporting her new hat.

As each rider was taking to the pen for their ride, Raylee recognized the winner from last year who'd just had another outstanding score and was sure to win the event again. It was devastating to her, watching helplessly from the sidelines. She could only imagine now how Cutter felt when he was banned from competition and had to sit out for three whole months for his fight with Tommy in Vegas. She had been sure that the agony of it would have been enough for Cutter and Tommy to put the bad blood to rest. But it didn't. The mutual hostility and friction had only escalated and the need for payback was almost consuming, especially since Raylee had entered into their conflict.

It wasn't until Raylee heard her name that her thoughts were brought back to the cutting.

"They've made a mistake," Raylee said quietly in her mother's ear as she leaned in close. "Don't they know I'm not riding?"

Evelyn caught on more quickly than Raylee did, touching her on the arm and pointing to Cutter and Aimee, who were making their way out to the corners.

"What?" she asked. "What's going on?" Raylee was confused, especially when she saw her father take up his position.

The announcer gave Raylee a huge welcome back, recalling her ride from last year and giving the colt an impressive introduction. When she looked for the rider, she could see the colt making his appearance... and Jesse?

What was Jesse doing taking her slot? Surely that was against the rules of competition, yet no one had picked up on it until the bell rang and started the countdown. Jesse was well into the mob when the officials sensed there was a mistake. Not to interrupt his ride, they let it continue, only for there being a perfectly good explanation at the end of it all.

The colt glided easily through the cattle, carrying Jesse forward like a professional. He looked like a young Cutter Jones, wearing his chaps and controlling the herd until he was down to one cow. His hand hit the horse and when the colt felt the reins fall loose, he all but took over.

Jesse received a big dose of reality when the colt made the break and shot after the cow in dramatic style. It was on. Every sprint was burning up the arena floor. Every turn was showing just how big his stops were, and as he dominated the pen and found a position low in the sand in the middle, the colt boogied with the cow for some explosive cutting action. It was entertainment plus.

When the cow gave up and turned away, Jesse had to restrain the colt and head him back to the herd, both eager for another cow.

The crowd were loving it. They had no idea who was in the cutting pen, as Jesse had everyone in the stands whispering and making wild accusations, none of which were even close to the truth. The officials were clueless as to who they had allowed into the pen, and when the President of the Association stood at the gate, Raylee knew they were going to be in deep shit.

Unaware of the commotion they were causing, Cutter was selecting the next cow and Jesse pushed it forward, fully focussed on driving it out from the rest. If the crowd hadn't already filled the arena with noise to overpower the loud music thumping out of the speakers, then they were about to raise the roof as he smashed his way through the second cow.

The colt never missed a beat. Consistently provoking the cow to take desperate measures to get past, he remained low and poised, ready to pounce on every move it made. Their connection was intense, while the run was lively. Jesse felt the power of the colt beneath him and was convinced that this was as unbeatable as his last bronc ride. Gripping the saddle and holding the horn tight, Jesse let the colt take full command of the cow and let him do his thing.

Bring it on. He had nothing to lose. As the seconds came to a close, Jesse finished with an impressive end to his run with the colt hotfooting on the spot, his tail sweeping the sand and his nose was down low. When the buzzer sounded, the crowd erupted. Cutter and Aimee came together in the center of the pen when Jesse pulled up the reins and sat. He was fully charged up and he looked around at the crowd, who were still unaware of who they were applauding. He put his hand down low and rubbed the colt.

"That was the best ride ever," Aimee overstated. "Sorry, Cutter, but it was," she added, looking past Jesse to her brother.

"Nah. I'll admit, it was pretty damn good," Cutter agreed.

They all rode together out of the pen. Aimee thought that she was dating the hottest cowboy in the arena after that ride and she couldn't stop smiling for him. When the announcer came over the speakers with a score of a two twenty-seven, his excitement was only marred by the identity of this cowboy. They had everyone talking.

They met Allan at the gate and he was equally impressed. "Not bad for a rodeo kid from Down Under," he said like a proud Aussie.

Their happiness turned back to reality when they were met by the officials in the loping area, while the cutting continued on. Cutter knew the President of the Association quite well and when Mike looked at him, he knew what was coming their way.

"Take those horses back to their stalls," Mike said to Aimee directly, before he turned his attention to Cutter. "And I expect a damn good explanation for this." Mike was furious, but since he was surrounded by three officials and an arena full of people who were still pumped up from Jesse's ride and leading score, it hardly seemed the right time or place to blow his stack. "You two, follow me."

Cutter and Jesse followed Mike to his office in silence, while Allan and Aimee took the horses back to their stalls, just as they were told. The boys kept looking sideways at each other and were keeping their laughter under control.

The plan had worked, just as Cutter had intended. With a zero score in the Open last year and a disastrous performance on him yesterday, the colt was losing credibility. Raylee couldn't show him due to her head injury and the last thing Cutter wanted, was to truck him home without giving him another chance to prove himself.

It couldn't have worked out better. Jesse not only gave the colt back everything that he was made famous by, but he had everyone in the arena wanting to know who he was. Now Mike was about to find out, so he could steal their thunder and rain on their victory parade.

"Sit down," Mike said with severity that Cutter thought was a little unnecessary.

"Now listen, Mike. I know what you're gonna say and before you do, we need to apologize for the mix up." Since Cutter knew him well, he would do the talking for the both of them.

"Sorry, Cutter. But that looked a little more than a mix up if you ask me. That was well orchestrated and you damn well know it." Mike was starting to wind up.

"Yes sir, it was. I admit. But we didn't hurt anyone, did we?"

"It's not the point. This is a serious competition, Cutter, and you just broke all the rules. You can't just throw anyone you like out there. We've got insurances and guidelines and rules to follow... And what about the other riders? Do you think they'll be happy when you bend all the rules to suit yourself and then you go out there and win the damn thing?"

Mike had seen the run and heard the score. He couldn't dispute that it was worth the winning buckle.

"What're you gonna do?" Cutter asked up front.

"I don't know," Mike said, rubbing his face, trying to provoke his thoughts. "But if I don't do something, then I'll have every other rider out there wanting your head, and to be perfectly honest, I can't really blame them."

"Take my points," Jesse offered. It was the first time he spoke and Mike heard his voice. "I only rode to show off the horse. The score doesn't mean anything."

"But Jesse, you're set to win a buckle," Cutter said to convince him that there must be an alternative way around this.

"I don't need a buckle to know that I won." Jesse was being quite decent about it. "Besides, it's your head they want, not mine. If you take the fall then you'll be out of the final."

"He's right," Mike agreed. "One of you has to take the fall and between you both, you need to work out who's got the most to lose."

It wasn't too difficult to figure out. Jesse had made his entrance into the sport in a big way and everyone would still be talking about that ride for many years to come. Not only from the thrill factor, but to go from the highest score of the week so far back down to a zero, would only add controversy to the scandal, and cause the rumor mill to go into overdrive.

Yes, the plan had worked very well. Everyone would be talking about the colt again.

They both stood up to leave. Mike had to give them one final warning to let them know he was just doing his job. "And if you ever pull another stunt like that again, you'll both be enjoying the view from the stands," he said. "And good luck for the finals," he added, before Cutter closed the door behind him and headed back to the stables.

The buzz around the arena was only hyped up by the colt's impressive run. While some competitors thought that Cutter should take a well deserved break and see out his punishment sitting on the rails for the rest of the show, others thought that it was worth the risk and were more impressed at how they'd got away with it.

Raylee, unaware of their game plan, was sitting on the fence. While she thought that it was a huge leap forward for Jesse, who was now well known from the stables to the stands, and from the officials to the President, she also knew that it was a huge gamble that could have easily backfired and nearly did. Jesse, on the other hand, didn't mind all the attention and when the reporters from the magazine caught up with him in the stables that afternoon, they were only too pleased to do a followup story. He was in the spotlight again. This time, for all the right and wrong reasons. It didn't stop him going about his business though, and he picked up the extra load with Raylee confined to either bed or the stands. She was cleared to ride again now, although she was still quietly doubtful if she should.

"Stay in bed," Cutter said, while he was pampering her some more. "If you're not feeling up to it, then you don't need to come over at all. Maybe have a day off." Cutter was only suggesting that she rest up before the start of the finals, yet Raylee wasn't sure if even by then she would make it back on a horse.

She agreed.

"And you know you're my first priority, but I do have to go and ride the mare. But as soon as I'm done, I'll be back," he promised.

"I'll try to make it over." Raylee wouldn't guarantee anything at that moment. Her heart was into cutting but her head wasn't.

Cutter reached down and kissed her. "I love you," he said, before he left her in the room to snuggle back in under the covers. Letting her thoughts drift into an idle state, she fell back into a healthy sleep again.

She was completely lost for time when a loud knock on the door brought her out of her deep slumber. It was her mother, with a smile that looked more hopeful than anything else.

"Did you take the test?" she asked.

"No, not yet." Raylee didn't return the smile and crashed back onto the bed.

"You know you can't avoid it forever. You have to know."

"Maybe I'll wait until I get home. I'd rather not know while the show's on."

Evelyn was more responsible than Raylee would have liked. "I know that you're scared, but you can't get back on a horse if you don't know."

Raylee knew what she had to do. She didn't want to take the test last night while they were in the room together, and now that Cutter was gone, she had to dig deep into the bottom of her bag where it was well hidden. She held it in her hand and stared at it. It frightened her to know. Without a word to her mother, she took it to the bathroom and closed the door behind her.

Another successful run on the mare saw another horse into a final. Cutter went into the second go-round of the Derby full of confidence and came out the other side with a guaranteed spot in the top twenty. He had pushed her hard to give her a good run, yet he still played it safe enough to secure her a place. His combined scores after two runs saw him fall back a few places and qualify him fourth overall. It wasn't anything to be disappointed in, as her run was spectacular in every way.

What he was disappointed in, was that he was missing his most valuable team member, as Raylee was noticeably absent from the corner as well as the stands. She'd missed it, and Cutter rushed back to the stables and let Aimee take over from there.

When he walked back into the room, Evelyn was sitting on the bed with Raylee and they were talking. He could see the leftover sandwiches and empty bottles of water on the bedside table, and her eyes were puffy, as if she had been crying.

"Hey, what's up?" he asked with care.

Evelyn stood up. "She's alright. She just needs you," she said, then she gave her daughter a kiss on the head and grabbed her bag before she made for the door. "You've got so much to talk about." Evelyn gave one final glance at the two of them sitting on the bed together before she closed it.

Cutter looked confused. "What was that all about?" he asked.

"I don't know," she lied with intent.

He looked closely into her face. "It looks like you've been crying."

"It's nothing, really." Raylee was avoiding the issues at hand. "How did you go? I'm sorry I didn't make it over."

"We're in the final. She was amazing," he stated. "You should've seen her." Cutter sounded pleased and Raylee didn't want to take that away from him.

She lifted up her smile. "That's great. I had every bit of faith in the both of you."

Cutter wouldn't let it rest and prompted her for some answers. "Are you upset that your mom and dad are going home next week?" he asked, trying to fill in the missing pieces.

Raylee jumped right onboard with it. "I'm going to miss them both. I loved that you asked my mom to come over, and I've loved the time with them. But it's gone so quickly."

"Well, with your mom going home and Marnie coming back after the show, we'll have everything back to normal," he assured her.

Or would they?

"Can I ask you something?" It had been playing on Cutter's mind and he needed to ask Raylee directly. He knew what the answer was going to be, yet he needed to look into her eyes and ask anyway.

"Sure," she said, hoping that he wasn't on the same trail.

"It's about the day you fainted."

Oh yes he was. As her heart raced, she played it cool. "What about it?"

"I need to know what you were doing with Tommy that day."

Her eyes filled up quickly again and she jumped to her own defense. "I wasn't with Tommy. No way. Why do you keep saying that?"

Cutter saw it for himself. Either Raylee had no idea or she was lying. When the tears started to roll, he regretted asking the question. "No... Don't cry. What're you crying for?" he asked, and he pulled her in close for comfort.

"Why would you accuse me of that?" she sobbed.

"I wasn't accusing you of anything. I just... Never mind. I just need to know that everything is alright."

Raylee confirmed that it was.

They spent the afternoon lazing around the room. Raylee finally got up and had a shower which made her feel better, while Cutter did everything he could to make her comfortable and entertained, constantly talking about the horses and bringing her food and drinks. She loved the fact that he was looking after her.

It was almost night when a knock on the door interrupted his retelling of his run in the cutting pen on the mare.

"Are you expecting someone?" she asked.

"It's probably Jesse and Aimee... Wanting to tell us that he's a pro trainer now and has picked up ten horses for next year and six sponsors." Cutter was only joking, and just the thought of it was enough to put a smile on Raylee's face.

He looked through the peep hole and got excited. "Are you ready for visitors?" he asked.

Raylee straightened herself out and sat up high on the bed, expecting to see the team walk in. When Cutter opened the door, she received a huge shock. It was Johnny and Emma, and the newest member of the O'Brien family.

"Hey, what're you doing here?" Cutter asked, and he immediately took the baby out of Emma's arms.

"I told you we were coming if you made the final," Johnny said, as if they shouldn't be surprised that he was keeping his promise.

When the baby arrived early, Johnny's parents had rushed home from vacation and were now back at the ranch taking care of everything. Johnny had been loaded down with work while they were away, and now he and Emma had taken the chance to get away as they both wanted to see Cutter ride.

"We heard you had a little accident," Emma said to Raylee.

Raylee touched her head where it was still tender. "I'm alright now. I only fainted but everyone's gone overboard with it."

"And look at this little man," Cutter said, as he walked around the room and held the baby in his arms, bouncing him while he slept. "Well he looks a lot cleaner than the first time I saw him," he added.

Cutter was a natural, and Raylee started to build up those tears that she thought had disappeared. If he loved Johnny and Emma's baby so much, then why wouldn't he be excited at the thought of having his own?

"You wanna hold him?" he asked Raylee, and without waiting for a reply, Cutter was handing her the baby.

She held him in her arms and looked at him. He was so tiny and was sleeping soundly, wrapped in a cotton blanket with only his face and little hand exposed. Raylee thought he was adorable, and could see the love in his parents' eyes. They were both in love with their son. Raylee looked up at Cutter. He didn't notice her emotional state as she did well to cover it up.

"So, we still don't know what you called him," Cutter said, as it had just dawned on him and he was now curious to find out.

Johnny and Emma looked at each other. "We named him after you," Johnny said, and he sounded well pleased with the decision.

It really wasn't sinking in so well with Cutter and a sense of confusion came across his face. "You called him Cutter?" he asked hesitantly.

They both laughed at their friend. "Come on, bro. We all know there's only one Cutter Jones in this world and those boots are way too big to fill," Johnny said for some fun. "And not to mention the size of your hat," he added, and Emma flicked him on the arm to stop the taunting.

Emma was always more serious than her husband. "His name is Jake...Jacob O'Brien," Emma said proudly. "Since you were the one who brought him into this world, we couldn't think of a better name than yours."

Cutter pulled back the cotton wrap from Jake's face so that he could look at him. He picked up his little hand and wrapped it around his finger, looking at how small and petite he was. Cutter hadn't been called that name since he was three years old and had moved to the ranch to live with Macca.

"I'm so honored," Cutter said. "What do you think, Raylee?" he asked, when he looked into her eyes.

They were so close now that she could see the fine dust particles still on his face from his ride earlier, and his eyes were shining brightly. "I think it's perfect," she agreed.

# Chapter Fourteen

It had been a week full of unexpected drama and controversy. No one on the team could have predicted the highest and lowest of scores, as they all found out that anything was possible in the cutting pen. While some of the results were disappointing to Cutter, he was more than happy with his two finalists.

The week had felt longer than it was and by the last day, the team were washed out and ready for it to be over. Except for Cutter. He always kept something in reserve for the end of a show.

The riders that had been eliminated as the week went on had found their way to the stands to watch or to the bar which overlooked the arena floor. It was a good place to quench their thirst with the hot days continuing and drown their sorrows for missing out on the finals. Mostly, it was a place where everyone caught up and horse owners exchanged phone numbers with trainers, and business was done the cowboy way... over a strong drink. Preferably a whiskey.

It wasn't a place that Cutter went to for business or for any other reason, after Tommy had accused him of bedding his girlfriend all those years ago and had taken out a revenge warrant against him. Wreaking havoc with the cattle in the cutting pen, brawling to the point that they were unrecognizable, and sitting out for three months when they were both banned from competition, it all started at the bar and Cutter had avoided going there at every show since.

It was also the place where the riders were divided in their opinion. Did Jesse deserve the points to be taken away and to miss out on a buckle, or should Cutter have been sat out for the finals? Either way, no one could dispute that the colt and Jesse had one of the best rides of the entire show, and if any other rider was going to take the title away from Cutter this year, then they'd rather it be settled in the cutting pen and not by default.

With Johnny now at the show to replace Raylee, the team was complete again. She liked that he was there to help Cutter in the finals and it was nice for the two of them to have another chance to ride together. It didn't stop Raylee going to the stables to make her presence known, and she delivered food and drinks, and brushed the horses down after they'd been exercised. She didn't want to miss anything and fulfilled her new role as if it was just as important as riding. It left everyone on the team to get on with their work and the rest of the family to go up into the stands, watching the finals of each event and being entertained as the day moved on.

Cassie finally convinced her mom and Evelyn to go shopping to buy hats for themselves, although it was more to keep Cassie quiet, as her persistence was becoming overbearing. When they all sat back down in the stands, they looked as if they belonged there, fitting well into the scene.

Emma was enjoying being in their company and she passed the baby around, each taking a turn of holding him, giving her a much needed rest. Little Jake was the highlight of the intervals and he was being spoilt by all their attention. Pete was silently pleased. He didn't know Johnny and Emma very well, and when he heard that his son's name had been given to this baby, he loved that the name had not disappeared altogether.

With the Classic final now over and the presentation done, the next herd was brought in and had to be settled. Many people in the crowd stood up to stretch their legs and made their way to the cafeteria to satisfy their hunger. It was overflowing with spectators wanting lunch. While the team were busy in the stables and sand yard, Cutter and Raylee went to the stands to see everyone. Beth looked at Raylee and tried to catch her eye, wanting to see if she gave her a glimmer of a hope. Raylee wouldn't give it to her. Or anyone else for that matter. But when Beth passed the baby to Raylee, everyone looked at her. When all eyes in the row turned her way, it was as if they were all thinking the same thing, and she wished they'd all just back off.

Cutter could sense it and even though no one asked, he gave them the answer anyway. "We're happy just the way we are, so don't even think about it. We don't need a baby right now, so you can all stop looking at us like that." He had his arm stretched out behind Raylee's seat and was looking into the baby's face. "Besides. I'll be busy getting this one into the saddle soon," he added, to make the serious comments that he had just dished out a little lighter.

If Raylee wasn't cut before, then she was now totally devastated. Cutter didn't want children just yet and he let everyone know it. She pulled herself together and felt silently humiliated, as she swallowed her pride and kept on smiling.

It was only a short break and Cutter had to excuse himself and head back down to the loping area to get ready for his ride.

"You wanna stay up here?" he asked Raylee.

"I might not be riding, but I'm not missing this," she said, and she handed the baby back up the row to his mother.

When the music suddenly stopped, the announcer gave everyone a welcome back and a long introduction to the next event. The Derby. He gave a quick rundown on the top twenty horses and qualifying scores. It was going to be a tough final, with a line up that was the best of the four-year-olds. There was not a horse that hadn't earned their position in the final, nor a trainer who was not up to the job. Cutter had just as good a chance as anyone else and if the mare's track record was anything to go by, then she'd be sure to steal the spotlight.

Cutter drew fourth out in the first herd and was quite comfortable with that position. He stood with Raylee at the rail in the loping area and put his chaps on, finding the buckles on the sides and he did them up.

Raylee was a mess inside. She had so much she wanted to say except that she knew the show had to come first. Everything that was weighing on her mind could wait one more day until they got home.

"Did you mean what you said?" she asked, just as Jesse was making his way over.

"I don't want everyone pressuring us," Cutter said. "It'll be our decision, and if that's two or three or five years away, then that's when it will be... Don't let them get to you."

They weren't. It was Cutter who was getting to her. She had poured her heart out to him while she was laid up in the medical room and he had dismissed what she'd told him. All she wanted was an acknowledgment. For him to say something. Maybe he was still taking it all in. Whatever Cutter was thinking, it was leaving Raylee to wonder.

He took to the saddle and she untied the horse for Jesse to ride. Cutter rode off, only to get his head back on track and she went to the fence to watch. There were still a couple of riders to take their turn and she studied their rides and waited for their scores, needing them to divert her attention.

Cutter took the mare into the prep lane, where the official seemed a little unhappy with him after the stunt they had pulled. He ran the mare up and down the narrow lane where he gave her a sharp kick of his spurs and was nearly turning her inside out.

With the team falling into their positions, Cutter was ready. He rode out into the pen along the fence line, listening to the announcer recapping his career highlights and giving the mare her long list of bloodlines. The cattle stood idle at the back of the pen and only started to move when Cutter and the mare slowly edged their way through. As each cow was finding its way back to the mob, the herd was down to four and he had to restrain the mare's eagerness to bust a move just yet. Johnny came in to help split them up and Cutter was left with his chosen cow. He lowered his hand. It was time to perform, when the mare stepped up with an arrogance and the chase was on.

Having been driven clear of the herd, the cow charged for a way back while the mare was committed to blocking it, creating an instant atmosphere that had everyone wooed from the start. She called the shots in the pen when she found her groove in the sand and was poised, quivering with anticipation for the cow to make a move.

It blasted across the pen, strong willed and determined to get through, as it sidestepped, looking for the lucky break. The mare was fully fearless and with every move gutsy, she tackled every stop and turn like the champion horse she was. Nothing would break her concentration. Nothing would contain her thunder. Except for Cutter, who pulled up the reins when the cow turned away and ran off towards the gate. As they walked back to the herd, Johnny and Allan quickly chased the cow on the loose and headed it back to the mob.

With a good first cow, Cutter wasted some time and brought the herd forward steadily, while the mare was hot for more.

Raylee was holding onto the fence. Her hands were sweating as she held on tight and her heart was pounding, keeping her eyes fixed on her cowboy when the pressure was back on.

The second cow was no challenge for the mare. Her provoking eyes tormented it and brought it to a position where it danced in the sand, looking for a way around. She blocked it, imitated it, and drove it to despair. It ran for the side of the pen and the mare defied any horse's ability when she recovered from her position low in the sand to pick up the speed and chased it down. She was on fire. Crushing the cow's spirit and reeling it back to the middle of the pen, the mare was stirred up and was unleashing her fury. She was overpowering that cow.

The noise of the crowd was sounding in Cutter's ears as every part of this ride was dramatic and every hotshot move from the mare was extreme.

The timing was perfect, as enough seconds had come off the clock when the cow turned away, leaving Cutter to look at what little time was left and he took the first unsuspecting cow from the side. Pushing it out and putting his hand down when they were clear, the mare stormed after the cow in spectacular style and sunk low into the sand for a little turn and burn in the five second countdown.

It was so thrilling that Cutter had the entire crowd shout out the final stages of his run, one second at a time, as they continued to tear up the arena floor until he heard the buzzer.

When Cutter pulled her up, his heart was still at full speed. He reached down to touch the mare, then looked around for Raylee. She wasn't there. Instead, it was Jesse who was making his way over to him.

"Not bad for an old bull rider," Jesse said smartly.

"You didn't do such a bad job yourself," he admitted, thankful that he had Jesse on his team.

They rode out of the pen while the announcer was wrapping up that ride and was giving the crowd a good reason to raise the roof. A two twenty-nine was enough to let the team think that he'd be unbeatable, even with another sixteen riders to go. He'd set the benchmark, and now every other rider who entered the pen had to look up to that score and know that the slightest of mistakes would see them out.

It was Raylee who was beside herself. She was just as fired up as everyone else and when Cutter landed in the sand, she threw her arms around him and had already begun the celebrations.

The wait was long and while every rider gave it their best shot, none came close to Cutter. His score seemed untouchable even from the best trainers there. He was looking safe, and when Tommy took to the pen to show off his impressive chestnut colt, he still finished five points under Cutter and was disappointed in his score, even though he had ridden well.

Cutter ran his hand over the mare and could still feel the heat. She was on a winning streak. First the Futurity last year, now the Derby. There was no denying it, she was classy and in a league of her own, just like the colt. She was devoted to her craft and was out there to perform.

Towards the end of the second herd, it was clear that no one was going to come close to Cutter on the score board. The points were coming down, not going up. When the last rider took to the pen, his off timing from the first cow was enough to secure the win for Cutter, and the team were all celebrating as they turned their back on the last ride and were giving their attention to the mare.

After another short wait while they prepared the arena floor, it was time for the presentation. When Cutter rode out, he looked into the crowd and could see a row full of happy faces from his well expanded family. He looked into the stands for Marnie. She wasn't in her usual seat and it played on his mind.

One down and one to go. If only the filly could rise to the occasion in the Futurity, then they would be celebrating well into the next week.

While Raylee was standing with the colt tied to the rail, she was watching Jesse ride the blue roan filly around in circles, feeling jealous because it should have been her. Cutter sat up on the fence and was studying the cattle with a watchful eye. He was dressed in his chaps. He was ready to ride. He was ready to win again, totally focussed on giving it everything he had in him. He was more than committed. Everything he had worked for with this horse was weighing on this very moment, and he wiped the sweat from his face and repositioned his hat to take the edge off his nerves.

Raylee didn't see Tommy walk up behind her and when he spoke, it startled her. "How's your head?" he asked.

"What?" Raylee replied, as she turned around and was surprised to see him.

"Your head... How is it?" Tommy asked again.

"It's fine... Thank you." Raylee would not be rude, though she wished him gone.

"Have you told him?" Tommy was being pleasant enough, although he wasn't making any sense.

Why is he talking to me, Raylee asked herself.

"Told who what?" she summed up quickly.

"Your news. Have you told him your news?"

Raylee nearly choked on his words and felt a hot flush all of a sudden. It didn't take her long to figure out the what and the who, but what she couldn't work out, was how Tommy knew. How could he possibly know something like that? Something so private.

"How do you know?" Raylee snapped back at Tommy, wanting a full explanation.

"You told me," he answered quickly, and it hit him right then, that Raylee didn't know that she had. "Don't you remember?"

"Remember what?"

"When you fainted, I took you to the medical room and that's when you told me."

"No... Did I? I don't remember..."

It was fast becoming clear. Raylee looked over at Cutter. He was still sitting on the fence watching the rider in the pen. She hadn't told him at all. He doesn't know. Tommy was sitting next to her in the medical room holding her hand and touching her tummy. He was the one who she'd shared her thoughts and her heart with, not Cutter.

"But you don't need to worry. I haven't said a word to anyone," Tommy said for reassurance. "Your secret's safe with me."

She started to breathe heavily.

"Hey, are you alright?" he asked.

"Yeah, I'm fine." Raylee gained back the control quickly and looked at him. She had laid her heart on the line and Tommy knew her deepest secret. He could have easily used it against them. Against Cutter. But he didn't. She was embarrassed at the same time as she was thankful.

When Cutter landed in the sand, he gave Jesse the nod to pull the filly over to the rail. He walked towards the colt and he saw Raylee standing against the fence having a close conversation with Tommy. His blood boiled, until she smiled at Tommy. Then it curdled. His rage was so deep, it would explode in front of everyone in the arena if he wasn't careful. She touched Tommy on the arm then he walked away.

Raylee looked up to see Cutter walking towards her and she gave him a smile. He didn't know. All this time he didn't know and she felt relieved... Then she saw his face.

No. This is not what it looks like.

For a private discussion, Cutter spoke louder than what was intended. "Do you wanna tell me what the hell is going on with you and Tommy?" he asked.

Jesse cut in. "Hey, Cutter, it's time."

Cutter wasn't listening. He had other things on his mind and cutting wasn't one of them.

"There's nothing going on with me and Tommy," Raylee defended. "But why didn't you tell me that he was the one that took me to the medical room when I fainted?" she asked.

"Because you were the one with him. I thought you knew," he threw straight back.

"I wasn't with him. I wasn't with anyone." Raylee was feeling the pressure again from all the accusations.

"I'm sorry, Cutter, but they won't wait all day for you," Jesse said firmly, to be the division in their untimely argument.

Cutter never took his eyes of Raylee. "Tell them I'm not riding."

"What? You have to ride. You're making a big deal out of this and you don't need to. You can't miss your ride over it," Raylee said unconvincingly.

"I'm not going out there," he repeated.

"Yes you are."

"No I'm not. I'm not going out there to make a fool of myself again when the last thing I can think about is cutting a damn cow."

The team all took their positions in the corners while Jesse stood there holding the horse, watching them throw their words at each other like a war was about to break out. If they hadn't pulled that stunt on the colt, then Jesse might have been tempted to ride the filly out into the pen and take the run for himself.

"Raylee, I'm not going into that pen and pretend there's nothing wrong unless you tell me exactly what's going on with you."

The official stepped forward to give them a hurry up. Jesse held up his hand to stop him, and gave him a sign to say that Cutter would be there soon. Although by the way it was looking, he wasn't holding his breath.

This wasn't the way Raylee wanted to tell him. To break that news just before he went out into the final. Couldn't it wait until after he had his run? She looked into his devastated eyes and could tell that nothing she could say at that moment would pick him up enough to face that final. Perhaps not even the truth.

"This is your last call," the official informed him.

Raylee heard his last chance call and had to decide if it was better to go into the pen without answers and the weight of the world resting heavily on his shoulders, to go back to the stables and face the client's long list of questions as to why he didn't ride, or rock his world in front of an arena full of spectators and other competitors.

"Please go out there," she pleaded.

"No." Cutter was adamant that he wasn't going.

"I need you to go out there."

"And I need you to tell me the truth."

"I'll tell you the truth after you take your run... Please take your run." Raylee was now begging, wanting desperately for Cutter to ride in the final.

The look he gave her was from a broken man. "You're lying. I know you Raylee, and I know there's something wrong," he said severely. "There's something you're not telling me."

"I promise you. There's nothing wrong," she insisted one last time.

"I'm not going out there."

She looked into his face. She was beyond in love with him and she hated to see him this way. He was hurting. She had to risk it. There was nothing to be jealous about and she let him know it.

"Cutter, the reason I fainted... is because we're going to have a baby," she said, before she started to cry a little.

The shock took the words right out of his mouth as he was stunned at the unexpected announcement. It wasn't processing in his head fast enough and her words were blurring his judgement. It was the last thing he was expecting to hear.

"We're what?" he asked cautiously, in case he misheard her.

"She's having a baby," Jesse said forcefully, and he shoved the reins into Cutter's hands and slapped him on the back. "Congratulations. You've put her in foal. Now get out there before I take your ride."

"A baby?" Cutter asked, still taking in the news and making sense of it all. "Are you?"

"Yes, she is," Jesse said, hoping to get him moving. "She just told you that. Weren't you listening?"

Raylee could only nod her head to confirm the question.

Before he put his boot into the stirrup, he reached over and kissed her, holding her face with both hands. "I love you, Raylee Jones," he added, before he took to the saddle and made his way out into the prep lane. Jesse rode ahead of him and sat in the corner, hoping he would follow. If he didn't take the ride now, he would be out of time. He took a few quick breaths to get his head straight. He was going to be a father. It was the last thing on his mind before this ride and right now, he had to decide whether the next two and a half minutes were going to be preoccupied with thoughts of the life changing news, or fully charge himself up for the ride that could take him to the top. The decision was his.

As he walked down the fence line, he looked at the mob, trying to get interested in the cattle. He didn't hear the bell ring to start the countdown. Focus. Keep your focus.

When he met Jesse in the corner, there was nothing between them except for cow talk. Jesse kept it professional and gave his few opinions. Cutter was still getting his head right, moving the herd forward and letting them fall away one at a time back to the mob, as Allan and Johnny came in to help him make a clear cut.

Raylee leaned on the fence and put her head down, hoping that Cutter could hold it together. Now was not the right time to fall apart. It had been the worst timing, but telling him the truth was the only way to get him out there to take his ride. She had wiped her face dry then shut her eyes tight to squeeze out the last unwelcome tear. It wasn't until she heard the whistles from the crowd bounce off the walls that she looked up. Cutter's hand was down and he had the filly sunk so low in the sand that when the cow charged sideways, she sprang up after it at full acceleration and matched it at the stop.

There was nothing but relief for Raylee. Her excitement outweighed her bundle of nerves and her eyes were now fixed on Cutter and the filly as they shot across the pen, only stopping to have a dance in the sand when the cow was stirred up with desperation to find a way past. There was no shaking the filly off its tail and she stayed on its heels with every short burst of runs and every draw back to the center.

The filly was switched on and was faithful to her training, doing everything right and letting her presence be known to both the cow and the crowd. Her ego was almost as big as the colt's. Her moves were equal to his. She was creating that same magic and when she got down low and jigged with the cow nose to nose, it was almost too much for the crowd who were letting it be known.

As the team sat in the corners and kept control of the mob, they were as anxious as everyone else for Cutter and the filly, who were giving a performance second to none. The filly read the cow's intended moves, responding with skill and fancy footwork, and keeping in sync with the cow's sprints across the pen and its sharpness in the turns. She used her presence to draw it back to the center of the pen where she provoked it into a spin. Both keeping their heads low, the cow was looking the filly in the eyes and their noses were only inches apart, then after one last hustle in the sand, the cow finally gave in.

When it turned and headed for Allan, Cutter pulled up the reins. It was shunted back to the mob and settled with the herd. Cutter looked at the clock. The seconds were coming down fast, but he still had enough time to add more points to his score and his mind drifted to Raylee.

A father. I'm going to be a father, he thought, and he had to recover his focus quickly as he headed for Jesse in the corner.

The stakes were high and Cutter needed to choose another cow equal to the first if he wanted to write his name in the history books again. The work was only half done. As he rode along the back wall below the clock, the beat of the music was pounding in his ears to a rhythm that was uplifting. He was fully determined to make it happen. When he pushed through the mob and was left with just one, he dropped on the cow, believing that the filly had enough cow smarts to see this through.

With her tricked-up footwork, she danced away in the middle of the pen, stealing the spotlight and brandishing her talents. The filly called the shots when the cow shied away and ran for fear, and she demonstrated her quick reflexes, pouncing all over it, and was sprinting into and out of the turns with athletic style and aggression. She was not letting that cow get one inch out of line and she mimicked it to perfection.

Was this the winning ride? It sure was impressive, as she rattled the cow into a frantic state. Running to the left. Racing to the right. The cow's sights were set on the mob and it did everything it could to make that breakaway back to the herd.

Unlike Cutter, the filly's attention on the cow was undivided and luckily for him, she took control of it and was responsive to every step. She was all over every stop. She steered out of every turn, and streaked across the pen while tearing up the sand behind her.

When the cow was on the move, the filly was hot on its tracks. When it stopped, there was a standoff, with the filly sinking low and shifting her weight, her ears laid back anticipating which way it would strike next.

She was like a woman possessed.

There was an 'ooh' from the crowd when the filly missed a beat, as the cow darted away from her when it saw daylight and made a break. The gap was wide but the filly was quick to pick up her feet and chase it down, instantaneously matching it in the corner for the return run. She was now all over it again.

Raylee looked at the clock. Cutter couldn't get off the cow and he had to keep up the pace and drive it to keep moving, as the seconds were down below eight.

Hold on. Keep it straight. Don't lose focus. Let the filly give it her all, and she broke out all the moves and pulled out all the stops, letting the cow know who was boss of the pen.

Raylee watched the last seconds disappear and at the sound of the buzzer, Cutter pulled the filly up. He reached down to touch her, feeling the heat. He gave it not another thought as he spurred her to move without waiting for his team. He hightailed it out of the pen and was gone.

When he saw Raylee waiting at the rail ready to tie up the horse, she had a big smile on her face.

"That was incredible," she said, praising that run.

Cutter launched himself off the horse and without words, he kissed her again. He wasn't celebrating that ride, he was celebrating his wife.

"Tell me again," he said, when he pulled away and looked at her closely.

For the first time that week, it made Raylee happy. "It's true... We're having a baby," she said quietly so that no one else could hear.

Cutter wouldn't be so quiet. He picked her up off the ground and twirled her around and gave a shout. They were now tangled up in the reins of the horse as Cutter still had hold of her. It was drawing attention from everyone, although it was presumed their celebrations were from that impressive ride.

The announcer came over the speakers to interrupt their celebrations. "A two twenty-three," he announced. "That's not gonna cut it for the winning buckle but that sure was a damn good ride anyway."

Cutter didn't care. The score and placings were irrelevant to him right then. He was so wrapped up in Raylee that he didn't care what was going on around him.

"Let's not tell anyone just yet," she whispered quietly, when the team pulled up next to them.

"Yes ma'am," he agreed. Jesse took the reins of the filly and led her away, but not before Cutter stopped him. "Thanks bro... You did a great job out there," he said. "And whatever you heard before..."

"I got it," Jesse said, and he led the horse away and tied her to the rail.

Cutter's focus went straight back to Raylee. "Why didn't you tell me before this?" he asked.

"To be honest, I thought I had... When I was in the medical room."

Cutter was trying to piece it together. "But you told Tommy instead?"

"Apparently," she confirmed. "I had no idea that he was there. I thought you were with me that day."

Cutter was taking it all in. Tommy was in the wrong place at the wrong time, and it was lucky for Raylee, that he was. He looked to the pen. Tommy was in the pen cutting cows and sending the crowd crazy. He must have been having a good ride.

"I promised I'd look after you and I didn't," Cutter said, totally down on himself.

Raylee wouldn't let him do that. "And you promised you'd make me happy and you do that every day."

"I can't believe it... We're actually going to have a baby." He was excited and Raylee was surprised.

"I didn't think you'd be this happy," she stated.

"Are you kidding? I've been taking the pressure off you all this time, thinking that you weren't ready for this."

"I'm not ready for it. I'm so scared," she admitted, and he could see it in her face and hear it in her voice.

There was a sudden realization and Cutter pulled her close. "I'm scared too. But hey, we've got a huge family now, so what's there to be scared about?"

Aimee joined them after she'd tied up the horse. "What are we celebrating?" she asked, after hearing the not so winning score.

Raylee looked at Cutter, desperate to keep it a secret. "We're celebrating the end of the show," he said, to throw her offtrack. "And now we can go home, and you can go off to college."

"Did you have to remind me?" she asked. "Actually, I've been thinking of dropping out and starting my new career with you."

Cutter laughed. "First of all, it's not a career. And secondly, you haven't even started college to drop out yet. And thirdly, your parents will kill me if I'm the reason you don't go."

Aimee laughed back at him. "Well for your information, you're not the reason I'm dropping out," she said in a matter of fact way. "Jesse is," she added, to let them both know her real intentions.

Cutter could only shake his head at his sister, as she untied the horse and walked away, back to the stables ready for the pack up.

"I can't believe she'd do that," he stated, as he watched her until she was out of sight.

The sound of the buzzer rang out and brought their attention back to the pen. Tommy's ride was over and he was leaving the pen with his team. He had an expression on his face that said just how happy he was.

"It's gonna shake things up," the announcer alerted everyone ahead of the score. The pause was only being filled in by the applause of the crowd, still appreciating that run. "Yes it is. A two twenty-eight puts Tommy Parker in first place with only four riders to go."

Deep down Cutter was gutted, at the same time he was ecstatic.

Cutter stood with Raylee and the filly as he watched Tommy with his team when they arrived back in the loping area. Tommy's grin was obvious, even from the other side to where they were standing. When he caught sight of Cutter and Raylee watching him, his grin mellowed, and he looked at them momentarily before he turned away and was accepting congratulations from the other riders.

"You were jealous," Raylee said, when she looked back at Cutter and brushed the dust off his face.

"No I wasn't," he said defensively. He looked at her and could tell that she didn't believe him. "Okay, so what if I was... Don't you want me to be?" he asked.

"I loved that you were. But you had nothing to be jealous about." Raylee was reinforcing her love and commitment to him. "And I think you might understand now how Tommy was feeling all those years ago," she said, to make him see that his reaction was no different to Tommy's.

Cutter wouldn't speak. He kept looking between his wife and his rival, hearing her words and trying to make it sound unreasonable in his head. He couldn't.

"He had the opportunity to even the score, Cutter, and he didn't." Raylee was only pointing out what he already knew.

Together they stood by the horse, waiting for the last cowboy to take his run before the leader board was final and they could get on with the presentation. It was the last ride of the week and the last chance to steal it away, except that his average ride and few mistakes secured the win for Tommy and his team, and the final was now wrapped up.

Cutter wasn't as bitter as he thought he was going to be, since Raylee's news had him on a high and he was consumed with other thoughts.

While he still had to go out and sit through the presentation, his fifth place was nothing to be ashamed of. The filly had everyone talking and had her owners over the moon, only equal to the news that was sitting silently in his own heart. She'd given an outstanding performance and only for an unfortunate slip up, it was enough to separate this elite group of horses.

He sat on the filly at the back wall of the pen after he'd gone through the presenting of his ribbons and prizes. He watched Tommy take position center stage, accepting more than he could carry, and another buckle to add to his collection. It was the title that meant the most. That would carry Tommy into the next season ahead of everyone else in the game and give him his pick of new horses coming into their early training years.

For Cutter, he thought about the year ahead. A baby. Training horses, running the ranch, and a baby. This time next year would be so different and he wondered about all the changes that were heading his way.

Allan took the filly from Cutter and headed back to the stables to get her washed and loaded, ready for the journey home. They were picking up the last of their things while the crowd were heading for the doors.

"I need you to do something for me," Raylee said.

"For you, anything," Cutter was quick to respond.

She looked at him and knew that she was asking the impossible, yet she would try it anyway. "I need you and Tommy to get over this bullshit and let everything go. None of it is worth it, and neither of you had done anything wrong to bring it on and you both know it now."

Deep down, Cutter did know it. He'd done nothing wrong all those years ago with Tommy's girlfriend, and Tommy had done everything right by Raylee when he could have been so revengeful. But his pride made him hesitate, after watching his rival take the victory while he was so close, yet he couldn't get those extra points to seal the win.

He looked at her. Her eyes were pleading. "If you can't do it for yourself... then do it for me," she said.

Only for the timing, it got Cutter thinking. It was the one chance to make this right. It would be now or never, with the opportunity close at hand.

"I can't do it, Raylee. I'm sorry, but I just can't do it," he said, fully believing it.

"Yes you can. You both have to realize now that it's over. It's in the past. You both need to get over it and move on."

Cutter looked between the two of them again. He was struggling with all the wrong reasons outweighing the right, and he was reluctant, waiting for it to hit him. He was trying to justify it in his head why he couldn't do it, until he looked down at Raylee, who was unaware that she was holding onto her tummy. He didn't speak. He didn't have to. If he couldn't do it for himself or for Raylee, then there was only one reason he would leave her standing by the rail and walk in Tommy's direction.

When Cutter grabbed Tommy on the shoulder from behind, his team moved in quickly for backup. He turned around and looked Cutter in the eyes. They were standing so close now that they could see they had matching scars on their cheeks, although Cutter's was less defined and that gave him a little more satisfaction.

It was tense, but Tommy put his hand up to his team to tell them to back off. They did, leaving the two cowboys with a bitter history between them standing alone.

"I wanna thank you for taking care of Raylee," Cutter said, and he held out his hand first.

Tommy was surprised. He looked at Cutter and was assessing the situation. The standoff was strained and not as long as it felt, while the two cowboys stood face to face and were equally suspicious of the other's thoughts. Tommy looked down at Cutter's hand, remembering the last time they were friends. It was so long ago now, that they'd hardly know each other as anything but bitter enemies.

Tommy put that aside and accepted. "You need to look after her," he replied, and Cutter knew exactly where he was coming from.

"I'm gonna do that," Cutter assured him.

"She's a great girl, Cutter, and you're one hell of a lucky son of a bitch," he said. "And if you're anything like your old man, then I'm sure you'll make a great father too," he added.

Macca had been a great support to all the cutting boys growing up and had seen them transition from their junior years through to pro level, and had been instrumental in bringing the young team together. They were dynamic on the way through but had let their egos and abilities get in the way of the real reason they were successful... Their love for the sport.

"Thanks, Tommy. That means more than you know." Cutter knew that Tommy respected his father, even after everything was said and done. There was not a person in the cutting world that didn't think that Macca Jones was a fair man. Unbiased and aboveboard. He was as straight as an arrow and would tell you exactly how it was. No bullshit. That was Macca's way and he had lived and died by those principles. He never let a personal vendetta against him change the honest man that he was.

"And congratulations... You deserved the win," Cutter was quick to add, before the words were buried too deep inside him to find their way out.

It was all that was needed to be said. It was quick and to the point without rehashing the events that got them to this sad and sorry state in the first place. They were young and totally full of themselves back then. Now they were men, and they could leave behind the anger and bitterness that tore their friendship apart all those years ago when Tommy believed that Cutter had broken the cowboy code.

"What did he say?" Raylee asked, when Cutter met her back at the fence where she was waiting patiently, giving them all the time that was needed.

He threw his arm around her shoulder and they started to walk off. "He said that I was gonna be a great dad," he said proudly, and Raylee could only agree. "But not as much as I think you're gonna make a great mom," he added.

Raylee threw a smile in Tommy's direction when they made for the stables.

"Now, let's go home," Cutter said, and they walked out of the arena for the last time that week.

The pack up was huge, and by the time Cutter and Raylee made it to the truck, Allan and Jesse had most of the horses loaded while Aimee had all the saddles away and was getting to work cleaning out the stalls. Johnny had hit the road, with Emma feeling weary from the long day and the need to get the baby home.

It was another show over. Another memorable show that Cutter would not forget in a hurry. They left Dallas with another life-changing family twist that only added excitement to their success in the cutting pen. While Cutter had fallen slightly short in the Futurity final, his win in the Derby kept his name in the spotlight.

Raylee was thankful it was just the two of them in the truck on the way home, so they could talk about everything in the open. Unlike Evelyn and Jesse, who had to remain silent about the good news and could only talk about the events of the week, while Aimee didn't stop bragging about Jesse's ride on the colt. By the time they arrived home, Allan was sick of hearing about it.

"You know, I liked it better when you were talking about the rodeo," he said to Aimee, when they stepped out of the truck and went to the float to unload the horses.

"Don't get her started," Jesse warned. "Do you wanna hear that magazine story all over again?" he asked.

"No." On second thoughts, Allan was quick to dismiss the rodeo too. He'd heard the article four times already.

Evelyn took her bags to the front porch where the light was on. Perhaps it had been left on all week after the power was cut from the storm. She was the first one to the house and realized that she had to wait for Cutter and Raylee to arrive home, as no one else had a key. Out of interest, she pulled on the handle anyway, expecting it to be locked. It wasn't. That's strange... Maybe they forgot to lock the door when they all left in a hurry, she thought, and she walked inside.

She looked around. There was nothing out of place except for eight cups sitting in a row on the kitchen counter and freshly baked cookies sitting under a net.

"Now that looks like it needs a good explanation," Evelyn stated to herself, trying to make sense of it.

It was late, yet the house had a few lights on and a homely feel to it. She wandered around the kitchen, thinking of how it was going to feel to go back to her house at the vineyard. She had missed her home, and was expecting that the return there would be more harmonious than it had been in years. It would be a new beginning for her and Allan, and an unexpected reunion for their boys.

When Cutter pulled the horse truck in behind the float, Raylee was still asleep with her head on his lap. They had talked most of the way home, although the last half hour she had started to yawn and felt the need to lie down. She tried to talk with her eyes closed and when she didn't answer his last question, Cutter knew that she had drifted off. He tried to wake her. Touching her on the shoulder and rubbing down her arm. "Raylee... Wake up. We're home." He was gentle with her. She stirred and sat up, looking tired and she took a huge yawn. "I'll help you to the house but I need to get the horses off first," he said.

"I'm alright. I'll come and help."

"No. I'll do it. You're tired. You should go inside."

"Cutter, I'm not dying. I'm having a baby," she reminded him.

He didn't need reminding. It was all he could think about for the entire trip. "And I wanna look after you every step of the way." He was still feeling the guilt that he wasn't there when she needed him the most and had vowed never to let that happen again. He picked up her hand and kissed it.

Raylee wouldn't let a little thing such as a baby get in the way of helping unload the truck. She wanted to be part of the team, helping them off with the horses while she left the heavy lifting to Cutter and Jesse, who would cover for her. When every horse was either in the barn or out in their yard, they made for the house.

They took their boots off at the front door and went into the kitchen, and they also noticed the cups all in a row.

"You look like you've got everything in order," Raylee said to her mother, who was sitting at the table, reading.

"Don't look at me," she said. "It was all here when I came in."

Cutter and Raylee looked at each other and the pause was almost too long. They were reading each other's mind, thinking the same thing.

"Marnie's home," Raylee announced excitedly at high volume. Together they rushed into the sitting room and found Marnie and Doug snoozing on the couch in that late hour of the night.

"Hey you two... Did we keep you up?" Cutter asked.

They woke with a fright. "We didn't hear you come in," Marnie said.

"Well I'll make sure I do a head count tomorrow," he replied. "Anyone could have come in and driven away with a hundred head of cattle and you wouldn't have known."

Doug stood up and shook Cutter's hand and gave Raylee a kiss. Marnie was slower to her feet and when she was up, she squeezed them both tight.

"What's with all the cups?" Raylee asked.

"When I got home, I knew someone had been sleeping in my bed and cooking in my kitchen... It wasn't hard to figure out," Marnie said.

"So you notice someone in your kitchen but not in my barn?" Cutter asked.

"Yes sir. It looks that way, doesn't it... Although all the Australian passports I found were a bit of a give away," she admitted, making them both laugh.

They were so pleased to see her. They were even more pleased to introduce them to everyone in the family. Marnie hesitated a little with Raylee's parents, although she settled well into their company when she saw how at ease Cutter was around them.

Over a hot cup of coffee, Marnie and Doug shared some of their adventures and where they had been for the last three months, while Dallas didn't quite make it onto their calendar. She received an update from Aimee and Allan about the local rodeo, as the two cowboys sat in silence and just listened to their over the top animated version of events.

Doug was curious to hear about the storm, since they had only heard about it on the radio while they were making their way home, and everything from the front entrance to the house had looked trashed with tree limbs and debris.

Raylee gave them a very descriptive version of the way Cutter had delivered Emma's baby, although she thought it appropriate to leave out the best bits, while everyone shared the events of the last week, each from their own personal experience and perspective.

Cutter sat at his table. There had been two more chairs added to accommodate the ever growing family. A lot had changed since the wedding and he looked around while he listened to everything that had happened since Raylee arrived back in Texas, and none was more surprising than Cutter and Tommy agreeing to put the past behind them.

As the talking slowed down, so did Aimee. She gave an uncontrollable wide-mouthed yawn that was enough to set Jesse in motion. They said their goodnights to everyone and headed out the door to the barn.

Marnie collected the cups from the table and took them to the sink. She had been home for a few days already and had taken her room back, leaving Allan's bags upstairs in the hallway, since she wasn't sure where else to put them. Allan had just been upgraded to the parents' room and for Cutter, it was a big deal.

It was late when everyone went to bed that night. Cutter had never had a house this full. Every room was bursting with people, except the small bedroom opposite theirs. Aimee had no intention of taking up residence in the house again and she didn't even take her bags inside to ease the pain for her brother. There would be no more sneaking around. Instead, Jesse took her bags into the barn. Cutter sucked it up and turned a blind eye. He knew that if it was Raylee, he'd do the exact same thing.

When they fell into bed that night, Cutter held Raylee in his arms. It was still quite hot and yet he needed to feel close to her. They didn't speak. Cutter touched her arm while he looked at her. He ran his fingers around her shoulders and down her sides, giving her a sensation that made her wriggle. It wasn't until he made his way down her body and rested his hand on her tummy, that she felt the need to say something.

She touched his hand. She was already hot and with the added warmth of his touch, it made her skin burn. It was comforting. "I love you," she simply said.

"And I love you," he replied.

He propped himself up on his elbow and looked down into her face, giving her tickles as he swirled his fingertips around her tummy. She smiled at his need to touch her there. She didn't say any more, just enjoying his undivided attention and being lost in his love for her.

Sitting up some more, he pulled the sheets back and looked at her lying on the bed. He was so in love with her. He reached down slowly to kiss her gently around her belly button and she closed her eyes, giving a playful giggle. Not from the tickle, but from knowing where he was going to kiss her next.

# Chapter Fifteen

Home was like no other place in the world.

When Raylee felt sick the next morning, she had the need to get up and start moving around. She made her way downstairs quietly and found some comfort in a piece of toast smothered in two layers of peanut butter. Doing her best to sneak around so as not to wake the rest of the house, she pushed on the screen door slowly and headed out to the porch. The squeak had gone. Raylee looked at it, and still holding the handle, she gave it a couple of quick pushes back and forth. Nothing. There was no squeak, and she could only put it down to one thing... Marnie and Doug.

They had arrived home a few days before the team and as Raylee started to look around, she noticed the small things. The house had been dusted down. The windows were sparkling. The garden had been weeded and the lawn was tidy. The debris from the storm had been cleaned up, and there was enough firewood chopped and sitting on the porch for the entire winter to come. All the little jobs that Raylee had noticed over the last few months, and some general maintenance they needed to catch up on, yet never had the time for, was all done in only a few short days. She was so happy to see Marnie and Doug home. Not only did Raylee miss their company, but she and Cutter needed them and were thankful for the help. Their thoughtfulness made a big difference.

She sat on the swing and began to sway. Taking the time to enjoy her surroundings, she looked over at the barn. It was still locked down. The horses in the yards were rugged and were picking at the grass and she could faintly see the cattle in the distance, grazing in the first pasture by the gate. Yes... there was no other place like it in the world and only the vineyard would come a close second in her heart.

After looking around, it became noticeable that the basket was gone from the front door. It was there when they left for the show last week and when Marnie returned home, she must have felt that it was time to take it away while Cutter was gone.

There would be many changes that were heading their way and this was just the beginning of them. The motion was making her feel uneasy again and was giving her a subtle reminder. She stopped the swing, stood up, and leaned on the rail overlooking the garden in case she felt the need to use it. A gentle breeze picked up and blew her hair across her face, giving her a warm feeling inside. She was happy... and she was happy to be home.

A kiss on the neck brought the smile out of her. She didn't hear the door open or the footsteps on the porch, but she knew those kisses well and his touch was always so welcome.

"How are you feeling this morning?" Cutter whispered in her ear while he was locked in close behind her.

"Do you mean after last night?" she asked.

He could only laugh as he spoke the honest truth. "Oh, I know exactly how you're feeling after that. I mean, how are you really feeling?"

She turned around. "I'm feeling fine."

"And when do you wanna tell everyone?"

She linked her hands behind his neck. "Tomorrow," she said. "Let's wait until tomorrow and we'll tell everyone together."

Cutter agreed. He'd have shouted it from the rooftops if it was up to him, but one more day wasn't going to hurt.

Raylee looked back at the view. "You know, I'd love to go out for a ride. Just the two of us."

"Oh no," Cutter said firmly, shaking his head. "No no no. You are not getting on a horse, no way." He was going to do everything he could to protect Raylee, and she could already see that it was going to drive her crazy.

"Just for a walk. We won't trot or anything," she said to convince him.

"Not even a walk. You'll be lucky if you make it behind the wheel of the truck," he said.

She gave him that look. That look that he'd seen so many times before.

"Okay, well maybe if you have to and only if I'm not available," he half agreed.

She didn't speak and her look deepened.

"Alright... But only if it's not raining," he added.

She still didn't say anything and she broke out into a subtle grin. He knew better than to boss Raylee Jones around, although he was just being extra cautious and she loved that.

"You're gonna do it anyway, aren't you?" he asked.

"Yes," she said, still holding his eyes with hers.

"And you're not gonna listen to me, are you?" he asked.

"No," she said.

"And the more I say you can't do something, the more you're gonna do it, aren't you?" he asked.

"You know me so well."

"Then you must also know that I love you and I need to take care of you."

It had not been twenty-four hours since Raylee had broken the news to Cutter and he was not taking care of her, he was suffocating her.

"Alright. I'm hearing you. But if you really wanna go for a ride, then we'd better get changed first," Cutter said, just to keep her happy.

Raylee was pleased that she had got her own way. When they went into the kitchen, there was still no sign of anyone. They crept up the stairs to get showered and dressed and when Cutter was ready first, he went back down to get prepared for their ride.

Raylee put her make-up on and did her hair, just to make herself feel better. It wasn't so much as helping, as it was covering up how she was really feeling. She tiptoed down the stairs again and snuck out through the kitchen. After she grabbed her boots and pulled them on, she looked up. Cutter was leaning on the side of the old Ford truck with her door open.

"Are you ready?" he asked.

She laughed at him. "I thought we were going for a ride?"

"Yes ma'am, we are going for a ride... In the truck."

He held her hand, helped her into the front seat and closed the door, then ran around the front and climbed in next to her and started it up. The morning breeze was warm as it flowed in through the open windows and as Cutter drove slowly, it was nice around Raylee's face.

They made their way out the front gate and turned onto the road in the opposite direction to town. The old truck chugged along and took the bends steadily and showed relief when the road straightened out and it could pick up some more speed.

Cutter pulled in under the big old oak tree and parked in the shade of the overhanging branches. There was a peacefulness about the resting place that even the road didn't disturb. He leaned down between the wires of the fence and stepped through, holding Raylee's hand when she followed behind him.

The surrounding pasture was down somewhat, with the thirty or so head of cattle that Cutter had let in to chew it out. It was the squeak on the gate that sent the chill up Raylee's spine, and it seemed to worsen every time they went there.

There were no flowers today. Just the two of them and the old Ford truck, and as Cutter squatted down on his heels, Raylee did the same and there was no need for words. It was another show done and Cutter knew that Macca would be proud.

He'd have been proud of the way the horses were going and with the results, and he'd have been more than pleased with the mare's performance. What he wouldn't have liked, was Cutter allowing Jesse to take the ride on the colt. Macca was as honest as the day was long and Cutter was sure that he'd never have seen the funny side of it. That was the cheeky side of Cutter that was unlike his father.

What Macca would have been more proud of than anything else, was that the rift between two close friends was finally put to rest. Although Cutter and Tommy would never get back to where they were all those years ago, they had settled their feud like grown-up men. Putting the past behind them, they could look forward from here on in and it was all because of one person.

The morning sun went behind a cloud and instantly faded their sight. They stood up, standing close.

"What are you thinking?" Raylee asked, wondering if they were thinking the same thing.

He was thinking of many things. Mostly about his mom and dad, but also about the show and how all the events that week were life changing. None more than Raylee standing next to him.

"I was just thinking of you," he said, still staring at the graves. "I know that you think I'm overprotective, but I've lost the two people closest to me and I have this need to look after you." He looked at her. "I'd never forgive myself if anything ever happened to you or the baby."

Raylee never knew Macca and Mary-Ann personally, but she knew enough to know how much it had devastated Cutter when they both died. The drive home was settling. They both needed to go there, and Raylee left the resting place knowing that Cutter only had her best interests at heart and that she would be well looked after. It was his way of showing her how much he cared.

The house was alive and bursting with everyone going about their morning duties when they arrived home. Jesse and Aimee had everything done at the barn. Allan and Doug were cleaning out the back of the float and horse truck, while Marnie and Evelyn had the kitchen in full swing, preparing the table and a banquet breakfast for everyone.

Cutter and Raylee stepped out of the truck and looked around.

"Looks like we've got the morning off," Cutter noted.

"And you'd better make the most of it, because it's not going to last long." Raylee loved the help. She was sadly counting down the days before her mom and dad would be going home. Before Doug would be heading back to his house in town and Aimee would be going back to Dallas to prepare herself for college. Everything would soon be back to normal and she hated the very thought of it.

The family all lined up at the kitchen counter to fill their plates full of every delicious breakfast recipe that Marnie had available to her. She had made all of Cutter's morning favorites and he went straight for the pancakes, stacking them six high and covering them with Marnie's secret creamy caramel sauce. He underestimated just how much he'd missed Marnie, until he took that first mouthful, and it took him back to his childhood when it was his regular Saturday morning breakfast special.

The rest of the day was more than relaxing since there would be no training of horses and nothing to do in the barn that couldn't wait. Allan wanted to take Evelyn out for a ride. She had not been on a horse since they'd moved to the vineyard and while someone had to check on the calves, it was Allan's idea to take his wife out for one last ride. Although, it was more to talk privately in the openness of the ranch.

Jesse and Aimee hid away for the afternoon, spending every last minute they could together in the loft, while Doug just pottered around doing odd jobs, as he had no ability to keep still.

With Raylee taking an afternoon nap upstairs, it left Cutter and Marnie to sit on the swing and catch up on the last three months. He gave her some of the highlights and they laughed-up the time together. While he was desperate to tell Marnie the good news, he knew that it had to wait one more day until the family were all together. Since finding out last year that he had sisters, and hearing Raylee's announcement yesterday, it had been playing on his mind to ask Marnie about his mother.

"Why did Mom and Macca never have children?" he asked. Marnie didn't reply straight away, which hinted to Cutter that she knew the reason. "Did they not want any?" he added.

"Of course they did. And you were always going to be Macca's son no matter what. But he wanted a little girl for your mom and a sister for you."

"Did they try?"

"Your mom didn't have more children from a lack of trying. She actually conceived many times in those first couple of years." Marnie had been there for Mary-Ann through every one of those times.

"What happened?"

Marnie had never been asked this before. It had never come up. She didn't look at Cutter when she spoke for fear of striking a painful emotion. "Your mom was pleased that you were too young to remember."

"Remember what?"

"What drove her to leave your father."

Cutter tried to recall. He couldn't. "I don't know what you're talking about."

"Then maybe you should ask your father... It's really not my place to say."

"Marnie..."

She patted him on the leg before she stood up. "Ask him. If Pete's the changed man that everyone says he is, then he'll tell you." She made her way to the door and went back inside. Cutter looked towards the barn but stared at nothing. Something had happened between his parents that drove the final nail into their doomed marriage, and he wanted to know what.

As the sun began its downward fall towards the west, Cutter grabbed Jesse from the comfort of the loft. They went out through the back gate behind the house and got to work for the rest of the afternoon.

"They're here," Raylee said with a happiness that was irritating to Aimee.

Pete, Beth and Cassie had just pulled up at the house and they went out to meet them. The thought of going home was devastating to Aimee, since college was the last thing on her mind and Dallas was so... citified. While Aimee still planned to come to the ranch for the weekends, it wasn't going to be the same.

Nothing could get her head into those study books and the thought of leaving Jesse behind was painful.

While Cassie was bouncing out of her skin at being back at the ranch, Pete and Beth were greeting Raylee with a hug. They knew she was the only reason they were standing on Double J Ranch after all these years and was welcomed into Cutter's life, and Pete felt indebted to Raylee for her support and persistence. He owed her so much.

Johnny and Emma's old green truck was making its way down the driveway and when Cutter saw it, he left the family to meet them. He went straight for the backseat, unbuckling little Jake from his capsule, ignoring his parents as if they weren't even there. He walked over to the barn.

"Oh, it's nice to see you too, bro," Johnny called out after him.

"Yeah, hey," Cutter said as he turned around. "We're just having our first lesson in the tack room," he said, and he left them by the side of the truck and went inside the barn. Emma was relaxed about it. Her baby was in the best care and there was no other person in the world that she trusted like their best friend. They carried their picnic basket to the porch where they met up with everyone.

Marnie and Evelyn were busy packing everything up and when they were ready, they all headed for the back gate. Never before had the picnic by the stream been opened up to so many people. It had always been a place for Cutter and his parents, and when Raylee came into his life, he had shared it with her. Even Marnie had never been there for any occasion and she was deeply surprised that it was suddenly opened to the wider family.

"Where's Cutter?" Jesse asked, when he turned around and noticed he was the only one missing.

"He'll be here," Johnny assured him. "Unless he's already progressed Jake from the tack room to the cutting pen."

Emma didn't think that was very funny at all and was more realistic. "One dirty diaper and he'll be back," she stated with certainty.

The sound of the stream was peaceful and the boys had done a good job of clearing the overgrown brush and making room for everyone to lay their picnic blankets down. Everyone was relaxing in the shadows of the trees, listening to the trickling water and the rustling of the branches blowing in the gentle breeze. Raylee looked around at everyone. She loved her family. They all had a special place in her heart and it gave her a warm sense of security that she and Cutter weren't about to embark on this new journey alone.

When the gate closed, everyone looked up to see Cutter walk through, holding the baby in one arm and leading the mare with the other. He was completely at ease with the two, and only handed little Jake to his mother when he needed to tie up the horse.

"Did you show him his saddle?" Johnny asked.

"I let him pick out his own," Cutter said. "He went for the best one in the tack room."

"That's my boy," Johnny added proudly.

It was a good time for everyone to catch up. Marnie and Evelyn were talking recipes. Allan was sharing details with Doug and Pete about the vineyard and complex. Jesse and Aimee wouldn't let anyone into their close entangled picnic for two, while Cassie was playing babies with Emma and Beth.

"It's time," Raylee whispered to Cutter while they were stretched out on the blanket. He was watching the clouds constantly changing shapes and they were entertaining his thoughts. It was the first time in three months he had taken a lengthy break and he needed it.

"Not yet," he said, and he rolled over and looked for his father. "There's something I need to do first." He found him, and he left Raylee on the blanket wondering what was on his mind.

"Hey, Pete," Cutter interrupted, to break up the deep conversation he was in with Allan and Doug. "Can I talk to you for a minute?"

"Sure." Pete excused himself and the two of them walked away.

Marnie caught sight of them wandering off downstream. She felt sick, and only wished that Cutter had chosen a better time than the picnic.

"Before you say anything, if you're gonna break the news to me, I already know." Pete wanted to get in first before Cutter had a chance to spill.

Cutter was surprised. "What? How do you know?"

"She told me. As soon as we arrived, she broke the news to us both. I'm not sure if she wanted to get it out in the open quickly, or if she enjoyed giving us the shock."

"She told you? She wasn't gonna do that until we told everyone together."

"I guess she couldn't wait."

"Well maybe she's more excited about this baby than she's letting on," Cutter said, disappointed that Raylee had blabbed, and happy that she was bursting at the seams to tell everyone.

Pete cut in straight away. "What? You're going to be a father?" he asked.

"Yes sir... Wait. What are you talking about?"

"Aimee told me she's dropping out of college."

He'd done it again. Only Cutter could be so involved in his own world that he forgot there were other things going on around him. He defended himself straight away. "Look, Pete. I've already told Aimee that it's a bad idea and you and Beth wouldn't let her do it. But it really had nothing to do with me." Cutter was making his disapproval clear and would let him know that he'd stand by Pete and Beth's decision to overrule their daughter's irrational behavior.

"Don't worry about Aimee... Raylee's having a baby?"

"Yes sir. I only found out two days ago," Cutter explained.

Pete's eyes filled up. He grabbed Cutter and put his arms around him, pulling him in close. It was the first time that he'd had a close encounter with his father like that and it was so unfamiliar.

Pete pulled away to look at him. "I'm gonna have grandkids?"

"Yes," Cutter confirmed again, and could only laugh at his excitement. "But that's not what I need to talk to you about."

Pete was overjoyed. It had caught him by surprise, even more so than Aimee's news. "What do you wanna talk about then? If you're asking me for some fatherly advice then I'm probably not the best one to give it to you," he openly admitted.

Cutter felt his honesty was genuine. He felt sorry for his father and nothing either of them could say about the past would change the outcome.

"Actually, I need to talk to you about Mom," Cutter said directly, and it took Pete aback as it was the third shock he'd received in an hour.

Pete put his head down, remembering Mary-Ann fondly, then looked up at his son. "Your mom was the most beautiful woman I've ever known, and I was the one who screwed it up for our family. I want you to know that I'll never get over doing that to you both."

Cutter could only accept his father's apology and agree. It was undisputed. There was no need to cut him down some more over what happened in the past. He had done it and was down on himself enough, that he didn't need Cutter to add to that now.

"I want you to tell me the truth," Cutter said.

Pete agreed. "I at least owe you that."

There was a long pause while Cutter was choosing the right words. "Why did she leave?" he asked.

His father kept it simple. "Because your mom had been through enough and she needed to get away."

"But why did she really leave?" Cutter asked again, looking at him and was expecting a fuller answer.

Pete could see his need. His son was going to become a father. He was going to be standing in those same boots, feeling the same love for a child and the need to provide well. Pete didn't want his son making the same mistakes as he had. It was now his chance to unravel the past to make the future clear. "What did she tell you?"

"Some things... Not everything," Cutter said. "She told me that you were once happy."

"I thought I was the luckiest man in the world," Pete said, as he recalled those early days and began to smile.

"Then why did you let it all go when you had everything?" Cutter asked.

"I didn't realize that I had everything, until it was all gone," Pete admitted. "When we brought you home from the hospital, you were so perfect. There weren't two other parents in the world who were more in love with their first child than we were. And one day soon, you'll understand that."

Pete looked up to see his reaction. Cutter looked pleased. He was wanted and he was adored, by both his parents. It was important for him to know that.

"She was such a great mom. She did everything right for the family and her life revolved around you. Around us." Pete choked up when he thought of his wife that way.

"So what went wrong?" Cutter asked.

Pete continued. "I wanted to make a good life for you both. I worked more and took on a second job so that we could buy our first house. I wanted your mom to have the gable roof and white picket fence and raise more children. I wanted the family dream. For both of us."

Cutter could tell that Pete only wanted the best for Mary-Ann. The best for his family.

"And we got it. I worked hard and we moved to a nice suburb and bought our first house, and we were happy, just like your mom said. But no one saw the financial collapse coming and the recession hit everyone hard. Factories were closing down. The banks were moving in, and people were losing their jobs everywhere. I was lucky to hold onto mine for a few months longer, but when my job went too, everything we ever owned and worked hard for was taken away."

"Is that when you started drinking?"

"It's when I started drinking more... It was killing the pain, at the same time it was killing the family. It was too late by the time I realized what was happening to us." Pete looked at his son, hoping for some understanding. "We didn't discuss it, but your mom thought that another baby would bring me out of the dark place I was in and pull us back together again. That I would straighten myself out. Her intensions were good, but the added pressure tipped me over the edge."

Cutter didn't need to ask the questions anymore, as Pete found it was the right time to lay it all out, and he took a deep breath before recalling his guilt.

"She was four months along when I came home drunk one night. She pleaded for me to stop drinking. To stay home at night with you both." He rubbed his face while he was remembering the night. "She said we should move away, find work somewhere else. She'd even been offered a part-time job down at the local store, but I was too proud to stay at home and look after you while she went to work and earned the money... We argued about it, and... I didn't mean to push her..."

It was those words that cut the most. Cutter was angry with his father at the same time as he was wanting to hear this out. He knew the outcome. He just needed to hear it from Pete, and Pete needed to say it, so he continued.

"She fell down the stairs and she lost the baby." Pete paused to think of what he'd done. What he was responsible for. "When she came home from the hospital, she packed her bags and left. It was the last time I saw her." He looked at Cutter. "I wanted to see you, but I knew I wasn't in the right state of mind and that wherever Mary-Ann was, I knew you were safe."

A tear rolled down Cutter's face. He had heard it for himself. Not only had his father expressed how much he was loved, but it was his desperation to make a better life for the family that drove him down a path of no return with Mary-Ann.

"Is that why she couldn't have any more children?" he asked.

Cutter needed the answers to questions that had played on his mind for all these years. There were only two people who could give him those answers now, and since Marnie wasn't about to, he needed to hear it from his father.

"I need to know," Cutter insisted.

Pete sat down on a rock. He put his head down in shame and rubbed his face again. He didn't speak for a time and Cutter let him sit there in silence while he was gathering his thoughts. The sounds of the running water and birds in the trees were peaceful and added calm to their discussion. If Cutter had heard this at any other time in his life, then Pete would have been lucky to walk away intact.

"I took that away from her," Pete admitted. His guilt was coming through in a string of confessions. "I'm the reason she couldn't carry another child. I'm the reason she left. And I'm the only reason our family fell apart."

It was enough to have brought it out of him and Cutter looked at his father and saw a broken man. He knew that the incident on the stairs only finalized all the scars that had appeared over time.

Cutter stood up in a hurry and went for Pete. Whatever he was going to do, Pete fully believed that he deserved what was coming his way. He stood up also, to take it like a man. But when Cutter threw his arms around his father, it was to comfort him. They shared the same pain and at that moment, all the bad blood and anger was gone. It was not something that Cutter would ever forget, but the resentment was not something that he could live with either.

As they walked back to the picnic area, the sounds of laughter and Johnny recalling the night of the rodeo came into earshot. He always talked much louder than was needed and his dramatic version of events entertained everyone.

"I want you to know that I loved your mom with all my heart, and it was my pride that got in the way." Pete was making it clear that he adored Mary-Ann, and from his reaction today, Cutter was sure that he still did.

"I know," Cutter replied, and he put his hand on Pete's shoulder and gave it a light squeeze. "And you have a great family now and two girls that think the world of you."

"But they don't know everything."

"And they don't need to," Cutter agreed. It was so long ago now and the girls didn't know their father in that way. There was no need for them to know every last detail from his past life.

Marnie was relieved when she caught sight of the two of them walking back close, side by side. Either that, or Pete hadn't been as honest as he should have been, leaving Marnie undecided.

Everyone had waited on Cutter and Pete to come back to the picnic so they could start lunch. The girls handed out the sandwiches and everyone tucked in. They shared their drinks and stories, and there was fun and more laughter all round.

When Raylee stretched out on the blanket and put her head on Cutter's lap, she looked up at the sky. The clouds were moving across the sky and the motion was making her feel as if she was spinning with the earth. She closed her eyes. Cutter was tempted to put his hand on her tummy, but for fear of drawing attention to her good news, it was best left until after the announcement.

They were relaxed, and when Allan came over and sat with them, he was as much at ease as everyone else. "I'm just letting you know that your mom and I had a talk yesterday, and we're giving you back your trust fund," he said like a businessman rather than a father.

It made Raylee sit upright with a brightness to her smile. "Really?" she asked.

Cutter interrupted. "Thanks, Allan. But we don't need it. We're totally fine."

Raylee's look said otherwise. "But Cutter..."

"Aren't you happy here with what we've got?" he asked, as if perhaps he hadn't provided enough.

"Of course I am. But do you know how much money that is?" she asked.

"No ma'am, and I don't care. We don't need it," he insisted. "We've got everything we need and more."

Allan sat back, letting them debate it. It was getting thrown back and forth between them and he wouldn't stick his nose in if it wasn't welcome.

"Tell him, Dad," Raylee said, looking in her father's direction for support.

Allan hesitated, not wanting to get on the wrong side of either of them. "Well, you could always put up a bigger arena, or extend the house, or go on a nice holiday if you want." He was only making some small suggestions as to what they could do with the money. "In fact, you could do all of that and more," he added.

"But I don't want a bigger arena or a bigger house," Cutter stated. "I'm more than comfortable with what we have."

Raylee immediately cut in. "But if we don't take it, then it will go to my brothers and that's not fair."

Cutter had seen first hand what the downside to a young struggling family meant. He had lived it. He could also see how too much money drove Allan and Evelyn apart and he didn't like that. He was most comfortable sitting in the middle with everything they needed. Cutter believed that's what made Macca and Mary-Ann so content in their life.

Allan got up to leave. It wasn't the response he was expecting and he'd let them sort it out alone. "Think about it. It's yours whenever you're ready."

"Thank you," Cutter said, grateful for the offer, yet convinced they wouldn't be taking it.

Raylee let it lie for now, but as far as she was concerned, it was far from over.

"Hey, Marnie," Cutter said, when she sat down on a corner of their blanket.

"Did you talk to Pete?" she asked.

"I sure did, and it's all good," he assured her.

Marnie wasn't backwards in coming forwards and she got straight to her point. "You know, it's only been a few months since you got married, and I thought you might want the house to yourselves."

"What?" Raylee said, and she sat up quickly again, devastated by Marnie's theory.

"What's brought this on?" Cutter asked, equally surprised.

"Well, Doug and I spoke about it on our trip home and we thought that you might want your own space. You're both so young and you need some time alone, which means you'll want the house to yourselves... All of the house."

"Where did you come up with that crazy idea from?" Raylee asked, still showing her disapproval.

"Just think about it. You don't want an old woman hiding around every corner while you're.. you know... married."

Marnie was good at sneaking around and Cutter was sure that she invented it. They'd only had the house to themselves for one week since they were married and it was most enjoyable. They could do whatever they wanted, wherever they wanted and whenever they wanted to do it. Yet they needed Marnie more than she knew, and Cutter played down those secret thoughts of having the house to themselves again.

"Now, Marnie, you don't hide around corners, do you? We've got nothing to hide," he insisted.

She laughed at them both. "I might be an old woman, but you're forgetting, I was married once," she said.

"Well it's open for discussion... And it's a discussion that I don't think you'll win," Cutter pointed out.

The afternoon was moving on and the baby had been doing the rounds with everyone. He was slowly heading in their direction. Raylee gave Cutter a nudge, to tell him that it was time. She couldn't wait any longer and almost had the need to blurt it out. He stood up and got everyone's attention. Cutter was out of his comfort, even though this was his family and friends and there was nothing to be uncomfortable about.

He cleared his throat and looked around at everyone. As he wiped his hands on the sides of his jeans, he noticed that he was sweating. Although it was a warm day, it was more from the sudden need to let all these people know how he felt about them.

"You know the reason we're here today is because it's another successful show over and I just need to say thank you to everyone on the team." He was off to a great start. "It's also a chance for us to say goodbye to Allan and Evelyn, who I'm pleased made the trip over... I must say, that I was quite surprised when I saw you standing in my kitchen, Allan, and I never expected that you would end up on my team. Raylee has loved every minute of your time here and she'll miss you both. But you'll have a place in our home whenever you visit."

Raylee's parents both looked thankful. It had been a successful trip in more ways than one.

"To my dad and Beth," Cutter said, and Pete looked at him with eyes that were slowly drowning in tears from his son's acceptance. "You have raised two beautiful young daughters and one of them especially has taught me more about being a brother than anyone will ever know." He then looked at Aimee. "Whatever you decide to do about college, Aims, you know where we'll be and you're always welcome here anytime." He gave her a warm brotherly smile as only the two of them would know the bond that would tie them together. "And Jesse. Thanks for being in my corner. You've done a great job with me in training and whether you decide to ride broncs or go cutting, I'll support you. You've earned the bro title, right Johnny?"

"As long as he knows he's the baby bro," Johnny called out, reducing everyone to laughter.

"And Johnny and Emma. You guys are the best friends anyone could ever want. You've been there for me when I needed you the most and I can't imagine my life without you." It was almost enough to bring him undone, especially when he saw Emma wiping her eyes dry. He controlled it. "And if you ever decide to go to town in the next storm, Johnny, and leave your pregnant wife at home, then you can consider her to be in good hands."

Emma blew him a kiss for everyone to see. She owed so much to him and she snuggled her baby close to her, knowing that Cutter was the only reason she hadn't gone through the experience alone.

He looked around and his eyes locked onto Doug. He'd never shared his personal thoughts with Doug before, and Cutter needed to let everyone know that he was a big part of his life growing up.

"I've known Doug since before I can remember, and he had to put up with me all those years ago, climbing all over his truck, inside and out. Asking him to take me for a drive and letting me push the cattle up the chute. Never once did he say no, and I'm sure I was a big pain in your butt... But what I really need to thank you for more than anything else, is for rolling your truck last year. You saved this ranch and I'll always be thankful to you for that."

Doug silently accepted his thanks with only a nod in return. While the accident last year was devastating at the time, it was only when Raylee lodged a claim to the insurance company for the loss of cattle that Cutter found out about Macca's life insurance policy. It was enough to stop the ranch from going under and Cutter was able to increase the cattle numbers and buy the new horse truck. That wild and stormy night was a turning point in their lives.

"And if there's one person here that has been with me forever, it's Marnie. You'll always have a place here with us and there are no family ties that are stronger than yours and mine. You don't have to be blood to be family. You just have to be with a person every day of your life to know that you can't live without them." Cutter couldn't live without Marnie and he would insist that she stay at the ranch for the rest of her days. She could barely remember a life away from the Jones ranch and always thought of Cutter as her own.

As he was winding down his thank you list, it was drawing everyone's attention to Raylee, that she was the last one. She waited anxiously for the words to pop out of his mouth, but they didn't.

"Allan," Cutter said, and everyone looked over at him. "Three months ago, the most incredible special event took place in my life and there was only one regret from that day... So if you don't mind, I'd like you to bring your daughter up to the front," he said.

Raylee was still lying back on her elbows, when her father stood up and held out his hand to pull her up. She looked at her father and linked her arm through his. Evelyn gave a sob that was catching on quickly, while everyone watched Allan walk his daughter through all the blankets, laughing as they stepped over the baskets, careful not to trip over or accidentally kick anything on the way through. When they reached the front, Raylee gave Cutter a thankful smile as she knew exactly what he had just done. She had missed out on her father walking her down the aisle and while it was not exactly the same, it meant so much to the both of them.

Allan reached out and shook Cutter's hand. He was thankful also, and was having a difficult time not letting it be seen.

"And I believe you all know my beautiful wife?" he asked. As he turned to look at her, he held her hands and gave a heartfelt sigh. "When I said 'I do' Raylee Tremayne, I meant that I do wanna be married to you for the rest of my life, and I do need to love you every day, and I do promise to take care of you as best as I can. So my promise to you in front of our family and friends, is that I will make you the happiest wife in the world."

Just like their wedding day, he reached down and kissed her, while everyone let it be known that they were right behind them. Evelyn's sobs were joined by Marnie's and Emma's, and they were now searching through the picnic baskets for the paper napkins.

He put his arm around her shoulder when they turned to look at their family. "So we just need to say thanks to everyone for helping us at the show and for believing in us."

He was done. He needed to let everyone know how he felt and had given them all the praise they deserved. It was not something that he normally had the nerve or the courage to do, and it only added to the buildup towards what was still to come.

Everyone was happy and appreciated his words. They gave a huge applause at the end and whistles from his two bros, as well as a few shouts of approval. Cutter and Raylee remained standing together until it all settled down. Just before it was expected that they would sit back down, Cutter made the announcement. "Oh, and by the way… We're having a baby."

"What?" everyone called out at the same time and they all scrambled to their feet in a hurry.

The news had just bowled everyone over. While the shock was setting in for some, for others it was a relief to know that the secret was now out in the open. The congratulations came in fast and none more than from Allan, who was first to throw his arms around his daughter.

It made for a very happy afternoon as everyone celebrated and shared in the good news. Many questions were being thrown their way, with Raylee's eventful week at the show now drawing suspicion and having everyone asking for more details.

# Chapter Sixteen

Over the next couple of days, the baby news had everyone on a high. The last thing Evelyn wanted to do now was go home and leave her daughter in Texas. While she was packing her bag that morning, there was no comfort in knowing that in a few more hours, she would be driving away from the ranch and leaving Raylee behind. She was looking forward to going home to the vineyard and unpacking her bags in her house again, but it was at the expense of breaking her daughter's heart. She'd made a promise though, to come back to the ranch when the baby was close.

It was Pete and Beth who were picking them up and taking them back to the airport, since Raylee knew how traumatic that final goodbye was going to be. They had agreed to let Aimee stay those extra couple of days at the ranch before she too needed to pack up and go home. The mood on the ranch had hit an all time high at the same time a low was unsettling everyone quickly. Jesse took Aimee out for one last ride over the ranch and they made their way to the back pasture to check on the calves. They were gone longer than was needed and when they arrived back at the barn, Cutter looked at his watch and could only imagine what other diversions they found along the way.

After the picnic, Doug had the need to go home. He had been away long enough and needed to pick up on some maintenance at his own house. He was expecting that Marnie would make her way into town over the next couple of weeks to move in, and he wanted to get everything in order beforehand. Unfortunately for Doug, Marnie was torn between the ranch and town, with her need to help raise the baby putting pressure on her decision.

She eventually concluded that she would spend her time between both, satisfying everyone as well as herself.

There was a thump on the porch when Allan dropped his bag from a height that was unintentional and it made Raylee jump. She had been sitting on the swing and was staring at the view. Allan had a long face and was just as deflated as Evelyn that today was the day. Cutter followed him out, and placed Evelyn's bag down in a much quieter way that was more in keeping with their surrounds.

"I want you to reconsider," Allan said to Cutter and Raylee, when he took up a position at the end of the porch for their final discussion.

"Look. I really appreciate what you're trying to do for us, but I'm telling you, we're fine," Cutter said again.

"I have no doubt about that," Allan agreed, and he looked around. He knew that his daughter and her new husband were most comfortable on the ranch. Between Cutter's training fees and prize money, and the turnover of cattle each year, they were doing exceptionally well. "So let me buy the colt from you. You can keep him here and ride him. Then you won't think that I'm just giving you the money."

"He's not for sale," Cutter said firmly.

"Well, let me buy the mare then. Obviously she'll stay here with you and you can take her to any shows you want, but..."

"She's not for sale either," Cutter added, cutting off every attempt to get past him.

"Well there must be something I can buy. There must be some way you'll take the money." Allan seemed desperate to make things right before he left to go home. It had been a very sore point over the last twelve months, when Allan had used Raylee's trust fund as a bargaining tool to win her over. Never did he expect that she was prepared to walk away from it all and give up everything, including her family. Allan had underestimated his daughter, and now he was all but throwing the money at them to ease his own conscience.

Cutter had done a lot of thinking about it over the last couple of days. While it wasn't sitting right with him to take the money from Allan, he wasn't comfortable either that Raylee was missing out on something that was rightfully hers and had belonged to her family. He was caught between a rock and a hard place and he could only come up with one solution. He called Allan to the rail and they leaned over, both looking beyond the barn and the yards, keeping out of earshot from Raylee and her mother. They stood close and Cutter pointed to the horizon.

"You see that out there?" he asked Allan.

"You mean the land?" Allan asked in return.

"All that land you see is ours. Mine and Raylee's," Cutter stated, and he took a moment to take it all in before he pointed to the east. "And do you know who owns that side?" Cutter asked.

Allan knew the answer to that one. "Johnny O'Brien," he said, as he was sure that it wasn't a trick question.

"And his family," Cutter added informatively. He then looked the other way and pointed to the west. "And do you know who owns that land out there?" Cutter asked.

Cutter had Allan stumped on that one, and not having a clue, he shrugged his shoulders. "I've got no idea," Allan answered, wondering where Cutter was going with all this.

"Well I'll tell you who owns it... You if you want."

Allan looked at Cutter and then to the west again. "What do you mean?" he asked, totally confused by Cutter's remarks.

Cutter went on to explain. "I've known the Cunninghams for most of my life. Been Macca's neighbors for two generations," he said, as part of his history lesson. "But I hear they might be selling out. Old man's gonna retire and the boys want their stake so they can buy somewhere else... Are you following me?" he asked.

"I think I'm keeping up," Allan said, while he was trying to fill in the missing pieces. "You want me to buy that land?"

"You and Raylee together... Of course, you don't need to be here. We'll take care of the cattle for you and oversee everything. It will give me more numbers to run through the pen and give you another reason to visit."

Allan liked the idea and it gave him an instant spark at the thought of it. He knew that Cutter would never accept his offer to just take the money and do whatever he liked with it. He'd turned down large sums of money for his horses. It wasn't his way. It wasn't what drove him. All Cutter ever wanted was to work hard and be comfortable, and he was already doing a damn good job of that.

Allan was still full of questions about the possibilities of the neighboring ranch when Pete and Beth pulled the car up in front of the house.

"You have my permission to pursue this," Allan said enthusiastically. "I want you to do a deal and get that land," he added secretly.

"I'll make the call today." Cutter put an end to their discussion when Raylee and Evelyn headed for the bags and Aimee popped her sad looking face out of the barn.

Cutter dived right in to stop Raylee from picking up her mother's heavy bag. "I'll get it," he said, and he took it out of her hand.

They all wandered down the steps. It was a heartbreaking moment for Raylee and her parents when they said their goodbyes at the side of the car, while Aimee still had her arms firmly wrapped around Jesse's neck and was struggling to let him go.

Cutter looked at them. "Oh, come on," he said dramatically. "You'll be back on the weekends," he pointed out, although Jesse and Aimee were not showing any kind of happiness at the thought of it.

He stood there and watched his sister peel herself away from Jesse only to give Raylee that same strong hold. Cutter loved that they were so close, as Raylee had been the only reason Aimee had lasted as long as she did on the ranch and wasn't sent home earlier.

When Aimee turned and looked at her brother, he looked back at her. From her grubby hat to her dusty worn boots, from her roughened hands to her faded blue jeans, Cutter had changed Aimee from the comfortable city girl to the rough and ready country girl that stood in front of him, and she totally agreed... She didn't want to go back to city life. But with a lot of persuasion from the family and extra encouragement from Jesse, Aimee had reluctantly agreed to start college. She would at least give it a go. Though she had it in the back of her mind that if it didn't work out then she would instantly drop out.

"I'm coming back," Aimee assured him, to let Cutter know that he would see her when he was home of a weekend and in the holidays.

Cutter took her hat off and kissed her on the top of her head, then she buried her face into his shoulder and hugged him tight. "I know you will," he said with certainty. "And when you do, I'll make sure I've got all the shit jobs lined up for you," he added, looking for a rise from her.

She didn't bite. "I love you," she said.

It immediately softened him. "And I love you too, Aims," he repeated, and he put her hat back on before she leaned down to get into the car.

It was almost too much for Raylee, whose flood of tears were interfering with her words. Beth was insisting they get on the road so they would make it to the airport in good time. The final goodbye was over and done, and Pete drove away before it was dragged out any longer than what was needed. It left Marnie on the porch waving after the car and Jesse standing alone looking completely lost.

It was always going to be a difficult day, and as Cutter walked towards the steps, he felt the same way as everyone else. His stride was shortened and his shoulders were sunken, as if he was carrying the weight of the world, and although he had everything to look forward to, it wasn't helping with the sudden empty feeling that was weighing him down.

Jesse was the last one to the door and when he pulled it open, the smell of Marnie's delicious freshly baked apple pie filled the kitchen and was spilling out towards the porch. It was the pick-me-up that they all needed. Guaranteed to take your mind off everything. As the four of them sat around the table, they shared in the laughter and the good times that they all had over the last while. Marnie was learning more about the sneaky games that had caused the stress levels in the house to rise and the fun and games that had followed.

There had been many changes in that short time. The unexpected reunion between Raylee's parents was the biggest surprise of all, while Cutter should have seen Jesse and his sister's attraction from the start.

But perhaps the biggest change was still coming their way. Cutter looked around the table. Everyone there was his family, yet his and Raylee's own family was just beginning. It was an overwhelming thought that this table and this house were about to welcome a new member to the Jones team.

A cowboy or cowgirl. A rancher, a cutter. Whatever he or she became, Cutter knew that a baby would be their greatest achievement to date. It would give him another reason to go to work each day on the ranch and in the cutting pen. He couldn't wait to buy that very first saddle and that very first pony, just like Macca had done for him all those years ago.

"So what's next?" Jesse asked, to bring him back to the now.

Cutter looked at everyone. "Well, I promised Raylee that we'd take some time out after the show. Just the two of us," he said, to make it clear that she was indeed his first priority. "And I'm gonna keep that promise. But after we get back, you can pack the truck and get your bags ready. The next show we're going to is in Vegas..."

# Acknowledgements

First of all I would like to thank everyone who has read The Cutter. It was an amazing experience for me to write it, and one that I will never forget. I loved every minute of it! I often hear authors say that they can't chose their favourite book between those they have written, as it would be like choosing between your own children. Now I know that feeling. The Cowboy Code is right up there with The Cutter and it was such a fun book to write.

I'd like to thank my mom again for taking the time to read the manuscript more than once. You have been there from the very beginning and I'm sure you know the story as well as I do… word for word. Thanks Mom, love you. x

To Cilento Publishing and the editing team. You have enabled me to turn my dream into something I can hold, so a huge thank you! I'm sure I didn't have as many mistakes or repetitive questions this time, did I? Or maybe I did, lol. Job well done, thank you. x

To Jessie. You have also been there from the very beginning, offering support and encouragement as The Cowboy Code was taking shape. And again you have brought the book to life with a stunning front cover! You always shine! Thank you. x

To Tyson. When I asked you to do a photoshoot for the cover, I thought that you would need a lot of persuasion, but you jumped in boots, chaps, hat and all, and I can't thank you enough. You smashed it! x

To Juliann. Your text message after you read the manuscript was simple, yet awesome. 'Finished. Loved it.' And that gave me the confidence that I was on the right track. Thank you a million times over! x

To Chanel. You have been so patient with me, thank you. You know when to be quiet, when to ask if I need anything, and you make great coffee too! And your photography is coming along nicely (see my Instagram for her handy work) You are an amazing, highly energetic, often dramatic piece of my life that I couldn't live without. I love you xx

To Marlene. I was able to fast-track The Cowboy Code into a book because of you. Your support means the world to me, as does our mother/daughter-in-law special bond, and I can't thank you enough for everything you have done in our lives. Our friendship is built on trust, loyalty, and our love for the same cowboy. Love you x

To Greg. It's been an incredible journey, from our first meeting to now, the things we've done, the places we've been, and the people we've met. But it's the horses that are the heart and soul of our special place and I love what we have created together. I'm so blessed that I get to do life with you. xx

And finally, to all the cutters out there, whether you're a cowgirl or cowboy, if it's your work or your play, if you're at the top or at the very beginning, put your hand down and keep the dream alive!

Linda x

# *Note to the reader –*

Thank you for reading The Cowboy Code. In the world of publishing, where millions of book titles are available online at the click of a button, it's extremely difficult to get noticed. However, the reader has the power to boost searches by giving a star rating and writing a review.

This review can make all the difference to the next potential reader. If you can take the time, please leave a review on Amazon (if you are a regular customer) and Goodreads (the reviewing website)

*Visit www.goodreads.com and register

*Search by title – The Cutter, and/or The Cowboy Code (The Cutter Series)

*Leave a star rating and review

And lastly, tell your friends. Word of mouth is still a great way to share what you have liked.


Thank you in advance!

Linda x

*Book Three in The Cutter series coming soon*

# Cowboy Rising

## By Linda Ellison

# Chapter 1

It's dark. The lights are out and the arena is deathly silent, in a state of complete blackness.

There is an atmosphere. A pause. A whistle. It's enough to start up the crowd who are anxious for the last ride of the night and they begin to shout and stomp their feet, all spurring on the last cowboy. The sound from the stands of five thousand pairs of boots drumming the floor is deafening. A lone spotlight highlights the chute and the applause goes over the top. The music thumps to the beat of a very fired up audience and the arena is lit up with a spectacular burst of sparks that shoot up high into the air. Colors of red, white and blue reach for the overhead lighting and fall gracefully, disappearing before they hit the ground, as the announcer fills the empty space with his voice to introduce the last courageous rider.

Raylee hates this. Wishing she was never there, she desperately wanted it over.

Rodeos had been a big part of her life growing up and had never bothered her before, until Cutter was hurt from a rouge bull that chased him down and slammed him hard against the rails, knocking him out cold and breaking his arm. Even though that was how they came to be together, she'd never look at rodeo the same and tonight was certainly no exception.

She couldn't take her eyes off the chute and as she slipped her hand into Cutter's and gripped it tight, she held her breath and wanted to look away. Her stomach turned over and her nerves came up into her throat, making her swallow hard, while her feet were now restless and her sweaty hands were shaking violently.

"Don't look," Cutter said.

"I can't. I have to look," she replied in a trembling voice, and Cutter put his arm around the back of her chair and pulled her in close to help settle her.

It was the longest wait of her life and added to the sickly feeling that was sitting silently in her heart. An explosion of colored lights filled the arena and the music hit an all time high when the cowboy gave a nod and the chute was pulled open. The bull launched forward. He was big, aggressive, and when he felt those spurs in his sides, his eyes widened and he went ballistic.

The cowboy was young and fearless, as he held on tight and sat high on the bull's back with no less than two thousand pounds between his legs. Balancing with his arm thrown back, the cowboy was being spun around in tight circles with every thrust of the bull's ferocious buck and twist. It was fast and perfectly in time to Raylee's heartbeat, and when Cutter felt her hand squeeze his, he was sure it was cutting off the circulation to his fingers.

The crowd were cheering him on as the seconds raced on the clock. The cowboy was hanging on for his life, feeling the full adrenalin of the bull who was now fully pissed at the rider on his back. He was unleashing every bit of fury he had in him to get that rider off, with an untamed strength of power and an eye that was deadly.

All eyes were on the cowboy, but when the timer reached the six second mark, the bull gave a vicious twist that caught the cowboy off balance and he was unable to recover, spitting him to the dirt.

It was done. He had given it his best shot, although tonight his best was not good enough. Landing clear of the bull on his knees, the cowboy immediately stood up and ran in the opposite direction away from danger as the bull was now being distracted by the two bullfighters, who were spectacularly encouraging him towards the gate.

Everyone in the stands raised to their feet to applaud him, even though he put his head down as he walked back to the chute, annoyed at himself and disappointed in that ride. Raylee released Cutter's hand and she stood up to join everyone in an applause that was long and drawn out.

The night was now finally over.

"Wooo," Cutter said loudly. He was pumped up and was applauding too. "That was insane," he said, pleased for the young cowboy even though he didn't reach his eight second target.

Raylee agreed with him. "Insane is right. In more ways than one," she added seriously.

The crowd remained standing, waiting on the official results to hit the big screen while the announcer was dramatically filling in the time with rambling commentary. Cutter and Raylee didn't need to see the results to know that it was another ride and another unsuccessful rodeo for Colton Jones.

"I'm so pleased it's over," Raylee stated, feeling the relief that her son had walked away in one piece. "That was way too close for my liking."

Cutter picked up on her relief. "Hey, you can start breathing now," he said, to help ease her mind.

It had been an intense night and now that it was over, Raylee turned to Johnny and Emma O'Brien, who had made the trip to Nashville with them. Their daughter, Avery, had tagged along with Colton and his sister, Dakota, for their first road trip together out of state.

Johnny reached over and grabbed Cutter on the shoulder. "He's still got a lot of work to do," he said in an honest but supportive way, and Cutter couldn't disagree with him, much to the complete disapproval of Raylee, who would rather her son rode cutting horses like his father instead of bulls.

When the presentation was done and the music had died down, the crowd dispersed slowly through the many exits and the bright lights of the arena came back on. The officials came in with tractors to prepare the sand while others packed down the extra rails and the presentation stand. Cutter and Raylee didn't rush. They were staying in town for the weekend and were there to surprise their son. After the crowd had thinned out, they made their way out of the arena to the competitor car park where they were sure to give Colton and the two girls a shock they weren't expecting.

They found his truck easily enough. It didn't take long, as Cutter had loaned his father's old blue truck for their first trip away and it stood out among all the other late models. It was only when his father passed away over twenty years ago that Cutter took it out of the garage and started to drive it. He'd looked after it for all those years and it held a personal value that couldn't be replaced.

Cutter pulled on the handle. It was locked and neither Colton nor the girls were anywhere to be seen. He asked around and nobody had seen them. The heads-up was that many of the riders from the rodeo were in the big tent out the back, and as the four of them made their way to the other side of the arena to look for their kids, when they neared, they could hear the music from the live band thumping out a song.

It was dark and late, and as they entered the makeshift club, it was full of drunk and disorderly cowboys and cowgirls, celebrating the success of the night or drowning their results. Everyone seemed to be having a good time on the dance floor, as it was packed to capacity. The lights were dim and it was smoky, with only a few colored spotlights to uplift their sight.

Cutter picked up Raylee's hand and unintentionally squeezed it. He never went to the bar after a show. He hadn't been to a bar for nearly thirty years since he knew that that was where all trouble begins and ends. It was an unwritten law in their house and it was the last place he ever expected to see his son. They looked around. Everyone was wearing the same thing. Jeans, boots and hats, and it made looking for their kids and Avery a little difficult in the seedy dark room.

"I can't see them," Raylee said loudly in Cutter's ear so that he could hear. He didn't answer and he kept walking around anyway, just to make sure.

They split up. Johnny and Emma went over to the bar while Cutter and Raylee walked around the outside of the dance floor. "Maybe they're back at the truck now," Raylee said only as a suggestion, as it seemed unlikely they would find them in this loose crowd of party goers. "Let's go back and look again," she added, although it was more so they could leave.

He didn't answer again and was beginning to think that Raylee was right. This wasn't where they were going to find their kids. It was more likely they had missed them in passing and were already back at the hotel.

Feeling uncomfortable about being there, they turned around and were heading towards the door to leave when Raylee stopped still, stunned by what she was looking at. Cutter pulled her by the hand to move and when she didn't, he looked up. He was completely floored.

On the dance floor was their daughter. Up close and very personal with a cowboy who had his hands all over her, touching her provocatively while he had his face buried in her neck. Dakota was clearly loving every minute of it, as she held her arms up high and rocked to the band while shouting out the words to the song as if it was hers.

Cutter and Raylee stood watching, unsure of what to do next. Should they turn around and walk away? Should they break it up? The reality of what they were looking at hadn't sunk in and their confusion was only added to when they saw Colton dancing next to her, beer bottle in the air with Avery hanging off him throwing back a whiskey. They were well on their way to being drunk and their public display of dirty dance moves looked more appropriate for a private dance party for two, behind closed doors.

No, this can't be happening, Cutter thought. Colton and Avery, both drunk? Dakota, dancing with some sleazy cowboy, allowing him to touch her that way? Whatever level of crazy thoughts were going through Cutter's mind as to how this was happening, was only taking a less priority over what he was going to do about it. His son didn't drink, let alone party. His daughter wasn't some cheap and easy flirt. His thoughts snapped back to the dance floor and as they were making their way through the crowd towards them, Dakota saw her parents coming and she froze. She stopped still. It was enough to put the fear in her while the others kept dancing, unaware that their party had just been seriously crashed. Cutter pushed through the crowd and had almost reached them when a fist came from nowhere and took his son to the floor.

Cutter looked up. It was Johnny who was standing over Colton. He had just laid Colton out with a fistful of anger that landed him on the ground. While Cutter thought his son may have deserved it and it had crossed his mind to do the same thing, it was his instincts that took over when he landed one in return on Johnny's cheek in Colton's defense. There was a scuffle on the dance floor and when all the cowgirls scattered to clear a way, a dozen fights broke out and no one knew who was fighting who and for what reason.

Emma grabbed Avery and pulled her to the side while Raylee took Dakota by the hand and led her away. The four girls stood watching helplessly and screamed at the boys to stop fighting, while the band didn't miss a beat and the bar was still in full swing, fuelling up the crowd for the long night ahead.

It was more of a wild brawl and every cowboy seemed to be more than willing to get involved. The security team was quick to the center of the dance floor and pulled everyone apart, and when they had Johnny restrained, Cutter leaned down to his son who was still lying on the floor, slowly coming around.

"Wake up," Cutter said forcefully, while he was slapping Colton on the side of his face.

Colton was on his back and moving. He had a gash across his cheekbone and the outside of his eye was glowing red. He lifted his head and rested back on his elbows, looking up into his father's face. He tried to focus but didn't speak, and he gave him a drunken smug grin that made Cutter fume, before another fist came from over the top of Cutter's shoulder and knocked Colton out again.

It was lights out.